DIVE AND FLY

DIVE AND FLY

A Novel

BY

WARREN CATERSON

 Winfield & Scott Press

First Printing, 2012

ISBN 978-0-9801568-5-0
LCCN 2001012345

Winfield & Scott Press
1497 Main Street
Suite 185
Dunedin, FL 34698

Cover Design: Thomas Broughton
Interior Design: Perseus Design
Author Photograph: Morning Glory Studios

Printed in the United States of America

To all of you who jumped off the cliff and built your wings on the way down.

CHAPTER 1

"PERHAPS IF we jump out far enough," he whispered to the young woman clutching his arm, "one of those tents might break our fall."

Billy Shakes eased up to the edge of the aircraft-carrier-sized roof and scanned the ground far below him—a broad expanse of finely manicured green lawns, massive chrome sculptures, and the billowing bright white tents of an upcoming celebration. A catering truck inched back to the curb. He turned and glanced at Eden, the girl beside him.

Hope danced in her eyes. "You think?"

The young couple teetered on a precipice more than 100 feet from the ground. The tips of their shoes curled over the keen edge of sharp-hewn, ivory granite. He wrapped his arm around her thin waist and caressed her side. She trembled in his grasp and he shared her fear. Or was that determination?

Billy tilted his head back and closed his eyes. The hissing brakes of sardine-can busses and the staccato blare of impatient taxi horns echoed off the buildings on Michigan Avenue to their left. And in the distance, the rumbling hum of afternoon traffic drifted up from Chicago's Lakeshore Drive. The sound of this urban symphony kneaded his tense muscles like the skilled hands of a Swedish masseuse and for one brief moment he felt relaxed.

Synesthesia. He felt the sound.

The crisp October breeze tousled his hair and the light of the midday sun warmed his face. He sighed and breathed in the salt air as it wafted in from Lake Michigan.

His eyes jerked open. Wait a minute. Salt? In the air? But this is a lake!

Billy started. He realized the salt air he was breathing was from his own perspiration. He ran a nervous hand through damp hair, and as he wiped the sweat from his hand on his pant leg an alarm pierced the air. He spun around. A door at the far end of the roof flew open and a gang of security guards spilled out as if the stairway had vomited them. As they bumped and stumbled around in the bright sunlight, one guard shouted, "There they are!"

Billy turned to Eden and snickered. "Here come the Keystone Kops."

"This isn't funny," she said.

"Sure it is. Just look at those—"

A shot rang out. Then another. And another.

The couple instinctively hunched and bobbed at the sound of each shot.

"They must be getting paid by the bullet," Billy said as he pushed her head down. "Good thing these guys can't aim or we'd be in real deep—"

Bam! He felt a thump over his left ear as if someone had pinged him with a knuckle. He stumbled forward.

She seized his arm and pulled him back from the edge. "Billy?"

"I'm—I'm okay." He regained his footing and touched the side of his head—it burned and he winced. He stared at his finger. Blood. Oh my God.

As the bright red fluid trickled down his knuckle, the sweet-sour taste of elderberry rolled over his tongue.

Synesthesia. He tasted the color.

He looked back over his shoulder. The security guards and their profanity-laden shouts were closing in. He turned to the young woman beside him. She was pale and unsteady. He tightened his grip around her waist and pulled her close. Sirens filled the air as three fire engines, a SWAT team van and an ambulance roared into a nearby parking lot off to their left. The banshee wail of the sirens pierced his skin like a hundred fine needles and he winced in pain.

As the rescue vehicles screeched to a halt, two TV news trucks rolled into the parking lot behind them. Firemen leapt off their trucks, snatching ladders and ropes. The back doors of the SWAT van burst open and a dozen black-clad men spilled onto the pavement, dark helmets gleaming in the sun. Female reporters skittered across the blacktop with camera-laden men in tow as the satellite turrets on their trucks rose and swiveled. A growing crowd of wide-eyed bystanders oozed across the lawn and parking lot. Pointing. Shouting.

Eden turned and searched Billy's eyes. "What now?"

He tried to reassure her with a look of confidence. He was bluffing. Did she notice?

"I have a plan," he said with tentative conviction.

Bam! A bullet zipped between them and out into the bright sky where it pierced a soaring pigeon in mid-flight. Gray and white feathers exploded and scattered into the air like a small fireworks display. They watched the mortally wounded bird tumble and toss in slow motion to the lawn below.

Eden gasped and shuddered at the sight.

"So it goes," she whispered. "So it goes."

Bam! Bam! Gunshot after gunshot shattered the calm afternoon.

Billy felt Eden's shoulders tighten and flinch at each report. They ducked and shifted as the bullets flew by. He placed his lips on the top of her head. Yep, so it goes, he thought as he gently kissed her hair. Twenty-four hours ago he was 1100 miles away, drowning his sorrows and feeding his senses at Art Walk. He glanced back over the edge of the roof.

But this?

Bam! Bam! Bam!

Everything has come to this?

Bam! Bam!

Shit.

CHAPTER 2

BILLY closed his laptop and placed it on the coffee table. He stood and raised his arms over his head, making that odd half-grunt, half-squeal noise men make when they stretch. He walked over to the large antique mirror hanging above the fireplace.

Four dead bodies. Seven suspects. No murder weapons. Yeah, chapter six is looking pretty good. Thirty-eight years old and you still got it. This book might pay the mortgage for a year. Hell, maybe two.

Billy stroked his stubbled chin and admired his reflection. 'Course, it doesn't hurt that you look just like that new James Bond fellah—what's his name? He leaned forward and studied his blue-gray eyes. The color filled his mouth with the taste of ice-cold December steel. Like licking the frozen flagpole in front of PS 19 back in the Bronx. Something he and dozens of kids from the neighborhood dared each other to do. Blue-gray eyes. Cold steel taste. It was the "condition." Synesthesia. Tasting color. Feeling sound. Odd. Odd as hell. But invigorating.

The phone rang and interrupted his thoughts.

"I got it, Ma!" He walked into the kitchen and flipped the cordless receiver in his hand.

"Yo, Billy, here."

"Hey, you mutant *trombenik*. How're we doing?"

Billy immediately recognized the whiney New York voice of his agent, Sy *Excuse-my-Yiddish* Greenburg.

"*Trombenik*?" He rolled his eyes. "Jeez, Sy, that's a new one."

"Means bum. Deadbeat. Look it up in the dictionary. Even has your picture next to the definition."

"Very funny." Billy grabbed a Granny Smith apple from a bowl on the counter and wandered back into the living room. Sure, Sy could be a pain, but he'd gotten Billy six lucrative book deals over the past decade and it wasn't like he has to have him over for the holidays. He took a juicy bite. They say absence makes the heart grow fonder, Billy thought. Jeez, Sy's absence keeps me sane. He cradled the phone against his shoulder.

"This isn't a collect call, is it?"

"What?! I make 15% off you so that I should make collect calls? Don't be such a *putz*."

"Last time you called collect. Nobody calls collect anymore. Except you."

"So, sue me. Listen, you making any headway on the new work?"

"Coming along." Billy took another bite.

"Great. Hey, listen, I just heard back from Angela at Worling Press. They're really anxious about *Daiquiri Taylor, Conch Republic President*."

"Ha!" Billy mumbled as the tart, green apple crunched in his mouth. "They should with the advance they paid me."

"Yeah...well—" Sy fell silent.

Seconds passed and Billy's shoulders stiffened. Sy was never at a loss for words. Ever. Billy swallowed hard. "But what?" He tossed the apple core into the trash and walked back into the living room. He plopped down in his overstuffed chair.

"They're concerned," Sy continued. "That's all I'm saying."

"Concerned?" He threw his feet up on the hassock.

"Angela said the numbers were down on the last two books. They want another hit like *Flying Fish and Turtle Kraals*. Y'know, movie options, international sales. All that shit."

"Don't rub it in." Billy picked at a loose thread on his jeans. "It's a slump. We all hit slumps. Even Hemingway—"

"Yeah, sure. Hemingway, Fitzgerald, Sinclair Lewis. Blah, blah, blah. Angela just wants this one to work. So she . . ." Sy paused. He never paused. Ever.

"Go on." Billy flicked the thread from his fingers.

"She wants you to rewrite chapter two."

Billy shrugged. "If it'll make her happy—"

"And four through eight."

He threw his feet off the hassock and bolted upright. "Is she crazy? That's the best part! No one's writing weird Florida stuff like that. Not Dorsey, not Shames, not even Hiaasen."

"And chapter ten."

"But—"

"And thirteen."

Billy leapt to his feet. "What?"

Sy coughed, then mumbled: "And sixteen through nineteen."

"That's ridiculous. Why I—"

"Listen to me. Are you listening to me?"

Billy marched across the room. "I'm listening."

"She said it's wooden."

"Wooden? Man, that's a load of—"

"Clumsy," Sy continued. "Unfocused. She said it's—" he paused as if to measure and weigh his words. "Lifeless."

Billy froze and stared off into space. Wooden? That I can fix. Clumsy? Piece of cake. Unfocused? I'll show 'em focus. He collapsed back into the chair. But...*lifeless?*

"Listen." Sy's voice caught his attention again. "I think she may be right. There *is* something missing. Chutzpah. Chutzpah and balls. It's got no balls. Where's the Billy who wrote *Zoot Suits and Toots?* Now that one had balls."

"Yeah, it did."

"Let me ask you something. You getting out? Y'know, having some fun?"

Billy looked up as his invalid mother passed by the hallway door in her electric three-wheeled scooter. She grinned and gave him a gentle wave. "Yeah, yeah, I'm getting out." He glanced down at the floor. "A lot."

"But are you getting laid?"

Billy leapt to his feet. "I beg your pardon?" He strode back to the fireplace and leaned on the mantel. Once again, he stared at his eyes. Blue-gray. Ice cold. Lifeless?

"You heard me," Sy's voice repeated. "You getting laid?"

He kicked a log in the fireplace. "That's none of your damn business."

"I guess that means no."

"Sy—"

"Listen to me. Are you listening to me? You wrote some of your best stuff when you took that oddball disease of yours and hit the road. My god, if I didn't know any better I'd think you'd become some kind of couch potato. A real *shlepper*. Keep this up and you'll drive both of us to the poor house."

"We're not going to the poor house." He glanced at the medical bills piled up on the writing desk in the corner. Specialist after specialist. And not a single one could diagnose his mother's problem or offer a prognosis. Why she couldn't walk was a mystery. A very expensive mystery for a mother and son without health insurance.

"I got alimony, Shakes! You gotta get out and have some fun. You *can't* let me down."

"For your information," Billy said as he turned and leaned back against the mantel. "I get out plenty." His mother motored back past the doorway and gave him another delicate wave. He smiled and returned her greeting with a nod.

"Okay, big shot. It's Friday. What're you doing tonight?"

Billy paused for a moment and panicked. He glanced down at the newspaper scattered and splayed open on the floor next to his chair. His eyes locked on the front page of the entertainment section. A stylized cartoon face with movie reels for eyes stared back at him. Written across the cartoon's chest: *Tampa Film Festival*. He smiled and snatched up the paper. "I'm going to the film festival." He cradled the phone against his shoulder and rattled through the pages to the schedule. His eyes fell on an ad. "The new Wim Wenders film."

"Wenders? Good. Very creative and edgy. Should get the juices flowing again. Who you going with? It isn't that country music fan I met last time I was down there. Talk about cottage cheese and cardboard."

Billy tossed the paper onto the chair and wandered back into the kitchen. "No, someone else. You don't know her."

"She hot?"

He rolled his eyes. "Pyrotechnic."

"She gotta name?"

Billy spotted a yellow bottle of dish soap by the sink. He read the label and broke into a grin. "Joy."

"Dammit, Shakes, you're lying to me. I can tell. If you were really getting some action, your writing wouldn't be so limp-dick."

"I gotta go, Sy."

"Now go on and get out. Take some goddam risks, d'you hear me? And get to work on that rewrite. She wants the first revision by—"

Billy replaced the receiver with a gentle click and ambled over to the open window. He breathed in the warm mid-September air and watched the rays of the setting sun dance along the broad green fronds of the sago palms. The tart-sweet taste of Key lime swirled across his tongue.

Sy's right. He had to break out of this slump. He thought of his mother. Gotta break out for her sake. He felt a gentle, misty rain against his skin as the whirr of his mother's scooter echoed through the house. No, for *their* sake.

A flitting, scattering motion off to his right caught his eye. It was Mango, his next-door neighbor's macaw helping himself to the last vestiges of water in Billy's backyard birdbath. The bright green bird with pomegranate highlights was a frequent visitor.

Billy walked back over to the phone and punched in a number. "Hey Ronnie. It's me. Mango's loose again. Yeah, he's at the birdbath. No problem. See ya."

He returned to the window as Ronnie, the diesel mechanic from next door, opened the wooden gate and tiptoed into the backyard. Mango noticed him immediately, shrugged the way parrots do, and returned his attention to the cool liquid of the cement fount. Ronnie crouched low, and with a baby-style inflection that Billy thought would annoy most babies, implored the large bird to "come to Papa." Mango looked over his shoulder, shrugged again, then continued to drink. Ronnie lunged and grasped at the bird. Billy thought Mango would jettison from his perch and soar into the sky, never to be seen again. But the bird didn't jettison. And he didn't soar. He wilted and tumbled into the hands of his owner like a falling hibiscus leaf. He was a beautiful bird, but he was not a stupid bird. Mango obviously knew where the food came from.

"Got him!" Ronnie shouted as he lifted Mango toward the window.

Billy thought he detected a smile and a wink.

Can birds do that?

The gate clacked shut and Billy glanced at his watch. Oh man, I'd better hop in the shower; it's almost seven. He turned toward the bedroom when he heard the whispering whirr of his mother's electric scooter grow close. Once again, the feeling of warm, misty rain washed over his skin.

"Plans for tonight, William?" she asked as she motored into the kitchen. She pulled her electric three-wheeler around the dinette and stopped next to the refrigerator. "I thought we were going to watch some videos?"

"Not tonight, Ma. I've got—um—plans. Film Festival. Downtown."

"Oh...? But what about my condition? I can't be left alone."

Billy leaned over and placed his hands on the handlebars. "I'm the one with the condition, Ma. Remember?"

"Yes." She shrugged her shoulders. "The one no one can pronounce."

"Synesthesia."

"Yes, synesth-amnesia. Tasting color. Feeling sound. I know how you struggle, Son. I always have. But—" she paused and looked down at her legs. "It's not as bad as not being able to walk."

Billy chuckled and stood back up.

"What's so funny?"

"How about the time I caught you running across the living room?"

"When?"

"Last Tuesday." He leaned in close and grinned. "You thought someone was at the door with your Publisher's Clearing House Prize, but it was only Mr. Shapiro from across the street."

"That was a miracle," she said as she steeled her shoulders and crossed herself. "Miracles happen, y'know."

Billy nodded and smiled. He knew how difficult it had been for his mother since his father passed last year. Up until that time, this feisty little Irish woman, the former Miss Caroline O'Malley, was the picture of health. But when her lifelong love was taken from her she lost something. Billy knew she'd get it back. Caroline Shakes wouldn't give up so easily. But he knew she needed some help. Billy insisted she move in with him knowing it would only be a matter of time 'til this Celtic firebrand of a woman would return to her normal world like a roiling North Sea storm. But for now, she was here, and she was welcomed. They spent many an evening watching the old movies they both loved. Though she spent most of the time commenting on the actors and actresses and their scandalous rumors gleaned from the celebrity magazines from Connolly's newsstand back home.

"Don't worry," Billy said as he pulled out a chair and sat down. "I'll call Mrs. Donaghee. She'll be more than glad to watch a movie or two with you."

"Oh, William, you're the world's greatest son." She crossed herself again. "God's gift."

He leaned forward and kissed her gently on the cheek. "I try."

She blushed and patted his hand. Then, as if embarrassed by this moment of sentimentality, she changed the subject and asked, "So, how's the book coming?"

"I think it'll be a winner."

"Why don't you write something serious for once?"

He leaned back and folded his arms. "And what's wrong with comic-thrillers?"

"Too much killing," she said, shaking her head. "And such god-awful killing. What kind of mind thinks of trussing someone up in barbed wire and freezing them alive inside a Good Humor ice cream truck?"

"So what kind of guy shakes down Good Humor men, Ma? He deserved it! Besides, his name was Delbert "Pop" Sickle." He looked up at the ceiling and chuckled. "I thought it was pretty funny."

She shook a bony finger at her son. "You keep writing that kind of nonsense and people are just going to laugh at you."

"I write comedy, Ma, people are supposed to laugh at me."

"Hmph. Your Uncle Eddie thought he was pretty funny. He made people laugh all the time." She frowned and shook her head slowly. "Now he's living on checks from the government."

Billy stood back up. "Uncle Eddie lost a leg in Vietnam, Ma. That's why he's living on checks from the government."

"See?" she said with a vigorous nod. "That's exactly what I'm saying."

"Sheesh. I've gotta get ready." He headed to the shower and chuckled at his mother's attempt to close down an argument. Whenever she knew she was losing she'd always throw in a *that's exactly what I'm saying* as if that should silence anyone. He dried off, and as he was pulling on a pair of Levi's the buzz of his mother's scooter caught his attention. She rolled into the room. A shopping bag hung from the short handlebar.

"If you're going out on the town, you might as well put this on." She slid the bag off. "I was saving it for your birthday."

He raised his eyebrows and took the bag.

"It's a new shirt," she continued. "Got it last week when Vera took me shopping at the Outlet Mall. Go ahead, put it on." Her eyes gleamed with pride and anticipation. "It's a genuine irregular. Two for ten dollars."

He rolled his eyes and removed the shirt from the bag. Oh no, not again. His mother bought clothes as if "irregular" was a brand name. He donned the shirt and looked down: shirttails dangled well below his knees.

"What's that look for?" she asked.

He stretched his arms out. "Why do you insist on shopping down there, Ma?"

"To save money."

"How does a shirt like this save money?"

"Easy," she said beaming. "You take the shirt tails and wrap them around your crotch, then you tuck the ends into your shoes. You save money on socks and underwear."

He grimaced and slid the shirt off. "I can't wear a shirt like this."

"Why not?"

"'Cuz people will laugh at me."

"See!" she said with a smile. "That's exactly what I'm saying." She gunned the electric motor, whipped the scooter around, and with a vigorous nod she cruised out of the room.

Billy tossed the tent-like shirt across the bed, then pulled a mint green cotton one off a hanger. He slipped his sock-less feet into a pair of loafers and walked back into the living room. His mother sat peering out the blinds of the front window.

"Another scandal unfolding?" he asked with a laugh.

She jumped at the sound of his voice and the blinds fell with a rattle. "This isn't funny! You should see this!" She leaned back over the handlebars and raised a metal slat. "Just look at how that woman is dressed. There's no modesty these days. No class. No style. Why I remember…"

Billy leaned against the doorframe and folded his arms. His heart melted as he looked at the frail woman reminiscing on the scooter. The late afternoon sun fell through the blinds casting bright lines across her cotton candy-pink Walmart jogging suit. He smiled at the yellow socklets with little pom-poms hanging over the back of gleaming white tennis shoes and the full head of pearl-gray hair tucked up into a crisp, new Mets baseball cap. Ma, when it comes to style, you got it going on.

"Women who dress like that just cause problems," she said as she shifted to get a better view. "They look like those cheap fillies in the girlie magazines. Tsk. Tsk. Nothing but trouble." She turned away from the window and let the slats fall with a soft clang. "You stay away from girls like that, you hear me, Son?"

"I'll try."

She frowned and took on the tone of motherly wisdom. "Remember what happened to your cousin Stevie. He spent way too much time in those girlie bars."

"Sports bars."

"Maybe so. But sports bars have cheerleaders in skimpy skirts."

"They don't have cheerleaders in sports—"

She cut him off. "If Stevie hadn't spent so much time in those girlie bars he wouldn't have gotten that dreadful SUV disease."

"SUV isn't a disease, Ma. It's a type of truck. Stevie got a new truck."

"See? That's exactly what I'm saying." She returned to the window and glanced between the slats. "Tsk, tsk, tsk, " she said shaking her head. "Will you just look at that?"

The doorbell rang and Billy's mother pulled away from her perch and puttered over to the door. She pulled it open and screamed with delight. A woman who was nearly as wide as she was tall greeted her with open arms. Fully erect, she nearly stood eye to eye with her friend on the scooter. The woman's bulbous, rosy-red face folded up into a smile. "Hello-o-o-o!" The singsong sound of her voice made Billy jump as if he just stepped on a bed of nails. A breeze blew past the short woman and filled the room with an aroma of carnations and liniment.

"Vera!"

"Caroline!"

"Come in, come in! My, my, look at you!" She closed the door behind her. "It's been so long!"

"Only yesterday," Billy chuckled as he took Mrs. Donaghee's more-like-a-bathrobe-than-a-coat and hung it in the hall closet.

Mrs. Donaghee removed a scarf from light blue hair piled high on her head like a loosely woven Easter egg basket. "Did you see that woman next door?"

"Boy, did I," Caroline said as she scowled and glanced at the blinds.

Vera snorted and shoved the scarf into the front pocket of her avocado green stretch slacks, creating a tumor-like bulge on her broad hip. "The women these days. No class." She stepped toward Billy. "And how's the literary world's most eligible bachelor?" She reached out and pinched his cheek. "Why if you weren't Caroline's own flesh and blood I think I could cover you in a million kisses."

Billy pulled himself away from her crab pincer-like fingers. "I'm out of here," he said as he leaned down and kissed the top of his mother's ball cap. "You two ladies have a good time. I've got some macaroni and cheese warming in the oven."

"Billy makes wonderful macaroni and cheese," his mother whispered to her friend. "It's like something from the Waldorf."

Mrs. Donaghee nodded as if hearing top-secret government information. "Mmm. Sounds delish!" she whispered.

Billy stepped past the giddy women, grabbed his keys off the end table and bounded out the front door. As he walked toward his midnight blue Jetta, he glanced over at the object of his mother's disgust. Ronnie's thirty-something wife stood in front of their home watering the small, thatched lawn with a garden hose. She held a thumb over the nozzle creating a haphazard spray. Her faded denim short-shorts and a white button-down shirt loosely tied just below her bra-less breasts made for an interesting and provocative PG-13 lawn display. Two twelve-year-old boys circled the block on their bikes hoping that at least one piece of fabric would give way.

"Big night tonight, Billy?" she asked with a wink.

"Film Fest, Danielle. Downtown. Wim Wenders," Billy replied as he unlocked the door.

"Vivienne, you say? Lucky, girl!" Her thumb slipped and a blast of water shot out, soaking her blouse. "Cripes!" she cried as her nipples stiffened and strained against the nearly transparent fabric. She threw down the hose and ran her hands over her sopping wet blouse. "Oh, just look at me!"

Billy obliged until he heard the sound of metal scraping metal. He looked up as Gordon Cromer, twelve-year-old number one, clipped the rear fender of Jay Summerlin, twelve-year-old number two. The bikes tangled and the two boys hit the asphalt, faces first, with a bone-jarring crunch. Billy sprinted into the street to the mound of aluminum and twisted limbs. Danielle yelped at the sight and ran to join them. With each bounding step the knot on her blouse loosened and by time she reached the boys her breasts, unknown to her, were nearly fully exposed and glistening in the late afternoon sun.

"Are you guys all right?" Billy asked as he knelt down beside them.

"Oh, man, did you see that?" Gordon asked as he sat up. "That lady's shirt turned invisible. Why I —" He stopped short as he came face to face with what would most likely be two of the most beautiful breasts that he would ever see in his life.

"Oh boy, did I," moaned Jay. He rolled over and took in the heavenly sight.

"I better get some bandages and ice," Danielle said as she started to turn.

Gordon grabbed the back pocket of her shorts. "No, no. Let Mr. Billy get it."

Jay vigorously nodded in agreement. "His house is closer."

Billy returned with a baggie full of ice to see Danielle kneeling over the boys. Each one pointed to suspected points of injury for her to inspect.

"Seems as if everything is under control here. I better be going."

"Thanks, Billy." Danielle stood and twirled a strand of hair with her finger. "Ronnie's working tonight. Maybe we can think of something to do."

"You can start by tying up your blouse. I think these boys have seen enough for today."

Danielle looked down, blushed and quickly tied up her shirt. The two boys glanced at Billy and scowled.

15

"I guess we're okay now," Gordon growled. He stood and snatched up his bicycle.

Jay struggled to his feet, wiped his nose with his forearm and steadied his bike. He bent down and picked something off the pavement. "Hey, Gordon. Is this your tooth?"

Billy climbed into his Jetta and backed out of the driveway. He looked in the rearview mirror to see the pouting face of his lovelorn neighbor and the upraised middle fingers of two prepubescent Casanovas. He stifled a laugh as he turned right on Seminole and headed downtown. Well, Sy, he thought, you want excitement? Hell, I can't even get out of the front yard without some serious sex and violence. What on earth could top this?

CHAPTER 3

"I**T'S FRIDAY**, Eden girl. Let's head downtown for a drink. Or two. Or three." Ginny Wheeler grabbed her purse from beneath the counter and danced across the floor to the front door of the shop.

Eden Myers smiled at her animated friend. Her identical twin. Identical twins from different mothers. She shook her head and laughed to herself. That's my Ginny. Twice divorced. Enough attitude to pave an interstate. My, my, how do you do it? The first marriage to an investment banker, now living in South America with $20 million dollars skimmed off his retiree clients. The last marriage to a respected gynecologist caught trading drugs for sexual favors from a cadre of nubile teenage girls. She chuckled. Talk about a good half-dozen episodes of Jerry Springer. Ginny lost the beach house and the one on the bay. The BMWs? Gone, too. Now she lives in a one-bedroom apartment above a garage in a transitional neighborhood and drives a '92 Toyota Corolla. Sometimes she can get the air to work.

"I don't know," she said. "I really should be getting home. Robbie will be waiting for supper."

"Screw him. Let him get his own damn supper for once." Ginny grabbed her by the arm. "C'mon, you know I don't like going to bars alone. It looks like I'm desperate."

"But Ginny, you *are* desperate."

"Am not." She released Eden's arm. "Desperate people take desperate measures. This isn't desperate. I'm going barhopping. That's not a sign of desperation." She paused and searched her friend's eyes. "Is it?"

Eden folded her arms and smirked.

"Okay. Maybe *it is* a little desperate. But if I'm going to find one of the Great Ones, I'm going to need a little back up." She grasped Eden's shoulders. "Besides, you owe me. Big time."

She backed out of Ginny's grasp. "Owe you? For what?"

"For all the advice I give you about Robbie and your jive-ass relationship." She threw her arms in the air. "Do you know how much I'm saving you in therapy bills alone? Hundreds. Probably thousands. C'mon. I want to get there early enough to get a parking space."

Eden shrugged. "Okay, but at least let me give him a call to let him know." She pulled out her cell phone and pushed the memory button.

"Hey, Robbie, it's me. I'm gonna be late… With Ginny…Downtown…I don't know…Open a can of tuna and make yourself a sandwich…"

Ginny glared at her. Arms crossed. Foot tapping the floor. "C'mon," she hissed as she tugged Eden's sleeve. "We gotta go."

Eden held up a finger and mouthed 'okay' then turned her attention back to the cell phone. "Opener's in the top drawer. . . next to the dishwasher…bread's in the fridge…"

Ginny stomped her foot then yanked the phone from Eden's hand. "Gimme that thing!" She held it to her mouth like a walkie-talkie and barked, "Gotta go. Bye."

She folded the phone and proudly presented it to Eden who stood with mouth agape. "Oh, don't look so morose. He'll cope. Let's rock. The Great Ones await us." She grabbed her arm and pulled her toward the door. "We'll take your car."

"Um. Okay."

"Great!" She said throwing open the front door. "Gimme the keys. I'll drive."

The 'Great Ones' was a concept Ginny and Eden picked up from one of their favorite old movies, *A Bronx Tale*. In this life you are only allowed three really great romances. That's it, just three.

"I got a good feeling about tonight," Ginny said as she hopped behind the wheel of Eden's Jeep Cherokee. "I read my horoscope today. Said us Geminis can expect the unexpected." She pulled her seatbelt across and adjusted the rearview mirror. "Tonight my dreams are gonna come true."

"Gemini?" Eden asked as she settled into the passenger seat. "But your birthday's in November."

Ginny tossed her hair back and shoved the key into the ignition. "Doesn't matter. I read all the horoscopes then pick out the ones I really like." She turned the key and revved the engine. She glanced at her friend. "You buckled up?"

Before Eden could answer, Ginny threw the gear into drive and burst out into the rush hour traffic like buckshot. "Yee-haa!" she shouted as she slapped the steering wheel.

They careened through Hyde Park toward downtown and Eden thought about how many of the Great Ones they'd already had. She knew Ginny's two ex-husbands didn't qualify, and she realized her fiancé Robbie probably wouldn't make the list either. She watched a tall ship drifting south toward the Sunshine Skyway. Was there anyone else in their past that qualified as a Great One? Will we meet one tonight?

Ginny pulled the Cherokee into a parking space and slammed on the brakes.

"Let's go," she said as she hopped out. Eden opened her door and reluctantly followed.

Ginny slipped her arm in Eden's and skipped down the sidewalk toward the oh-so-hip Fly Bar like she was going down the yellow brick road. "The Great Ones await."

* * *

"What do you think about that hunk over there?" Eden nodded to a late twenty-something in a blue polo shirt and freshly pressed khakis. He leaned on the bar and nursed what looked like a Manhattan.

"Hunk? Hunk of what?" Ginny eyed the young man and pointed to a belt that missed not one, but two loops. "Oops, guess mama didn't dress you right this morning."

"Then how about that guy over there?" Eden pointed to a tall blonde in a group of impeccably dressed young men. His broad shoulders shook as he laughed and traded barbs with his friends. Her eyes briefly locked on his tight buns. She blushed and averted her gaze, then stole another glance. "Now that's what *I* call a hunk."

"Maybe." Ginny wrinkled her brow and grinned. "Except for two things. His personality and his voice."

"Wait a minute." Eden set her drink down. "OK, I can see how a tall, strapping, Scandinavian god might not appeal to *you*. But how can you tell what his personality's like just from looking at him?"

"Already know him," she replied then sipped her cosmopolitan. "His name is Roger Belkins. Roger Welkin Belkins."

Eden coughed into her drink then said, "Belkins? Why that's not even close to Scandinavian-"

"I used to work with him," Ginny continued. "Couple of years ago. Between my first and second marriage. He took me out once. Promised he would take me to the stars. He took me to the stars, all right." She paused for a moment then looked down at her drink and chuckled. "We wound up going to a lecture on cosmology at the University."

"Yikes." Eden looked back at the bar. But those buns! She looked away.

"Yikes is right." Ginny stirred her drink. "He kept hounding me so I told him I was just diagnosed with Merkle's disease."

"Merkle's disease? What's that?"

"I don't know." She smiled a devilish smile. "I made it up."

"Ginny, you're horrible."

"Hey, it worked." She picked up her drink then grabbed Eden's hand. "Don't look now, but he's coming over."

Roger Welkin Belkins swaggered up to the table. He ran a hand through thick blond hair and thrust his hips forward. The girls exchanged glances at this primitive courting gesture and giggled.

"Hey, Ginny, long time no see."

Eden's mouth dropped open. That voice! A cross between Porky Pig and Billy Bob Thornton. She raised a hand to her lips and stifled a laugh as Roger continued, "You sure look great. Especially after your bout with that disease."

"Hello, Robert," Ginny said flatly.

"Roger."

"Oh, yeah, Roger." She winked at Eden.

He pulled up a nearby chair and sat down. "Mind if I join you?"

"As a matter of fact, we do." Ginny glanced around the crowded room. "We're waiting on two guys."

He scooted his chair closer and looked from one girl to the other. "Anyone I know?"

"It's certainly not Porky or Billy Bob ," Eden whispered, hiding a smile behind her margarita.

"Probably not," Ginny replied as she continued to search the room. "They're two of the Great Ones."

Roger picked up his drink and leaned back in his chair. "Great Ones?" He took a sip. "What's that all about?"

Ginny looked down at her drink and sighed. "You wouldn't understand."

"Hey, listen," Roger said with a wink. "I understand." He pushed his chair back and rose. "Now that you're feeling better, Ginny, maybe you and I can go out again. There's a great documentary on the Industrial Age showing at the Museum of Science and Industry this weekend. It oughta be a hoot."

"I don't think so, Rodney."

"Roger."

"Yeah, that's right. Roger."

He turned his attention to Eden and rested his hand on her shoulder. She stiffened at his uninvited touch.

"How 'bout your friend here? Maybe she'd like to join me for an exciting evening of—"

Eden cut him off. "I'm spoken for, but thanks anyway."

"That's right, you're waiting for one of the "Great Ones," too."

"Yep."

Roger shrugged his broad shoulders. "Your loss, ladies." He sauntered back to the bar where he was greeted with guffaws and a few punches on the arm.

Eden turned to Ginny. "*Oughta be a hoot?*"

Ginny took a generous sip and said, "What'd I tell you?"

"Definitely not one of the Great Ones." Eden shook her head. "And that voice! Porky Pig meets Billy Bob Thornton."

"Really? I was thinking Donald Duck meets Jimmy Carter."

Eden coughed in her drink then wiped her nose and mouth with a cocktail napkin.

Ginny raised her glass and added, "Here's to the Great Ones."

"To the Great Ones," Eden said as she raised her own glass and glanced around the room. "Wherever the heck they're hiding."

* * *

Billy pulled up in front of the Tampa Museum of Art. A colorful twenty-foot banner fluttered in the breeze announcing the new Wim Wenders film. A hand-lettered sandwich sign out front announced that the show was sold out.

Damn, just missed it! He pulled the car away from the curb and turned left on Ashley toward the Tampa Theatre. The marquee advertised two films he hadn't heard of. It'll do, I guess. At least the Festival after-party will be held there. That should make for some interesting conversation.

He pulled into a parking lot across the street and fell in with a crowd spilling out of the Fly Bar and heading to the historic theater. The conversation around him was lively, boisterous and obviously alcohol infused. His toe caught the heel of one of the identical twins in front of him. The girl barely glanced over her shoulder and barked. "Watch it, bud!"

"Sorry."

"I'm sure he didn't mean it, Ginny," the other girl whispered.

He backed off as the crowd approached the theater.

Yes, he thought, as he stepped up to the ticket booth and slid a crumpled ten-dollar bill to the attendant. This should make for some interesting conversation.

* * *

Billy wandered into the lobby after the end of the second film. He waited a minute or two for his eyes to adjust then walked up to the bar and ordered a glass of white wine. High above him, little white lights twinkled in the sky-blue plaster ceiling. Over in the corner, two guys with skinny black ties and Buddy Holly glasses hovered over a stack of electronic equipment. Thumping, bass-heavy trip hop emanated from the large speakers that flanked them and the monotonous drone hurt Billy's scalp. He noticed that the two men were the only ones who seemed to be enjoying their selection of music - like the aural equivalent of family vacation slides. He wandered over to the far end of the lobby and joined a black-clad group of colorfully tattooed people. The glint of numerous piercings sparkled like sequins on a movie star's gown. They stood in a circle and discussed the film in overly articulate voices. But instead of symbolism, camera angles and pacing, they talked about the style of clothing and lack of gratuitous sex and violence. Billy sipped his wine and listened in silence. When there was a lull in conversation Billy piped in and offered, "I thought the last film was very Capra-esque."

"What exactly does 'Capra-esque' mean?" asked the young man to his left. He was a head taller than Billy and his tousled ebony hair looked like an explosion on his head. A leather jacket hung from his bony frame. *Dixie Discount Air* read the embroidered patch to the right of his lapel. And below that, a tag: *Manager.*

Hmm, Billy thought, Dixie Discount Air, one of Florida's most notorious airlines. Just read about another near miss at Tampa International. Well, it seems they certainly don't spare any expense on staffing. He scanned the circle of pale, blank faces and tasted chalk. "It reminded me of Capra. Frank Capra. You know, the director."

"Is he new?" asked a woman with flamingo-pink hair. Her arms were completely covered in a swirl of tattoos.

"Um, no. He's a legend, actually."

"Wasn't she that famous tennis player who went bonkers back in the day?" chimed in another girl whose fluorescent green hair fought for the attention her friend's hair demanded. When the others stared at her with a look of surprise she added, "My parents made me take tennis lessons at the club when I was a little kid."

"No, you're thinking of Capriati. Jennifer Capriati," Billy explained.

"Didn't she get stabbed?" asked a chubby man with multiple facial piercings. Billy watched the young man sip his drink and wondered if he would leak. When the others looked at the boy with similar looks of disbelief he said, "My parents made me take lessons, too."

"You mean the director got stabbed?" asked the flamingo girl. "That is way too cool!"

"No," explained Billy. "That was Monica Seles, another tennis player."

The girl pouted then sipped her drink.

Billy sighed and continued. "I'm talking about Frank Capra, the famous director."

"Hmm," said the tall man. "He can't be too famous. *I've* never heard of him." He raised his glass and took a sip.

"Me neither," added the chubby boy. The girls nodded in agreement.

"Never heard of Capra?" Billy asked. "What about *Meet John Doe?*"

"John who?" the tall man asked.

"Or *Mr. Smith Goes to Washington* or *It's a Wonderful Life?*"

His question was met by a chorus of shrugs.

"Oh, come on now. What about the celebration of the human spirit and all that?"

Silence.

Billy was taken aback by their complete lack of film history knowledge. Of course there were always folks who showed up at events simply because they were events. No intention of seeing the film, appreciating the art, enjoying the music. They were there to be seen—the foci of attention. Obviously he had stumbled upon one such group. Generation Y, look at me.

They all stood motionless as if time had come to a screeching halt. The quiet was broken only by the occasional clink of ice melting and slipping in their drink glasses. The surreal scene reminded Billy of old Jerry Lewis movies where the actors froze after Jerry created a major faux pas. He glanced around at the blank faces and felt the awkwardness of being older and well informed. A restroom door opened and yet another black-clad girl emerged. She locked eyes with his.

"Billy! Is that you?!"

"Nicole?" Billy asked in surprise. Yes. Nicole, the artist. She attended his lecture at a writer's festival in St. Pete a couple of years ago. She cornered him after his talk then followed-up with what seemed like hundreds of gushing e-mails. Then she started attending all of his signings and lectures. Clearwater, Sarasota, Orlando. When his mother moved in, it curtailed his schedule and he hadn't seen her around for a few months. In fact, the last time he saw her was at an art opening in NoHo back in early spring. Nicole was one of eight exhibiting artists. He vaguely remembered her piece. Something created from two-by-fours, bent aluminum tent poles, and Jell-O. Multimedia she explained to him at the time. No, he'd seen her since then. At the Whole Foods, Walgreen's, that gas station on Fowler, even the driver's license bureau. What are the odds?

"Fancy meeting you here," she said with a wink and took her drink from the chubby boy.

Billy managed a smile and raised his glass in greeting. "Long time no see. Still working on that Jell-O thing?"

"Nah. I've grown so far beyond *that*." She flipped her jet-black hair off her shoulder. "I'm into roofing tar and broken glass. Now I become one with the art."

Billy raised his eyebrows then wished he hadn't.

"See," the chubby boy explained, "she mops gobs of roofing tar on a four-by-eight sheet of plywood and sprinkles it with shards of broken glass. Then she strips butt-naked and rolls across it."

The others in the group gaped at him in amazement. He met their questioning gaze and murmured. "Least that's what she told me." He spit a broken ice cube back into his glass. "She won't actually let me watch her work."

"Pierce is right," she said, nodding to the boy. "I take off all my clothes then roll around on broken glass and get jagged little cuts all over me." She raised her glass and took a long, slow sip. "My blood mixes with the tar and I become one with the art."

Billy shivered. "Sounds painful."

"Art *is* pain," she said as she stared at him over the rim of her glass. A dark, penetrating stare. She shook her hair back. "Why don't you come by and watch me work. I could always use an assistant. You know, someone to help me out of my clothes and rub me down with mineral spirits when I'm done." She closed her eyes and seemed to relish the thought of Billy's hands caressing her body. She opened her eyes. "Roofing tar's a bitch to get off your skin." She looked down and picked at one of the small dark scabs that were scattered like freckles across her milk-white arms. Then her visage suddenly changed to giddy as if someone had flipped a switch. She looked around at the group. "So, what are you guys talking about?"

"That stupid movie," the flamingo girl said smirking at Billy. "Did you know it was 'Capra-esque'?"

Nicole scrunched up her nose. "The old-school tennis player?"

"As I was trying to explain to your friends," Billy said, "Capra was a—"

"Well, I thought it was *very* Capra-esque." A sultry voice washed in from behind him and caressed his shoulders.

He turned and caught his breath as the woman stepped closer. Mahogany hair—vibrant, wild and untamed. Sparkling blue eyes. Broad ruby lips revealing pearl-bright teeth. Mmm...Peppermint. Billy's eyes roamed over her lithe figure and feasted on her. Bronze, glowing skin. He savored the flavor—crème brûlée. Is she Caribbean? The lilt in her voice seemed to indicate that she was.

"The way the film explored the innate goodness of the human spirit," she continued. "The conquest of the self and the elevation of virtue. I thought it was the perfect homage to Capra."

My, my, my, he thought as he savored the cool flavor of her eyes. A clean refreshing taste washed over his tongue. Pinot Grigio? Perhaps.

"Look," she said, interrupting his silent veneration. "You're almost out of wine. Let me get you another glass." She put her arm through his and led him across the lobby toward the bar.

"But...Billy..." Nicole pleaded after them. "What about *me*?"

He looked back over his shoulder. "Don't worry. We'll catch up at the next poetry slam. I promise."

Nicole drained her glass then turned to her friends and scowled. "Let's blow this hell-hole. We saw the movie and it sucked farts." She slammed her glass on a nearby table and stormed toward the door. "It all sucks!" she shouted to the theater's starlit ceiling.

The chubby boy took one last sip. "Well," he mumbled. "*I've* never been sucked."

Billy watched the black-clad group tumble out the door and disappear into the night.

"Friends of yours?" the bronzed woman asked.

"Met them tonight."

"Didn't look like your type anyway."

"And what exactly is my type?"

"Let's refill our drinks and we can discuss it." She led him up to the bar. "What's your pleasure?

"Is that a trick question?" he replied with a gleam in his eye.

"What do you mean by that?" she asked, but her coy demeanor told him she knew exactly what he meant.

"I could go for something light. Something sweet. Something. . .blue."

She cocked her head to one side. "Something blue?"

"I'll take the Pinot Grigio."

She turned to the bartender. "Pinot Grigio. Two, please."

They found two empty chairs by a front window. Outside, a river of people drifted by to cars that would take them to homes in the suburbs.

Billy sighed as he watched the exodus. "It's not like in the old days. No one lives downtown anymore."

"Do you?" She sipped her wine.

"No, I have a bungalow in Seminole Heights. You?"

"Davis Island."

"Nice." Actually, more than nice, he thought. The Island was home to some of the city's priciest real estate. Especially by the Bay. Old money. Much of it earned when the city gushed money from the nearby phosphate mines, cigar factories and local land speculators. But this woman doesn't look like Davis Island stock. Complexion is too dark. Too easy going and playful.

She shrugged. "I guess it's ok." The woman crossed her long, lean legs. The hem of the summer dress slid up her shimmering thighs.

Billy struggled to maintain eye contact. "So, you admire Frank Capra?"

"Yes, but he's not my favorite. I really enjoy Otto Preminger, and, of course, there's Bergman and Hitchcock."

"No kidding?" He leaned forward. "Me, too. In fact, I appreciate all the classics. Especially those in black and white. I find them less distracting than the color films."

"You mean you love the subtle moods the black-and-white genre evinces?"

"No." He turned and looked out the window. "It's just that I have this. . .condition."

"Condition? What kind of condition?"

Billy hesitated and glanced down at his drink. An awkward moment of silence filled the air between them. The woman leaned back

27

in her chair and crossed her arms. She studied him for a moment then raised her eyebrows as if to say, "Well?"

"My senses are mixed up." He paused. "I taste color. I feel sound."

A look of concern crossed her face. Or was it empathy?

She sat in silence and waited for him to continue.

"It's very rare and misunderstood," he explained. "Hell, I'm not sure if I completely understand it." He waited for a moment. Gauging her reaction. Was that a smirk? A raised eyebrow?

She nodded thoughtfully. "Hmm, I see." She leaned forward and gently touched his arm. "You have synesthesia."

He started and sat upright. "You've heard of it?"

She nodded. "Of course. It sounds fascinating and you must tell me all about it." She looked down at her diamond-encrusted lady's Rolex. "But not tonight. It's getting late."

Billy glanced at his own watch, a Seiko from Target. It was nearly one a.m.

"I'll walk you to your car."

"I wouldn't have it any other way, Mr.—"

"Shakes. Billy Shakes." He offered his hand as they rose. "And your name wouldn't happen to be Joy, would it?"

"Why do you ask?"

Billy chuckled. "Just curious."

"No. My name is Maureen." She cradled his hand in hers. "Valentino."

"My pleasure, Ms. Valentino."

"Maureen," she said with a scolding smile as her thumb caressed the back of his hand.

"Maureen it is." He held the door open and they stepped out into the cool Florida night.

"I hope I didn't spoil your evening. Were you expecting to find Joy?"

Billy grinned. "Aren't we all?"

"Yes," she replied pensively. "I suppose we are."

They walked along the now nearly deserted sidewalk, the air unusually thick with humidity for this time of year. The cadence of their footsteps echoed off the glass and brick of dark and empty storefronts. They drew close. Their shoulders occasionally touched and it gave him chills.

"We must have lunch sometime," she said as they arrived at her Jaguar. Billy admired the flawless, classic curves. Streetlights glinted off the soft, pewter-like finish. He tasted something bittersweet. *Sloe gin?*

He took a step closer and placed his hands on her hips. He was glad when she didn't recoil from his touch. "Do you really have to go? I know this great little place over on Armenia. We could drop in, have a few drinks, then—"

"Why don't I give you a call?" she said with a coy smile. "What's your cell phone number?" She pulled a fountain pen and a small leather notebook from her purse.

"I don't have a cell phone."

"Oh?"

Billy shrugged. "I guess I'm the last of the Luddites. Sometimes I feel like I'm riding a little red tricycle on the information superhighway. My laptop is a '96 Apple. I was still buying record albums in the late 80s. I don't have cable." He looked around, leaned in and confessed in a whisper, "And I still lick 'peel and stick' postage stamps."

Maureen tossed her head back and laughed. "My word, you are a Luddite! But you do have a car, don't you? Or are you one of those horse-and-buggy types?"

Billy chuckled. "Of course, I'm not that primitive."

"Good. Now about lunch, Mr. Billy Shakes the Luddite. Any days open next week?"

"How's Tuesday? I'll meet you at Rennie's Pickapepper in west Ybor. Delicious Caribbean fare."

"I adore Caribbean!"

Bingo. Knew it.

"I'm from St. Kitts." She playfully poked him in the chest. "So, it better be good."

"It's authentic all right. Rennie's from Jamaica and he's got the cuisine down pat. I often go there for inspiration."

She cocked her head to one side. "Are you a chef?"

"Writer. I find a lot of character possibilities in places like Rennie's."

Maureen folded her arms and leaned back against the rear fender. "A writer, you say? Interesting."

He opened the car door and placed his hand against the small of her back. She slipped into the driver's seat and turned the key in the ignition.

"A writer and a film buff with synesthesia," she said as the Jaguar idled and purred. "I believe we'll have much to talk about at lunch, Mr. Billy Shakes."

At that, she closed the door and pulled away from the curb. Crimson taillights reflected off the shimmering, dew-covered street then disappeared in the rising mist. He stood silently for a moment then turned and walked to his own car around the corner. Well, he thought, I think I just met the woman of my dreams.

* * *

Eden Myers drifted across a barren, hardscrabble field. The few tufts of prairie grass that struggled up from the earth seemed half real. More like white filament than something organic. Her nightgown dragged the ground and kicked up wisps of dust as she moved forward. The towering specter ahead motioned to her. Imploring her to follow. The spirit reminded her of a photograph negative. Details hidden and obscure. But she could make out six—or was it eight?—terrible wings. Eyes that should have been black glowed with a brilliance equal to the stars. She wanted to turn away and run. But where? She looked over her shoulder at barren fields that faded into the distance until they melded with the heavy sky. She turned and continued, lured by the spirit's siren song. It led her to the edge of a cliff. They stood over what appeared to be an entirely different world. Above them the grey sky was swallowed up into a brilliant blue. Below, sunlight danced across a rolling field of emerald treetops. Snow-covered mountains rose like titans in the distance. Beyond that—a shimmering, crystalline sea.

"It's yours," the spirit whispered. "Step out and receive it."

Eden looked down and shuddered. The façade of the cliff tumbled thousands of feet to the valley below. "I—I—can't."

"You must." The spirit began to shimmer and fade.

"Don't leave me here." Eden glanced back at the withered landscape. "Not alone!"

"You won't be alone," the spirit whispered. "Dive and fly. Others will find you in flight." Then, like a candle that had reached its end, the specter vanished.

"Don't leave me here!" Eden shouted to the empty sky. "Don't leave me! Don't—"

She bolted upright in her bed. Shaking. Covered in sweat. She glanced at the clock on her night table. Two a.m.

Eden ran a trembling hand through her hair. "Oh, my god," she said through heaving breaths. She slid her feet off the side of the bed, swallowed hard and stared at the ceiling. "Oh my god, this has *got* to stop."

A hand grabbed her shoulder and she jumped.

"Another nightmare?" Robbie asked, his voice filled with sleep. "Come to Papa." He reached around, grabbed her breast and pulled her back down on the bed. "It's just a stupid dream."

She tore his hand away from her chest. "What are you doing in my bed?"

"The couch was getting lumpy."

"Aaargh." She pried herself away from his grasp and pulled the covers over her.

"Yes," she mumbled to herself as she nudged Robbie's semi-comatose form toward the edge of the bed with her hip. "This has *got* to stop."

CHAPTER 4

BILLY leaned against a large plate glass window in front of Rennie's Pickapepper Cafe. The midday sun warmed his skin. He glanced at his watch. Ten past noon.

I wonder if Maureen will show up. He looked up and down the busy street. A bike messenger sailed by with a whoosh. He checked his watch again. Eleven past. Well, it sure wouldn't be the first time someone seemed fascinated about my condition. Then doubts would rise and suspicion would set in. Story of my life.

He dug his hands into his pockets and watched the midday traffic rumble by. Exhaust assaulted his nostrils. He pulled his hand out of his pocket and glanced at his watch again. Twelve thirteen. He looked down and kicked a dented Dr. Pepper bottle cap across the sidewalk. It rolled to the curb then teetered on the edge before falling into the gutter. Would she actually give this thing a shot? Man, I hope so.

Across the street, a curbside hot dog vendor began to scuffle with what appeared to be a used car salesman. The salesman was nearly twice the size of his adversary.

"You don't know shit," cried the vendor as he shoved the obese salesman away from his stainless steel cart.

"I'm telling you, butt-for-brains, this ain't Dijon!" The salesman turned away and hurled his hot dog over a chain link fence. It landed with a splat on the cracked windshield of an abandoned Yugo.

The vendor took two menacing steps forward. "You owe me for that dog!"

The used car salesman glanced back over his shoulder. "Put it on my tab, Peewee."

"I'll take it out of your goddam hide!" The vendor leapt over his cart and on the salesman's back and the two men tumbled to the ground in a heap.

Billy clenched his fists and cheered for the vendor as they rolled across the sidewalk, off the curb and into the street. Then he caught himself. Here I am again watching the action from a distance. Always in the distance. He shook his head. Man, I can get this down on paper; I just can't live it. He watched the vendor drag the salesman back onto the sidewalk by his tie and Billy was engaged again.

"That's it old man. Whoop his slimy used-car butt!"

The vendor grabbed a fistful of dogs off the cart and shoved them into the gagging salesman's mouth. Billy thrust a victorious fist into the air when a smoky voice interrupted his excitement.

"It's so good to see you again, Mr. Shakes."

Billy froze at the familiar sound. Again, his shoulders felt a gentle caress. The shouting from across the street faded up into the noon sky.

He turned around to see Maureen strolling up the sidewalk. Her steps were long, fluid and full of grace. She wore a pale green skirt and a bleached-white cotton top. The simple outfit complemented her soft, bronze skin. Her hair pulled back. Her eyes seemed to dance.

He caught his breath. My word, she looks even more radiant now than in the dreams I've been having since that first night we met. "Hi, Maureen." He smiled and extended his hand. "I'm so glad you could make it."

She ignored his outstretched hand and moved in close. "I've been thinking a lot about you, Billy." She softly kissed his cheek. Her warm lips lingered. He returned her sensual greeting with a nervous smile.

"What's all the commotion across the street?" she asked with a nod.

"Just your typical proletarian class struggle. Blue-collar versus sleaze-collar."

A resounding 'You want some Dijon with that, fat boy?!' echoed off the midday traffic and bounced across the street as the vendor crammed two more dogs into the strained, red face of the salesman.

Maureen nodded. "I hope that hot dog guy wins."

"He will."

"How do you know?"

Billy grinned. "I can taste it."

He put his arm around Maureen's waist and opened the front door where a cheerful hostess greeted them with a "Welcome to Rennie's" and guided them to a small table for two. Next to them a four-by-eight-foot painting hung by chains from the ceiling. It was one of a dozen suspended and scattered throughout the room as makeshift dividers between the tables.

Maureen seated herself and looked at the large canvas beside them. Fluorescent green palm trees flanked a yellow shotgun cracker shack. "Interesting."

"This used to be an automobile repair shop," Billy explained as he pointed to the bank of four garage doors across the front and four across the back. A cool breeze blew through and caused the paintings to swing gently back and forth. "When the weather's nice, Rennie has the busboys roll up the doors."

"I see," Maureen said as the painting brushed up against her shoulder.

"Told you, it's a great place for inspiration."

She pushed the canvas away and glanced around the room. "I can see why."

In addition to the enormous paintings suspended from the ceiling, several dozen smaller canvases hung on the exposed red brick walls. The lunchtime crowd was an unusual mix: business people, blue-collar workers, bohemians and, according to the slogans splashed across their t-shirts, a few anarchists. A wooden bar the length of a Greyhound bus filled one end of the restaurant and it was packed two deep. At the other end, a steam-filled, bustling kitchen spewed a torrent of glorious aromas into the dining room - roasted red peppers, coconut, garlic, cumin and allspice. Waiters, waitresses and busboys entered and exited the two kitchen doors like the precisely animated figurines of a Bavarian cuckoo clock. An outdoor seating area lay just beyond the open back doors where chatty diners sat at stainless steel café tables under billowing umbrellas the size of flying saucers. Back inside, the sensual voice of Tanya St. Val drifted down from hidden speakers like a misty Caribbean rain.

Maureen picked up her menu. "What do you recommend?"

"I usually order the skirt steak with mango salsa," Billy replied.
She set her menu back on the table. " I'll have the same."

A cheerful teenage waitress approached their table. "Hey, Billy!"

Billy froze. He recognized the jet-black hair and pale white skin
immediately. "Nicole? I didn't know you worked here."

"Just started." She nibbled the end of her pen. "I'd see you here a
lot, working on your stuff. Right over there." She nodded to a table
across the room. "So I told myself, 'What the hell? If I'm gonna hang
out here, might as well get paid for it.' Makes sense, huh?"

It didn't make sense to him. Not even remotely so. He was con-
vinced that the young girl looming before him was more than the
tortured and angst-ridden artist she played herself to be. He decided
to make light of the situation while determining to find a new café
to frequent. "Guess you're keeping busy then?" Billy did his best to
sound interested.

She wiped her brow and looked around the room. "Ha! What do
you think?"

"Busy place like this must keep you on your toes," Maureen
offered.

Billy wasn't surprised as Nicole ignored Maureen's attempt at civil-
ity. The young girl's dark eyes remained riveted to him. He instinctively leaned back further in his chair, adding a few more inches of
distance from her.

"It was great seeing you at the Film Fest last week. Too bad you had
to leave." She cast a snide glance toward Maureen, then continued,
"Say, are you going to the slam at Sacred Grounds next Friday?"

"Thinking about it."

"Another chap book in the pipeline? Cuz let me know and I'll be
the first to buy one."

Maureen smiled and chimed in, "I'm afraid that won't be
possible."

"Oh?" Nicole planted her hands on her hips and turned to Maureen. "And why's that?"

"I already have an order in for the first ten copies."

Billy turned to her and raised his eyebrows.

"Remember, Billy?" She pointed out with a slight nod.

"Oh, uh, yeah."

Nicole pouted. "Rats."

Billy turned his attention back to their waitress intending to placate the situation. "You two haven't been introduced. Nicole, this is Maureen."

The young girl smirked. "Hey."

"Nice to meet you, Nicole," Maureen said. "I hear you're a big fan of Billy's."

"Oh, yes!" Her eyes lit up like Fourth-of-July sparklers. "I buy all his stuff and go to all his readings."

Maureen leaned forward on her elbows and stared at Billy. "So do I."

He raised his eyebrows again. Oh, really?

"That's funny." Nicole scratched her head with her pen. "I've never seen you at one."

"I try to stay in the background. After all, it is Billy's night."

Nicole nodded slowly. "Makes sense. . .I guess." She shifted her eyes from Maureen to Billy then back to Maureen. "So are you two, like, a couple?"

"Well, not exact—" But Billy couldn't finish.

"I adore this man." Maureen gave him a look that reminded him of a cheetah stalking its prey. He nearly fell off his chair.

"Why don't you order," she purred. Or was that a growl?

He composed himself and turned back to Nicole. "We'll have two skirt steaks with mango salsa, grilled corn and a pitcher of Sangria."

"No problem," Nicole mumbled as she scribbled on her pad. She turned with a sulk, then bobbed and weaved through the crowd like a slow motion human pinball.

Billy shrugged and sighed. "She comes to all of my readings. Always gushing and fawning, making sure everyone around her knows that she's my friend. I seem to bump into her everywhere. The grocery store, the gas station, the Saturday Market in Hyde Park..."

"Don't forget the Film Festival," Maureen added.

"Yeah, and the film fest." He leaned forward. "You know, a few months ago I ran into her when I was waiting in the doctor's office? What are the odds?"

Maureen shivered. "Sounds creepy, if you ask me."

"Must be because I'm a successful writer," he said with a laugh. "We're like rock stars—except we have less charisma."

Maureen folded her arms. "So you're telling me groupies come with the territory?"

"I guess so. But please don't hold it against me."

"I can think of better things I'd like to hold against you." She reached across the table and held his hands. Tanya's voice continued to drift down from the rafters. Maureen's shoulders gently swayed in time to the music.

"I like this," Billy said. "It's so earthy and sensuous."

"Laissez-moi vous montrer ce que signifie sensuelle." Maureen winked.

"Looks like I'm going to have to learn me some French," Billy said with a smile.

Nicole returned with a pitcher of chilled Sangria and a basket of warm Cuban bread. She glared at the hands clasped on the table. "Steaks will be out in a minute."

"Thanks, Nicole." His kindness appeared to lift her spirits. She winked, turned and floated back to the kitchen.

Billy poured two generous glasses. "Cheers."

Nicole returned and carefully laid Billy's plate in front of him. "Enjoy, sweetie." Then she turned and gave Maureen a frigid nod. "And I hope you like it, too." She dropped the plate on the table. Salsa splattered across Maureen's blouse.

"Oops, my bad," Nicole said with obvious mock concern then spun and faded back into the lunch hour rush.

Billy offered Maureen his napkin. "Sorry about that. I'll talk to her."

"Don't worry about this old thing." Maureen dipped the napkin in her water glass and daubed her blouse. "Kind of young, eh Billy?"

He smiled. "Like I said, she's the one who's been following me."

"And like *I* said, it's kind of creepy." She picked up a new napkin and placed it on her lap. "At least she has good taste."

Billy felt himself blushing.

"And speaking of taste, synesthesia-man." She tore off a piece of bread and with a devilish look asked, "What do I taste like?"

He leaned across the table and whispered, "Crème brûlée."

Her eyes sparkled. "I hope you like crème brûlée?"

"Love it."

She shimmied in her seat and smiled. "I was hoping you'd say that."

He took a sip of wine and for a few awkward moments, they ate in silence. He was thankful for the surrounding din. So much noise, he felt numb.

"Tasting color," she finally said between bites. "That must be an exhilarating sensation. In a way, I envy you."

He shook his head. "Not every color is a pleasant experience. There's one particular shade of red that is absolutely searing. A habanero burn. They told me that when I was a baby my Aunt Lucille bought me a stuffed animal—Fred, the Red-Haired Bear. It was exactly that shade of red. Evidently the mere sight of Fred would fill my mouth with Louisiana hot sauce. I wailed uncontrollably whenever someone put him in my playpen or crib. When I was finally old enough to toss him out, I did, just so I could get some sleep. At first they thought I had a severe case of colic. They took me to pediatricians and specialists. They had a priest come and bless my room with holy water. My Aunt Lucille even hired a psychic. That lady spent hours in my room, trying to detect some sort of presence."

"Did it help?"

"Help? She only helped herself to my dad's liquor cabinet and my Aunt Lucille's wallet."

Maureen laughed. "Tell me about sound. You *feel* it?"

Billy nodded. "Yes. But I'm not the only one. I remember dating Elaine. We met at a synesthesia support group back in the early 90s. I asked her to dinner and the symphony."

"Sounds rather quaint and romantic."

"That's what I thought. See, I've always loved listening to classical music; it bathes me in the warmth of a tropical spring. But there was something about Elaine I didn't know: when she listened to classical music, especially baroque, it was an intensely erotic experience."

Maureen opened her eyes. "Now that sounds *really* interesting."

"One evening we attended a performance featuring the best baroque composers. Elaine was completely overwhelmed. Before the orchestra finished Pachelbel's Canon she had already experienced multiple orgasms. By the end of the evening she was slumped in her seat, nearly unconscious. I leaned over and whispered, '*Elaine, that was absolutely magnificent.*'

"*Billy*,' she moaned, '*you have no idea. . .*"

"I gathered my coat and began to move down the row of seats. When I looked back over my shoulder, she was still slumped in her chair. I walked back to her and asked, '*Elaine, are you coming?*'

"She smiled a dreamy smile and sighed. '*Not anymore. . .*'

Maureen dabbed her lips with her napkin and giggled.

"We became members of the symphony," he continued. "I even bought some CDs. Unfortunately, all that classical music began to take a toll on the poor girl. She often missed work and avoided friends. Seemed tired all of the time. She finally realized something had to change and started to make excuses whenever I suggested we attend a concert. One night I came by after work, enthusiastic about the evening's performance."

"*Elaine*," I asked. "*Aren't you going to get dressed? We only have an hour.*"

"*Not tonight, Billy. . . I have a headache.*"

"She did her best to avoid symphony performances just to maintain her sanity." He sipped his wine. "I haven't seen her for years, but I understand she is doing fine now. I heard she's taken up bluegrass music."

Maureen laughed. "And what about Billy? Any unpleasant sounds?"

"When I hear sirens I feel like I'm being pierced by hundreds of sharp, fine needles."

Her eyes grew wide. "Sounds painful."

"Believe me, it is. Of course, the fact that my family lived next door to Ladder Company 39 on West 233rd Street didn't do much to let me enjoy my early childhood. Several times a week I suffered excruciating pain. I was a human pincushion."

"I guess when I suggest a place to dine," Maureen paused and grinned. "It'll be blocks from a fire station. After all, I wouldn't want to be accused of death by perforation."

Billy laughed and shook his head. "I feel like such a *putz* doing all the talking."

Maureen wrinkled her brow. "*Putz?*"

"That's from Sy Greenberg, my agent. It's Yiddish for jackass or some such. He's a good guy but he's been on my case. Wants me to push the edge of the envelope. Take more risks, cast caution to the four winds. Says it'll help my writing."

She looked down and ran a finger around the rim of her glass. "Someday," she softly said, "I'd like to push the edge of the envelope." Her glass began to ring and Billy shivered as if a chill breeze blew through the room.

"So, what about you?" he asked as the glass continued to sing under her touch. "I know you're from the islands and you love old movies. What else?"

"I don't suffer from any rare conditions, if that's what you're asking."

"No, no. I mean, tell me a little about yourself."

"I was born in St. Kitts and came here to study interior design at Florida State. Then I came here to work at a major firm. Eventually I opened my own studio. That's where I met my hus—" she paused and bit her lip, "—um, many friends."

"Do you still work in design?" he asked.

"No, I sold the business a few years ago. I guess you could say I'm semi-retired."

"Is there someone special?"

She lifted her finger off the rim and the ringing stopped. "You mean, am I in love?"

"Well, yeah."

Another breeze wafted through the restaurant. The painting brushed up against her shoulder. She nudged it aside, paused and looked away. "No."

Nicole came by and laid the check on the table. "See you around, Billy," she said with a wink before spinning away toward another table.

"Thanks," he said to her back. He turned to Maureen and raised his glass. "Here's to old movies, great conversation, and death by perforation."

She clinked her glass against his. "And here's to the most fascinating man I've ever met."

"And," he added before taking a sip, "to the most fascinating woman I've ever tasted."

Then behind him, just off to the left, Billy was sure he heard the vicious whisper of his most rabid fan, Nicole.

"Die, bitch."

CHAPTER 5

Over the next two weeks, Billy and Maureen met for lunch every three or four days. They took turns choosing the restaurant. Always local. Never a chain. And in keeping with the promise she made to him, she never suggested one that was near a fire station. Today they opted for Tex-Mex in West Shore. They found themselves at a corner table nursing two margaritas and nibbling crisp, warm tortilla chips.

"Any of your waitress-girlfriends work here?" Maureen asked playfully.

"No. But I wouldn't mind asking her out." Billy nodded to a petite server with honey-blonde hair balancing a tray full of burritos and fajitas.

Maureen reached across the table and slapped his hand. "You're so bad."

"Hey, you're the one who asked."

"Speaking of dates, when are you going to ask me out?"

"What? I thought our lunches were dates." Billy sipped his margarita.

"No, these are lunches. I'm talking about a real date. Like a play or a movie. Dinner maybe. They're showing the old *Raiders of the Lost Ark* over at the pier in Clearwater. Movie under the stars. Might be fun."

Billy thought for a moment. He didn't really enjoy modern adventure movies. The cacophony of color splashing across an enormous screen and the bone shaking surround-sound created sensory overload. "Raiders? I don't think so."

"That's right, your condition."

Billy shrugged. "Sorry."

"I've got an idea!" Maureen said, sitting up. "Let's watch a movie at my house. A classic. It'll be a little more quiet and intimate. Why don't you come by after work Friday?"

Billy leaned back in his chair and crossed his arms. "Okay, but under one condition."

She arched her eyebrows.

"You won't try to seduce me. I've got an all-day workshop in Sarasota on Saturday. I'm going to need all my strength."

"Promise," she said as she crossed her fingers under the table and smiled.

* * *

Billy stopped by the wine shop after he was done for the day and picked up a bottle of Shiraz, then drove over to Maureen's Davis Island home. Towering palm trees stood like sentinels along the road. The setting sun cast dark purple shadows across yards of lush tropical landscaping.

He marched up to the heavy oak doors of her flamingo pink Mediterranean home. He pushed the doorbell and heard the toning of bells echoing inside, then the rapid tap-tap of shoes on tile as they approached. Maureen pulled the door open and greeted him with a warm kiss and a hug.

"Billy! Make yourself at home." She led him into the living room. "I'll get some glasses."

Billy settled into a supple leather couch and looked up at the high oak-beamed ceiling. Two large Tiffany chandeliers hung suspended above him. Leaded glass windows filled one wall; the others were light-pink stucco showcasing three Winslow Homers and two Turners. A Mary Cassatt hung above the stone fireplace. He stood back up and strolled around the room admiring the artwork.

Mmm. Not prints. He placed his hands on his hips and surveyed the cavernous room. Well, Toto, he whispered under his breath, we're not in Kansas anymore.

* * *

Across the street, nestled under a sleepy canopy of bougainvillea and river oak, sat a piss-yellow '85 Pontiac Bonneville with missing hubcaps and a broken antenna. *Black Flag, Fugazi,* and *Hüsker Dü* stickers plastered the cracked rear windshield, revealing the driver's penchant for old-school punk. Inside, a Bic lighter flicked, illuminating the end of a Camel cigarette and the pale-white face of a teenage girl in a waitress uniform. She tossed the lighter onto the seat then reached over and turned up the stereo. The Circle Jerks. Acoustic guitars, barely tuned, and an upright base. A bourbon-nicotine voice bitching about assholes, two-timers, and painfully violent deaths.

"Oh, yeah," she said softly. "The oldies." She pulled the cigarette from her lips and stared at the tangerine glow of the tip. "Man, they don't write 'em like that anymore."

She raised the Camel to her mouth and inhaled deeply, then blew a billow of smoke out the window. She tapped the cigarette in the dashboard ashtray, stared at the sprawling Mediterranean across the street, and mumbled, "Billy, how could you do this to me?"

A dog barked in the distance.

She took another long drag and exhaled. "Sure, she has nice tits," she mumbled as she looked down at her champagne-glass breasts. "And to think I had these babies pierced for you." She shuddered. "God, did that hurt." She looked at herself in the rear-view mirror and brushed her hair away from her forehead. "Hell, she might be rich and pretty." She leaned in close and glared at her reflection. "But Billy, you're an artist. And dammit, *I know art!*" She smacked the mirror askew, slumped back behind the wheel and took another heavy drag. She let it settle in her lungs for a moment then blew another blue-white cloud out the window where it faded into the moonlit sky. "But I guess your kind's not good enough for you, eh?"

She flicked the butt out onto the pavement and watched the sparks dance across the asphalt. "But there's more than one way to skin a two-timing fuck. And his rich-bitch as well."

She jammed her key in the ignition and the Bonneville coughed and sputtered to life. She threw it in gear and two bald rear tires chirped on the pavement. The Clash blasted from ragged speakers, shaking the leaves off the stately oaks of the upper-class neighborhood.

"Rock the Casbah. Rock the Casbah."

* * *

Maureen returned with two crystal glasses and a corkscrew. "This way, Billy." Then she led him down a serpentine hall toward the home theater.

"What's on for tonight?" he asked as he watched the fluid rhythm of her hips.

"*North by Northwest*," she replied over her shoulder.

They entered the dimly lit, walnut-paneled room and she motioned to the sofa. Billy sat as Maureen opened the bottle of wine. She handed him his glass and snuggled up to him on the sofa. He laid his arm behind her and took a sip as she picked up the remote and turned on the high definition monitor. He always enjoyed the company of Bacall, Hepburn, and Gary Cooper. And he loved it when Jimmy Stewart, Bogie, or Marlene dropped by. Tonight he relished a visit from Cary Grant and Eva Marie Saint in one of Hitchcock's best. Even better with Maureen nestled by his side. The movie started and every few moments he'd run his fingers through her hair, sometimes caressing her neck. He cast a furtive glance toward her, gauging her reaction. Her eyes were riveted to the flickering blue-light glow of the television screen and her stoic expression caused him to rethink his advances.

As Eva Marie fell into Cary's arms, Maureen moved her hand from her lap to Billy's knee. He looked down and lost interest in the movie. He caressed her neck and she gave him a gentle squeeze. Each time he brushed her neck, she slowly moved her hand up his thigh. They continued this game—a brush against her soft and supple neck, a gentle, short caress along his thigh. He swallowed hard and stole another glance. Her eyes were still entranced by the movements on the screen, but now she was wearing a devious smile. He leaned into her and placed his lips on her neck. She closed her eyes and moaned, "Yesss…"

Then—

"Maureen?!" A bellowing voice rumbled down the hall and into the room like a small avalanche. "Maureen? You home?"

Billy started and Maureen bolted upright. She snatched her hand off his thigh and placed it on her lap. The sound of the man's voice fell on Billy's chest like a heavy stone and he gasped for breath under its weight. An enormous form filled the doorway, creating an ogre-like silhouette. The scent of Old Spice and bourbon filled the room.

"Is that you, Maureen?"

"F-F-Frank? What are you doing here? You're not supposed to be back until Sunday."

Billy turned to Maureen and mouthed, "Frank?" Then scooted to the end of the sofa.

"Man, it's good to be home." A beefy arm reached into the room and switched on the light. Billy turned to the voice and met a ruddy, pockmarked face peering into the room. The hulking form stepped forward and two beady eyes glared at the couple. "Who's this, Maureen?"

"His name's Billy."

"Oh?"

The pressure on Billy's chest grew heavier.

"He's a writer, Frank."

His eyes narrowed. "What, for newspapers and shit?"

"No, Frank. Novels—"

"Novels?" He raised his eyebrows. "Like fiction novels?"

Maureen rolled her eyes. "Yes, Frank. Fiction novels."

Billy glanced at Maureen and started to rise. She waved a hand and he eased back down. "And poems. He's a poet, too."

Frank rubbed his five o'clock stubble. "A poet you say?" Then he turned to Maureen and raised an eyebrow. "So he must be—" He held up his hand. It fell limp and he winked.

She reached across the sofa and patted Billy's knee. "Yes, Frank. He certainly is."

The big man nodded and smiled. "And he's here for what?"

"I was scared the other night, and with you being gone for so long I thought it would be a good idea if Billy came by for a bit. It made me feel a little safer. And since he's—well, you know—I thought you wouldn't mind."

Frank rubbed the back of his neck and appeared to ponder this new information.

"You're right, Maureen. It was a good idea." Then turning to Billy he said, "Well, little poetry-man, thanks for keeping an eye on her for me. I'm on the road a lot and I worry about her. You're welcome around here anytime." He reached in his pocket, pulled out a set of keys and tossed them to Billy. "Here you go. Mi casa, su casa."

Billy snagged the keys in mid-air and nodded slowly. "No problem."

Frank stretched. "I'm beat. I'm going to hit the sack. Don't stay up too late, okay?"

"We won't," Maureen replied. "Goodnight, Frank."

The burly man turned and lumbered down the hallway to a master bedroom located somewhere in the bowels of the house.

As the last footstep faded away, the heavy weight on Billy's chest lifted. He turned to Maureen and whispered, "Frank?! Who the hell is Frank?"

She heaved her shoulders and sighed. "My husband."

"What?" Billy jerked upright. "You didn't tell me you had a husband!"

She looked down and picked at a finely manicured fingernail. "You didn't ask."

"Yes, I did."

"No," she said as she looked away. "You asked me if I was in love."

"Same difference."

She met his gaze. "Not really."

"Where's your ring?"

Maureen held out her left hand and admired it. "I only wear it when I don't want men bothering me."

Billy stood and began to pace in front of the leather sofa. "Man, oh man." He ran his hand through his hair. "I'm up for taking risks, but not on this scale."

She grabbed his hand and pulled him back down to the sofa. "I'm a trophy wife. He's never loved me." She stopped and looked away. "Although at one time, long ago, I think I once loved him."

"But he's your *husband*." Billy touched her cheek and turned her head. He searched her eyes and noticed tears welling up. Something inside him began to melt.

"Husband? I guess," she replied as she stared past his shoulder. "But he's so controlling and abusive." She turned back to face him. "He's got an incredibly hot temper."

"Don't tell me he's hit you."

She slid her dress straps off her shoulders, letting them fall. She shyly covered her breasts with her arms then turned to show him the dark purple bruises that blanketed her lower back and ribs.

"When he gets mad, everyone in the neighborhood knows about it. And he punches me where it doesn't show." She pulled the straps back up onto her shoulders. "Thankfully, he's gone most of the time, visiting one of at least six girlfriends he has scattered around the state."

"So, that's why the bastard was so quick to give up the keys. I'm his ticket to paradise."

Maureen nodded.

"Why don't you just leave him?"

"I've thought about it. Really I have. But where would I go? I have no family here and no real friends." She looked away and scowled. "Frank has seen to that."

He slowly nodded. "I see."

Maureen whimpered and her shoulders began to shake. He placed his hand on hers.

"What does Frank do that he's gone so much?"

She shrugged and giggled through her tears. "He thinks he's in the Mafia."

He released her hand and jumped back across the sofa. "The Mafia?!"

She wiped away a tear and managed a smile. "Don't worry." She grabbed his hand and pulled him back close to her. "I said he '*thinks*' he's in the Mafia. He actually sells heavy construction equipment to contractors around the state."

"B-but, the Mafia?" Billy swallowed hard.

"Well, to be honest, rumor has it there may be some mob connections." She picked up her glass and sipped her wine. "But you know how it is. Whenever anyone with a vowel at the end of their last name is successful, rumors begin to fly. And I think Frank encouraged these rumors. He probably felt the reputation would help his business."

"So you're telling me there's no *real* mob connection, right?"

She scrunched her eyebrows and nodded slowly. "No, I don't believe so."

Billy let out a sigh of relief.

"However, there was an incident a few years back." She raised her eyes and stared at the ceiling, deep in recollection. "He took a fall in a bribery trial involving a state representative and construction kick-backs on a toll road in Pasco County."

Her eyes returned to Billy and met his wide-eyed gaze. "Frank walked out with a big fine and time served. I think the Representative is still making license plates up in Raiford. Frank filed for bankruptcy, but his friends rewarded him handsomely. Within a week, Frank's company was up and running again under a different name." She paused to sip her wine. "So there *was* that meeting in an Ybor City bar, but he doesn't have any *real* mob ties."

"You're sure, Maureen?"

"Yes, pretty sure." She glanced around the room and waved her arm. "Frank Valentino earned his fortune the old-fashioned way. Over-charging his customers and cooking the books."

Billy looked away and stared at the snow on the bright white screen of the television. The hiss of the stereo system echoed in his ears and he felt like he was being pelted with small stones. Maureen set her glass down and reached out to hold his hands.

"Billy," she said softly. "You told me you want to take risks. Do you really? Or is that just in your books?"

He turned and searched her eyes.

She leaned forward and squeezed his hands.

"Then take a risk on me."

CHAPTER 6

BILLY gathered up the dinner dishes and turned on the faucet. "Don't worry, Ma. I'll only be in Chicago for a few days."

"Another writer's conference?" she asked as she helped herself to another slice of blueberry pie.

"No. Vacation. I was thinking about asking Maureen." He scraped his dish into the sink. "You remember Maureen, don't you, Ma? She came for dinner last week." He flipped the switch on the disposal and watched the scraps disappear down the drain.

"Oh yes," she replied. "A very classy girl. And such a nice tan." She swirled a bit of pie in the blueberry juice on her plate, then placed it in her mouth and nearly swooned. "This is so good."

"That wasn't a tan. She's Caribbean."

"Caribbean, Presbyterian, Episcopalian. As long as she believes in God." She crossed herself then placed another juicy piece into her small mouth. "Mmm. Such good pie."

"I'll get Mrs. Donaghee to come over. She'll keep you company while I'm gone."

"Wonderful! We can shop and we can watch movies and we can invite the Shapiros over for a round of canasta and we can—" she stopped with her fork midway to her mouth and frowned. "But what if something happens to me while you're gone?"

"Nothing's going to happen," he said as he wiped his hands on the dishtowel. "I've left the number of the hotel by the phone. Call me if you need anything."

She looked up at the yellow post-it note and smiled. "I'm glad you're going, son. Sy's right. You need to get out more often."

"How do *you* know what Sy said?" he asked as he squinted his eyes in mock interrogation. "You weren't listening in on the extension again were you?"

"I picked it up 'cuz I thought it might be for me."

"And you kept listening? Why?" he asked with a wry smile.

She shrugged. "I'm old, my reflexes aren't what they used to be."

"Sheesh," he said as he draped the dish towel on a hook by the window.

"Anyway, Sy's right." She scraped the last bit of pie off her plate and placed it in her mouth. "You spend too much time at that desk of yours."

"Writing pays the bills." He lifted the whistling kettle off the stove. "More tea?"

"No, no. I'll burst." She drained her cup and set it on the saucer. "But it's good for you to get away. Especially with a pretty girl like Maureen."

"I'm glad you like her, Ma," he said as he picked up her dessert plate and carried it over to the sink. "She's a very special girl."

She dabbed her lips with a napkin. "And such a nice tan."

* * *

Maureen stepped out of the shower and the phone rang. She quickly wrapped a towel around her and padded across the bathroom leaving little pools of water on the white marble floor. She always thought a phone in the master bath was a bit much, but Frank insisted.

"I do most of my strategic thinking when I'm sitting on the can," she remembered him telling her. *"I need to have access to a phone in case I gotta put together a deal."*

"Sure, Frank." She snatched up the phone before the third ring. "Hello," she sang as shimmering beads of water dripped from her hair and tap-tapped to the floor.

"Hi, Maureen. It's me."

Her countenance brightened. "Billy?"

"Are you sitting down?"

She glanced at the sleek, bone-white toilet and bidet. "No."

"Well, you might want to."

Again, she pondered the porcelain fixtures and grimaced. "I don't think so. What's up?"

"We're going on a trip."

"A trip?" She tightened her grip and pulled the towel snug around her. "Where? When?" A twinge of excitement crept up her spine. She quickly paced back and forth in front of the long granite vanity.

"To Chicago. The film festival. Next month."

She stopped and stared at the ceiling. "Oh, Billy! Are you serious? Please tell me you're not joking!"

"You told me to take a risk on you. Well, I did. I've got it all arranged. Just you and me. First class on Air Deco and a room at the Hotel InterContinental."

For one brief moment, Maureen stood silent and stared at herself in the misty mirror. Her eyes grew wide and an exuberant smile filled her face. "Yes!" she squealed as she threw her arms into the air. The soft cotton towel tumbled to the floor.

* * *

Nicole pulled her Bonneville up in front of a chipped-brick storefront down by the docks; the one Psycho-Benny suggested when she put out the word that she needed a weapon—no questions asked. She climbed out of her car and glanced up and down the ghost-town-silent street. A crumpled plastic shopping bag skipped across the road like a small tumbleweed. She looked at the plywood sign above her, paint peeling off in fine slivers from the constant heat and afternoon showers. *Doc's Emporium.* She marched up to the entrance and pulled on the steel-mesh-covered black glass door. It didn't budge. She stepped back and noticed the makeshift intercom system: a scuff-rusted black speaker bolted to the bricks beside the door. She pushed the red button.

"Yeah?" the speaker cackled.

She stood on her tiptoes and leaned into the intercom. "I need a gun."

"We're closed."

"Psycho-Benny sent me."

The door buzzed and she yanked it open. Flickering overhead fluorescents and the sunlight filtering through the grime-covered windows cast an eerie and unearthly glow throughout the room. It took a moment for her eyes to adjust. Then she noticed a bone-thin young man in camouflage fatigues sitting behind a display case filled with an array of gleaming knives and bayonets. He was hunched over a comic book, lips moving as he read.

"Ahem." Nicole coughed.

"Hold on," the man said as he waved his arm and continued to read. "I'm almost finished with this page." He looked up and paused, then slid the comic book off to the side. He wore a patch over one eye and his one good, jaundice-yellow eye ogled the girl in the white tank top, black-as-midnight jeans, and scuffed Doc Martens. He broke into a crooked smile that made his pockmarked face morph into a desert relief map of ravines and small craters. He sat up and ran a pasty hand over the shiny dome of his head.

"Look what the cat drug in," he said in a subterranean voice. He licked his lips. "Or should I say...*pussy.*"

She rolled her eyes. Great, she thought. A perv.

She strode up to the counter and scanned the array of handguns and rifles hanging on the walls. "I need a gun," she said matter-of-factly.

"We got lots of guns." He waved his arm around the room. "What you need it for?"

She thought for a moment. "Hunting."

He pulled a weapon off the wall and cradled it in his arms. "This here's a Groza bullpup assault rifle. With armor-piercing bullets this sumbitch can take out a Humvee at 300 yards." He raised the rifle to his shoulder, aimed at a target somewhere in his imagination and pulled the trigger.

Click.

Nicole flinched.

He lowered the gun and admired it. "Doubles as a grenade launcher, too. Talk about owning the fuckin' neighborhood."

"Too big. Gimme something smaller." She walked over to a collection of sawed-off shotguns. "But not too small. It's got to kill in one shot."

He walked around the counter and joined her. "Big game hunting, eh?" He rested a hand on her shoulder.

She shoved it off. "Sorta."

The man winked at her with his one good eye. "Listen. I can see from your clothes and tats that you're one of us." He motioned to the stained canvas tarp hanging in the doorway behind him. "This way."

Nicole glanced from side to side then shrugged and walked around the counter. He pulled the tarp back and ushered her into a dimly lit room. A clammy wet-dog smell hung heavy in the air. Tattered Nazi flags and Civil War pendants hung from the rafters like clumps of Spanish moss. An enormous framed picture of Adolph Hitler glared down at them from the back wall.

"I got just the ticket," the man said as he unlatched the rusty hasp of a rat-gray trunk. The heavy lid creaked as he lifted it open. He pulled out a matte black submachine gun. A glistening bead of drool fell from his lower lip as he unfolded the shoulder stock.

"Brügger & Thomet MP9," he said as he wiped the spittle off the barrel with his thumb. "Ain't she a beauty? High-impact resin polymer. Rotating-barrel locking system." The words tumbled out in a steady stream. "Ambidextrous load. Fully adjustable low ghost ring sight and rail. Transparent magazines. Integrated vertical fore grip." He paused to catch his breath. "Here, what d'ya think?"

She took the gun and weighed it in her hands. Hmm. Lighter than she thought it'd be. Not too bad. She raised it against her shoulder and peered through the sight.

"Watch it!" He wrenched the gun from her hands. "It's loaded."

"I'll take it. How much?"

"Well since you're one of us, $750."

"Second time you said that. What the hell d'you mean, 'one of us'?"

He looked over his shoulder and nodded at the picture of Hitler. "You know. One of us."

"Whatever." You Nazi piece of shit.

"Might need some more ammo," he said as wandered back over to the trunk. He pulled out a small cardboard box, shook it and smiled at the metallic rattle. "These clips should do for awhile."

"How much for the ammo?"

"No charge. I'll throw it in on account of it's Kaltenbrunner's birthday." He nodded to another faded black-and-white photo on the wall.

She rolled her eyes. "Thanks."

He tossed the gun from one hand to the other. "Say, do you know how to shoot one of these babies?"

"Um, no. I've never had a gun before."

"Ha! Didn't think so. Come with me." He opened a door beneath the picture of Hitler and they entered a narrow cinderblock room. He flipped a switch and a half-dozen bare light bulbs filled the room with a dull glow that sent large roaches scampering into the shadows. Spent shells and fossilized wads of chewing tobacco crunched under their feet. Nicole stared at the poster targets hanging from the ceiling at the far end of the room. A black man in overalls, a Jew, complete with yarmulke and oversized nose, and a nondescript white man wearing horn-rimmed glasses and an ill-fitting business suit.

"What's up with Clark Kent?" she asked, pointing to the last target.

"That's my father." The young man yanked the cartridge out, checked it, and then slapped it back in with a click. "I hate my father."

He raised the gun to his shoulder, took aim, and pulled the trigger. The sharp, staccato blast caused Nicole to jump back against the door. Acrid smoke filled the air as a rage of bullets shredded the businessman and the Jew beside him. The young man released the trigger and a wet smile crawled across his face.

"Here, you try," he said, handing her the warm weapon. "Hell, you don't even need to aim. Just point it in the general direction and pull the trigger. Go ahead, kill the nigger."

Nicole frowned at the target. "Don't you have any other pictures?"

"Like what?"

"Any girls?"

The man paused and scratched his head. "Yeah, I think I got one." He pulled a string to his left and a full-color poster unrolled from the ceiling. "We get some good targets at Wal-Mart. Cheap too. 'Specially when you steal 'em."

"That's that Hilton chick. She's as blond and blue-eyed as they come."

"Yeah, I know." He turned his head and spat on the floor. "Then she went and made that sex tape. God, how I hated that."

"Was she doing a Jew?"

"Nah. It's 'cuz she wasn't doing me. Now you gonna shoot the skinny bitch or am I gonna have to waste her myself?"

She raised the weapon and her shaking finger pulled the trigger. The gun erupted and slammed against her shoulder sending her sprawling across the concrete floor. The Nazi-boy dove for the corner and covered his head with his hands. Nicole's entire body convulsed as a torrent of bullets shredded the poster then climbed the cinderblock wall and raked the ceiling. Chunks of concrete and wood rained down like large hailstones. Sawdust and plaster filled the air and her lungs. She released the trigger, coughed, and propped herself up on her elbows. She took a few deep breaths and stared at the weapon lying across her lap. White wisps of smoke, like the ghosts of snakes, slithered from the end of the gun barrel.

The man scrambled back to his feet and exploded into laughter. "Great shot," he managed to shout between guffaws. "You not only killed the bitch, you nailed the fuckin' wall!" He looked up. "Haw! And the goddamn ceiling too!"

Nicole struggled back up to her feet, straightened her shoulders and glared at him. "I'll take it." She shoved the warm gun against his chest with a thud.

"Sure," he coughed. "No problem. Let me wrap it up for you."

They left the target room and the man laid the gun on top of the trunk. He pulled a burlap bag out of a nearby crate and began to wrap the weapon.

"So what happened to your eye?" Nicole asked as she watched him work.

He turned around. "Oh, this?" he said lifting the black patch. "I wear it for show. Makes me look like a badass, don't it?"

Hmph, more like dumbass.

The man replaced the patch and handed her the bundle. "Here's to the Second Amendment."

"Whatever," Nicole said with a snort. She turned to the doorway and pulled back the tarp.

"Hey, listen," he called after her.

She turned and scowled. "Now what?"

He took two steps forward, dug his hands in his pockets, and shrugged. "We have meetings here. Every Friday night, nine o'clock. You should come."

"Can't." She turned, drew the tarp back, and stepped into the front room.

"Oh, that's right," he said with a twitter. "You're going hunting."

"Yeah," she said over her shoulder as she thought of Billy's half-breed bitch. "Hunting."

He followed her into the front room and stepped behind the display case. "That'll be seven-fifty." He opened the register and paused. "But if you show me your tits," he added with a leer, "I'll knock off two-fifty."

Nicole rolled her eyes and laid the burlap bag on the display case. She reached down and lifted her tank top.

The man lifted his patch and his eyes grew wide at the sight of her pert, champagne-glass breasts. "Damn! Those babies are pierced!"

Nicole looked down at the small stainless-steel hoops dangling from her nipples. She stifled a yawn. "You noticed."

The man wiped his mouth with his forearm and continued to stare. She pulled her shirt back over her breasts, reached into her jeans, and pulled out a wad of money. She peeled off five bills and slapped them in the man's clammy palm. "There you go."

"Thanks!" He licked his thumb and counted the bills. Nicole picked up the burlap bag and turned to the door.

He looked up. "Just so you know, it comes with a money-back guarantee."

She pushed the door open, then stopped and turned. "Can I ask you something?" she asked with a devilish smile.

"What? You want another discount?" He broke into a grin that exhibited rows of corn-kernel teeth. "I could drop it another couple of hundred bucks—if you drop your pants."

"Oh?" She ran a finger across the top of her jeans and let it linger on her belt buckle. "And I get my money back if I'm not satisfied?"

"Damn right." He licked his lips and stared at her tight crotch in obvious anticipation.

She heaved her shoulders and sighed. "Well, in that case. . ."

She leveled the gun, clenched her teeth, and pulled the trigger. The man's chest exploded in a flurry of bone and blood as he flew back against the brick wall. He collapsed in a shredded mound on the cold concrete floor, thick blood pooling around him. Nicole stepped behind the counter and snatched the wad of bills from the man's limp hand.

"I want my money back," she said to the lifeless form at her feet. "Killing you wasn't as satisfying as I thought."

She threw the weapon over her shoulder and yanked the front door open. "Is this world full of fuckin' weirdoes?" she asked herself as she stepped out into the bright Florida sun. "Or is it just me?"

CHAPTER 7

O N the day of their long-awaited trip, Billy stopped by Maureen's during lunch to see if she needed anything for the trip. He sat at the kitchen table while she prepared a Caesar salad with grilled chicken. Billy opened a bottle of Sauvignon Blanc and poured a glass for each of them.

"So," she said between bites. "This Hotel InterContinental. Is it as nice as they say?"

"Oh, my, yes. Particularly the older building. The indoor pool looks like it came right out of a Busby Berkeley movie. It'll be like starring in our own Hollywood production. I figured we'd check in then grab a bite to eat and head to the film festival."

She leaned forward on her elbows. "And after that?"

"Maybe head back to the hotel for some coffee and dessert."

"What will you have for dessert?"

He detected the sparkle in her eye. "Why, crème brûlée, of course."

"I was hoping you would say that." She reached over to caress his cheek then pulled away as her husband Frank blundered into the room. He grabbed a cold beer from the fridge and joined them at the table.

"So, you two kids ready for your big trip?" He twisted off the cap and tossed it towards the stainless steel trashcan. It bounced off the lid with a ping.

"Matter of fact," Billy said, "we were just discussing details." He winked at Maureen.

Frank leaned back and shook his head. "Man, I wish I could go to a fag fest." He chortled then raised the bottle to his lips.

"Film Fest," Maureen said with a look of disgust. She rose to clear the table while the men stood and stepped through the French doors to the flagstone patio.

"You're a good man," Frank said as he patted Billy on the back. "Even though you are, well, you know."

"Yeah, Frank." Billy sipped his wine and smiled. "I know."

"She's been looking forward to this trip for weeks. It's all she can talk about." Frank took a generous swig and continued, "Yeah, I think you kids are going to have a great weekend in Chicago. Did I ever tell you about my time in Chicago?"

"Sure," Billy lied. "Just last week."

"That's what I thought. I guess you'll be in your element, what with all that movie star shit. Heh, heh, there'll probably be a lot of 'your kind' there as well, don't ya think?"

"Could be."

"But, hey," Frank said with a playful nudge. "Don't get distracted and lose track of my wife."

"Oh, she'll be in good hands." Billy chuckled at his unintended double entendre.

Frank took another swig and wiped his mouth with his sleeve. "I gotta say, you two really seem to hit it off. I can't tell you how much I appreciate you taking the time to be with her. You know, sharing her interests and all that. 'Specially with my travel schedule being what it is."

"No problem. No problem at all."

A soft breeze blew in off the bay and rustled the leaves of the river oaks overhead. A thick cloud of Old Spice rose from Frank's ruddy cheeks and wafted toward Billy, causing him to stifle a sneeze. The two men were silent for a moment as they looked out over the green expanse of the well-manicured backyard toward the glistening ripples of Tampa Bay. Billy felt a gentle buzz from the wine.

"Yeah, she's a damn good woman," Frank said proudly as he rocked back and forth on his heels.

"And she tastes like crème brûlée," Billy muttered into his wine glass.

"That she does, my friend. . . " Frank froze; beer bottle halfway to his lips. "Hey, wait one damn minute." He slowly turned his head. "What do you mean, 'she tastes like crème brûlée'?"

Billy shuddered. Oh shit. He turned to look at Frank's molten red face. Veins pulsed in his thick neck. Steam and ash appeared to rise from his shoulders. The ground beneath them seemed to tremble. "No, you see, what I mean is. . ."

Frank slammed his bottle to the ground and it shattered, sending shards of glass helter-skelter across the patio. Billy continued to stutter as two massive hands clamped around his neck and lifted him off the ground like a forklift. Legs dangling and kicking. Gasping for air. Ripping and clutching at the human vise-grips crushing his throat.

A few seconds later he found himself tumbling through the air like a six-foot Raggedy-Ann doll. He landed with a dull thud and slid across the lawn—an Olympic bobsledder without his sled. When he finally came to a stop, he shook his head to get his bearings. Confusion filled his addled mind. Was it from the wine? The lack of oxygen from a nearly crushed windpipe? The crash landing? He rubbed his neck as bleary eyes turned to a booming voice rumbling down from the crest of the small hill. Was it a beast? A monster? A man? He could only make out bits and pieces of Frank's tirade.

"You faggot, home-wrecking, mother-fucking. . ." The profanities rolled across the lawn like angry ocean waves. Billy steadied himself and rose, swaying back and forth. He reached into his pocket. "Hey, Frank!"

"What, scumbag?"

He held up a shiny key ring. "Does this mean you want your house keys back?"

"Why you little piece of shit!" Frank stormed forward and snatched the keys from Billy's hand then put his massive shoe against his chest and sent him sprawling backwards.

"Now get outta my face before I get mad," Frank said then spun and marched back to the house.

Billy staggered back to his feet. "Hey, you big Sicilian ox!"

Frank spun around. "Yeah, fag face?"

Billy teetered and managed a smile. "Who you calling 'little'?"

Frank took one step forward and Billy flinched. Frank mumbled another string of creative profanities then stormed back to the house, slamming the patio door behind him. Two panes of glass fell out and shattered on the patio flagstones.

Billy glanced at the kitchen window and noticed Maureen peeking out. He managed a smile and offered a faint salute. She blew him a tender kiss then slowly bowed her head and released the curtain. He turned and limped to his car. He sat against the front fender and pulled the airline ticket confirmation from his pocket. So much for taking risks, he thought. He began to tear it up, then stopped. Maybe I'll just go alone. No, I'd only think about the fact that Maureen wasn't there. He looked toward the house. But now I have Frank to deal with. Can't go home now. He'll know where to find me. He folded the confirmation back up and put it back in his pocket then climbed behind the wheel. He looked in the rear-view mirror and ran his fingers through his hair. So, you had to go and mention the crème brûlée, didn't you? He picked out a few stray blades of grass and tossed them over his shoulder. Art Walk's tonight. Maybe I'll head downtown. The walk, the art, the drink. . . yes, especially the drink, might do me some good. Then I can decide what to do.

Billy put the Jetta in reverse and backed down the twisting driveway onto Riviera. He shifted to first and with a chirp of the wheels headed downtown. He decided to visit the Wilson-Peale Gallery. Always engaging. Always delicious. When he arrived in Ybor, he circled the block and pulled into a vacant parking space. Well, Sy, he thought as he walked to the corner, so much for taking my condition out on the road. Get out, he says. Get laid, he says. Hell, why don't these relationships ever work out? He considered Julia, Elaine, Brenda, Lori, Nicole, and now Maureen. Too young, too intense, too emotional, too clingy, too psycho, too married. He thought about the characters in his books—full of life, adventure and possibilities. How can I describe something so well when I can't seem to live it myself? He shoved his hands into his pockets. A cement mixer growled and grumbled by. What's holding me down?

He looked up as if expecting a reply. His lips puckered at the blue, yet tart-as-apple-cider sky and was greeted by sunshine and silence.

CHAPTER 8

EDEN Myers picked up her sales slips and carried them to the office at the rear of the shop. Her best friend Ginny sat at a paper-strewn desk and pored over a pile of receipts. Eden placed the slips into the bright metal inbox and reached for her diet Coke. "I hate inventory." She slumped against a gray filing cabinet. "I feel like I worked all night."

"We nearly did," Ginny said as her fingers danced across the keys of a calculator. Click. Click. Whirr. Click. Click. Whirr.

"Coming in at midnight and working 'til 11, I guess we did." She sipped her Coke. Yuck. Lukewarm and flat.

"Any big plans this weekend?" Ginny asked without looking up. Click. Whirr. Click.

"Boy, do I. Robbie and I are going over to Cocoa. We'll get in some surfing. Maybe some beach volleyball. Moonlight walks on the beach."

"Liar."

"And just what do you mean by that?"

Ginny raised an eyebrow. "Surfing? Beach volleyball? Moonlight walks? With Robbie? As in Robbie Renfro?"

"Yeah."

"Like I said." She returned her attention to the mound of receipts. "Liar."

Eden crossed her arms. "How can you say that?"

"'Cuz you two don't do anything together anymore. He's got you in a rut."

"You're being ridiculous."

"The bum's living off your kindness and generosity. You're not going anywhere."

"We have plans." Eden took another sip of warm soda and grimaced.

Ginny pushed the calculator aside. "You've been engaged for what, two years?"

"Three."

"Like I said, you're not going anywhere."

"You know that wasn't the original idea. We had a date."

"Oh really?" she asked with a smirk. "Then what happened?"

"You know darn well what happened. Robbie postponed it. He said there was no need to rush into such a big decision. Said we need financial stability."

"Now here you are, three years later."

Eden sighed and drew small circles in the dust on the top of the filing cabinet. "You're right. The rush to wedded bliss morphed to a walk and then to a crawl." She stared at her smudged fingertips. "Now I think rigor mortis is setting in."

Ginny leaned back in her chair and popped her gum. "So what are you gonna do, wait another three years?"

"We're gonna get married as soon as his career in the transportation industry takes off. And that'll happen any time now."

"Transportation industry? Hah! Doesn't he drive a forklift for some freight company?"

Eden thought about the time she dropped off his lunch at Mallory Shipping and Logistics. A warehouse as big as the Westshore Mall. Robbie, one of a dozen forklift jockeys scampering through aisles as deep and wide as canyons, like hamsters in a maze. Before that, a professional pooper scooper and the relentless pressure he put on all their friends who were just as happy to clean up their own dog poop, thank you very much. Then his foray into a multilevel marketing scheme that left her with a closet full of laundry soap and alienated what few friends they had left. Oh, then his stint as a yellow pages rep. Cable installer. Timeshare salesman. Jiffy Lube manager trainee. All this from a political science major. So much promise. He was even an aide to Senator Furst. Too constricting, he said. Need to be my own captain. She sighed. Yeah. Forklift captain. She stared at her shoes and scraped a toe across the white-flecked tile. "That's what he does when he actually shows up."

Ginny lurched forward and spread her hands out on the desk. "How many times have we been through this? He can't hold a job.

He couldn't afford his own place so you let him move in. You pay the bills, cook the meals, do the laundry—"

Eden looked back up. "At least I'm not sleeping with him. I'm saving myself—"

Ginny leapt to her feet and walked around the desk. "Oh right. I forgot. The last great American virgin."

"Someone's got to carry the banner."

"Don't change the subject, Miss Goodie-Two-Shoes. If I were you, I'd dump that chump."

Eden thrust her hands out to her side. "Some people change, y'know."

Ginny rolled her eyes. "And some don't."

"He might."

Ginny grabbed her shoulders and searched her eyes. "Maybe you're the one who needs to change."

"Me?"

"Think about it, girl. You're too nice. You fawn over rude customers, you help old ladies across the street, you rescue lost puppies and bring them home—"

"It wasn't a puppy. It was a ferret."

She turned and threw her hands into the air. "Ferret-shmerrit. You're out to save the whole frigging world. But, girl, some folks don't want to be saved."

"Robbie?"

Ginny planted her hands on her hips and nodded. "There's a word for people like you."

"Codependent?"

"Doormat. Now listen to me. You gotta dive and fly, girl. Leave the jackass."

Eden froze. "What did you say?"

"I said leave that jackass."

"No. Before that."

Ginny shrugged her shoulders. "Um, dive and fly?"

"And just what do you mean by that?"

"Hey, don't get your panties in a wad. I just meant you have to spread your wings. Y'know, find someone new. Sheesh." She stepped back behind her desk and snatched a paper from her printer. "Here, I did a little net surfing for you. Check it out."

Eden took it and scanned the page. She peeked over the top. "Hot Tampa Bay Singles?"

Ginny shrugged. "Why not?"

"It's seems so. . . contrived." She leafed through the pages. "It's just not organic."

"Jeez, don't tell me you're into vegan dating now!" She popped the paper with her forefinger. "Someone in there has to be better than that inorganic, lard-ass excuse for a fiancé."

Eden glanced back down at the paper and frowned. "Gee, I don't know."

Ginny walked around the desk and opened the office door. She turned and paused. "Do me a favor, okay?"

Eden looked up from the paper. "What?"

"Promise me you'll do something for yourself for once. Something wild and crazy, ok?"

"But—"

"Live it up a little, will ya? You only go around once, right?" She snapped her fingers for emphasis then turned and let the door click shut behind her.

Eden stood silent for a moment then tossed the paper on the desk. She turned to look at herself in the full-length mirror propped against the wall.

"You don't look too wild and crazy," she whispered as she pulled her hair back into a bun. "You look like a nice Jewish girl—a nice Jewish girl from Boca." She walked around the desk and plopped down in Ginny's chair. She stared at the printout for a moment then snatched it up and scanned the entries.

Me Tarzan. You Jane. Tarzan white. 42 seasons. Me want to bungle in the jungle. No monkey business. Tarzan nice.

Yikes!

Sleek antique roadster in rare condition. 1938 model. Some wear and tear but very road worthy. Well equipped. Seeking classic model with copious front bumpers and enormous tailfins. Hop in my rumble seat and we'll. . .

She shook her head. No. No. No.

I'm a sex-crazed drunken pirate who would love to check you for scurvy. We'll sail the Caribbean on my love boat. Let me fondle your casabas and I'll let you squeeze my limes. Arrgh, it's the pirate's life for me.

"Arrgh is right!" She crumbled the paper into a ball and hurled it into the trashcan. The chair creaked as she leaned back and stared at the ceiling. Leave Robbie? For these losers? At least I know where I stand with *my* loser. He'll come around. She jerked the seat back upright and turned to face the mirror.

"I know," she told her reflection. "We'll talk about the future tonight over New York strips and garlic mashed potatoes." She spun the chair around and around. "He loves garlic mashed potatoes." She set her feet down and the chair skidded to a halt. "I'll even whip up dessert. Something exotic."

She stood and smiled, then gathered up her things.

"Maybe some crème brûlée."

CHAPTER 9

MAUREEN peered out of the kitchen window and watched Billy struggle to his feet. She bit her lip and whispered, "I am so sorry."

Billy pulled out the airline confirmation. He stared at it and shook his head. Maureen caught her breath and felt her heart sink. He's going to tear it up. Please, don't! He paused and stared at the paper. She breathed a sigh of relief when he shoved it back into his pocket. He's going. I know he's going! I'll have to—

Bam! Crash!

She jumped at the sound of a slamming door and breaking glass.

"What a goddam fucking loser." Frank lumbered back into the kitchen, wiping his hands on the front of his shirt. "If a man's gonna steal someone's wife, he shouldn't tell the husband about it, you know what I'm saying?"

Maureen spun away from the window. "I can't believe you did that."

Frank held out his hands in supplication. "What'd I do?"

"Threw Billy out on the lawn."

"Don't tell me you're all worried about that lying, two-timing, fake faggot. Jesus, Mary and Joseph." Frank walked over to the fridge and grabbed another beer. "Y'know he wasn't even gay?" He unscrewed the bottle and took a swig. "Sure had you fooled. But not me."

"You had no right to treat him like that." She took a step toward him.

He cocked his head to one side and frowned. "What are you saying, Maureen?"

"Billy was my friend, Frank."

"*Was* is right."

She planted her hands on her hips. "And just what do you mean by that?"

"I'm saying *'was'* is the perfect word."

"Are you telling me I can't see Billy anymore?" she asked, taking another step closer. She was only inches from him now.

"You got that right."

"You can't do that."

"Just watch me." He raised the bottle of beer to his lips and took a generous pull.

"Why you. . ." Maureen clenched her fists and pounded Frank's burly chest but her blows fell like snowflakes on granite. He quickly set his beer on the counter and grabbed her wrists. He grinned as he held her arms out in front of him.

"Stop it, Frank," she said, as she jerked and pulled in his grasp. "You're hurting me. Let me go."

"Now just calm yourself down," he said with a fatherly smile.

She slowly stopped her writhing. Muscles tense. Dull throb across her brow.

"There, there, that's my girl." Frank pulled her close and whispered. "Listen, baby doll. What can that guy give you that I can't?"

She pushed herself away and glared into his eyes. "For starters?"

"OK, yeah, for starters."

Maureen stroked her chin and stared at the ceiling. "Let's see. He gives me his attention—"

"Attention? Hah! I can give that in spades. Why I could—"

"And affection, and consideration, and laughter, and understanding, and honesty, and compassion, and a zest for life, and—"

"Whoa, whoa, whoa. Hold it right there. I give you all those things, Maureen."

Her eyes challenged his. "No you don't."

"Well I give you most of those things."

She shook her head.

"Some of those things?"

"Nope."

"How 'bout the time we went to Cancun? We had a wonderful vacation! Why, in that one weekend alone I gave you all of those things. It was like being in heaven."

Maureen scowled. "Sorry, Frank. That wasn't me."

"No? But I thought—"

"I've never been to Cancun, Frank. You must be thinking of someone else."

"Jeez, I coulda sworn that was you." He scratched the back of his head and stared off in the distance. "What about that trip to Aruba?"

"Nope."

"But I thought. . ."

"You've only taken me to Vegas and Reno. Oh, and those business trips to Teaneck, New Jersey and Gary, Indiana. We never really spent any time together on those so-called vacations. You gave me a handful of credit cards and told me to enjoy myself while you went gallivanting with who-knows-who to who-knows-where."

"But—But—" he stammered then finally blurted out, "Well, I let you hang out with that bozo Billy. That shows I give you consideration. Hell, I was even going to let you two run off to that fag-festival in Chicago."

"I told you it was a film festival."

He picked up his beer and took a swig. "Like I said, fag festival."

"But you sure changed your mind quick enough, Frank. He was the greatest thing that ever happened to me." She spun on her heels and walked away.

"Don't you turn your back on me."

"Screw you."

"Maureen! Wait!"

She waved her middle finger over her shoulder.

"OK, Maureen, now I'm starting to get upset."

A beer bottle sailed across her shoulder and shattered against the wall. She jumped at the sound then spun around. "He *was* the greatest, Frank." She wiped an angry tear from the corner of her eye. "You could learn a thing or two from someone like my Billy."

"*Your* Billy? Dammit. That's the last straw. I don't want his name mentioned in this house again!"

Maureen planted her hands on her hips and smirked. "Billy," she said spitefully.

"What did you say?" Frank's temple twitched.

73

"You heard me. Bill-y," she repeated, stretching out his name.

"Watch it, Maureen." The twitch turned to spasm and the veins in his neck pulsed.

She cocked her hips from side to side chanting, "Billy, Billy, Billy."

"I'm warning you, Maureen." His shoulders heaved and tiny beads of sweat appeared on his brow.

"Billy, Billy, Billy, Billy, Billy, Billy. . ."

"That's it," he said as he rolled up his sleeves. "Now somebody's gonna get hurt."

Maureen took two steps backward and spat out, "Bill-lllly."

Frank lunged.

"Leave me alone!" she yelled as she bolted from the kitchen and down the hallway.

"Come back here, you slut!" Frank stumbled over a kitchen stool. "Damn it!" He kicked the chair across the tile floor and raced down the hall. Maureen turned a corner and dashed into the hall bathroom. She slammed the door and quickly turned the lock.

"Open up, goddam it!" he yelled as he threw himself against the door.

She pressed her back against the door. "Leave me alone!"

"Don't make me break this door down!" Frank's pounding sent tremors through her body.

She braced herself and pushed her shoulder against the door. "Leave me alone you big Italian ape!"

"Oh, so now we're getting personal."

"I'm gonna scream!"

"Go ahead. See if I care."

"Yiiiiii---eeeeee-----iiiiii"

"Maureen. Stop that! The neighbors!"

"Help me, someone!"

The hammering suddenly stopped. Maureen put her ear to the door.

"This isn't working," she heard him whisper to himself. "Gotta change strategies."

He tapped on the door. "C'mon baby doll, you know I love you," he cooed. "Open up and give daddy a great, big hug."

Maureen whimpered and bit her lip.

"Baby doll?"

"HELP ME SOMEBODY!"

"Jeezus! I think you shattered my eardrum! That's it, no more foolin' around." His voice trailed away. "Now you're really gonna get it."

She pressed her ear to the door and heard her husband's heavy footsteps fade down the hall. She cracked the door open and caught a glimpse of his back as he disappeared into the kitchen. Whew. The coast is clear. She turned the button to lock the door and eased it closed. Then she grabbed her purse off the side table and slipped out the front door, padding across the lawn to her car.

* * *

Frank stormed down the hall and through the kitchen toward the garage. She thinks she can defy me? We'll see about that. I'm the king of this fucking castle. He burst into the garage, eyes scanning the room. Aha! He wrenched a rusty pickaxe from the wall and marched back through the kitchen and down the hall to the bath. He jiggled the door handle. Locked.

"I warned you, Maureen! Now I'm coming in!" He took a step back and spit on his hands. He raised the pickaxe over his shoulder then slammed it through the door. Shards of wood sailed through the air as the door splintered down the middle. Frank reached in through the jagged hole, turned the lock, and shoved what remained of the door open. He stormed into the room and raised the pickaxe over his head. "You want some attention, Maureen? Well, I got your attention right here!"

His eyes scanned the quiet, empty room. What the hell? A bead of water dripped from the faucet. Shplit.

He eyed the linen closet door and grinned. He grasped the doorknob and took a deep breath. He yanked it open.

"Aha! Gotcha, bitch!"

A wall of soft pink towels and washcloths stared back at him in silence. Two rolls of toilet paper fell off a shelf and bounced silently across the floor.

"What the. . ?" Frank lowered the pickaxe. It hit the ceramic tile with a ping. Where the hell did that woman go?

He started at the high-pitched squeal of tires and jerked his head around.

"Why that dirty…"

He ran down the hall and burst through the front door to see Maureen's silver Jaguar backing wildly down the long, twisting driveway. Frank bounded down the steps and sprinted across the front yard leaping over small shrubs and lawn ornaments. He reached the end of the driveway ahead of her and raised the axe like a lumberjack on crack. The Jaguar barreled toward him kicking up loose asphalt and dust. Frank planted his feet. Adrenaline coursing through every vein. Maureen's eyes grew wide as she glanced over her shoulder and screamed at the sight of her husband. She jerked the car to the left and Frank dove to the right. The Jag spun across the lawn and jolted to a stop in a thick stand of hibiscus.

Frank stumbled to the driver's side window. "And where the hell do you think you're going?" he shouted between wheezes.

Shaken and hysterical, Maureen glared into his eyes. "I'm going to Chicago with Billy!"

"Over my dead body!" He hoisted the pickaxe high over his head. Maureen slammed the gearshift into first and fishtailed out from beneath his downward swing. The pickaxe pierced the trunk of her car with a thud that stung his hands and sent violent tremors up his arms. The handle ripped from his hands as the Jag screamed down the driveway and out onto the road, where it was followed by a piss-yellow boat-of-a-car that seemed to appear from nowhere.

He heaved a sigh and examined his throbbing hands. God, that hurt. He looked up to see his elderly neighbor peeking over the hedges, eyes as wide as paper plates.

He forced a smile. "Why, hello, Eunice. Nice day for some yard work, eh?"

The old woman nodded in slow motion.

Frank continued, "I just came out to aerate some of the hydrangea beds."

She furrowed her brow and frowned. "Oh, Frank. What was all that screaming and yelling. . . and tires squealing. . . and that crashing sound. . . and oh my, what's this about dead bodies and running off to Chicago. . .?"

"Eunice."

"Yes, Frank?"

He raised his fist and shook it. "Why don't you shut the hell up and take that wrinkled little ass of yours back inside and mind your own goddam business."

"Oh, my!" She lifted her dressing gown then scampered down the flagstone walk and disappeared into her house.

"Chicago, huh?" Frank muttered. "We'll see about that." He shrugged his shoulders, pulled at his collar and ambled back up to the house. "Yeah, we'll just fucking see about that."

* * *

Maureen careened down the boulevard toward the interstate. When she took the entrance ramp to I-275 a yellow Bonneville pulled up beside her but was forced back as the ramp narrowed to one lane. Idiot, she muttered, wait your turn. She was still shaking as she merged onto the highway and pushed the accelerator to the floor. Light poles flicked by and billboards became a blur as the Jag approached 80.

"I've got to talk to Billy."

She grabbed her purse and pulled out her cell phone. A Dodge minivan with Kansas plates swerved and blared its horn as Maureen's car drifted from her lane. "Sorry!" Maureen jerked the wheel and waved an apology. She juggled the phone and did her best to steer.

"Dammit! He doesn't have a cell phone!" She hurled hers across the seat and threw her head back. Arggh! She looked back down and froze. The traffic in front of her had come to a crawl. The red and blue lettering on the back of a FedEx truck rushed toward her and filled her windshield.

"Shit!" She slammed on the brakes and wrenched the steering wheel to the left. The car shuddered sideways and slid down into the grassy median. The tall weeds slowed her down, but not enough to keep her from skidding up and into the northbound lanes. A chorus of angry horns filled the air as oncoming cars braked and swerved. She yanked the wheel to her right and spun the car back into the median where it came to a jolting halt.

* * *

Four cars behind the speeding Jaguar, Nicole gritted her teeth, cursed the interstate traffic and chain-smoked Camels.

"This is too intense," she spat out as she weaved from one lane into another. "I gotta relax."

As her Bonneville crossed the bridge over Dale Mabry she pulled a joint out of the center console and hung it on her lower lip. She touched the bright red ash of her cigarette against the twisted end and took a deep drag. Sweet, thick marijuana smoke filled her lungs as she tossed the Camel out the window. She patted the matte black submachine gun lying beside her. Okay, here's the plan: follow the bitch, pull up next to her, pull the trigger. Shredded wheat. Simple as that. She pulled out from behind a lumbering garbage truck and sped past. She shook her head and took another deep drag. No. Not on the interstate. Too many witnesses. And with this traffic, hell, I'd never get away. Better wait 'til she stops. She's gotta eat—or piss—or shop—or something. Then let her have it on the spot. Yeah. That's it.

She smiled, took another hit, and glanced down at the gun. "Don't let me down, my friend," she whispered as she caressed the smooth barrel. She looked up and screamed—the traffic in front of her shuddered to a jolting halt. Four cars ahead, a silver Jaguar spun wildly across the median. Directly in front of her, an eighteen-passenger van fishtailed, sending plumes of smoke out from beneath locked-up rear wheels.

Nicole slammed on her brakes and plowed into the back of the van with a bone-jarring, metallic crunch. The submachine gun struck the dashboard and discharged, blowing out the Bonneville's windshield and the rear windows of the passenger van in front of her. Nicole felt the wind go out of her as the steering wheel smashed into her chest and sent the still-smoking joint sailing across the hissing, crumpled hood of her car. She collapsed back on the seat gasping for breath. Through half-opened eyes she watched two-dozen short, bronze men in baggy jeans and tank tops leap out of the van, over the guardrail, and dash down the embankment shouting, "I-N-S! I-N-S!" She heard more screeching rubber and glanced up at the rear view mirror to see the front grill of a garbage truck climbing up and over her trunk. The force of impact jerked her neck backwards then sent her flying forward again. Face hitting the steering wheel like a mallet. She bounced off in slow motion and her limp body slumped against the door. A thick warm liquid oozed over her eyelids and down her cheeks. She tasted metal mixed with blood as she slipped into darkness.

* * *

The Jaguar spun completely around and slid to a shuddering halt in the median. Horns screamed, tires howled and metal crunched and crumpled behind her. Maureen clenched the steering wheel and sat still for a moment, body trembling, heart beating in her ears. She swallowed hard and eased the car off the grass and back into the crawl of the westbound lane. She looked in the rear view mirror at the jumbled, steaming mess behind her. An enormous yellow car sandwiched between two trucks. Hmphh. Serves you right. Shouldn't have been following so close. The cars ahead sped up and pulled away from her, easing the congestion. She flicked her turn signal, checked her mirrors and veered into the middle lane. She soon hit sixty.

Her arms still shook and her hands gripped the steering wheel as if she were afraid it would bail on her. She swallowed hard and took a deep breath. A traffic update on the radio warned of a massive multi-vehicle pile-up on the interstate, one mile north of the city. At least two-dozen cars and trucks. Multiple injuries. Gunshots. Rescue vehicles on the scene.

Sure glad I missed *that*. She looked at herself in the rearview mirror and pulled her hair back with one hand. OK, calm down now and think. You have to get to Chicago. She slapped the steering wheel. "I've got it!" She snatched up the phone and steered with her elbows as her fingers pushed the small buttons. Beep, beep, beep, beep.

"Information. What city, please?"

"Chicago."

"What listing?"

"The Hotel InterContinental."

"One moment please."

CHAPTER 10

A s Eden Myers drew closer to home she had a gut feeling that something wasn't quite right. She did her best to stifle the instinct when she turned off Fletcher Avenue into her apartment complex. Gravel crunched and popped beneath her wheels as she drove her Jeep Cherokee into the parking lot. She noticed the light green Dodge Neon straddling two parking spaces at the end of the lot.

Yep, his car, all right. But what's it doing here at noon? He should be at work. She pulled her Jeep into an empty parking space. Maybe he hitched a ride with a friend. Yeah, that's it. He carpooled. She turned off the ignition and sighed. Nope. He didn't hitch a ride. He didn't car pool. He didn't go to work. . . again. Third time in the past two weeks.

She drummed her fingers against the steering wheel and stared out the window. Take a deep breath. That's it. Now breathe out. . . slowly. Good. Keep your cool. It could be worse.

She got out and slowly climbed up the stairs to her apartment. She placed her hand on the doorknob and took a few more deep breaths. She eased the door open and looked down. Sneakers. Four pairs. They weren't there when she left for work late last night. Not a good sign.

She stepped inside and scanned the foyer and hall. In addition to the pile of sneakers, she counted two t-shirts, three gym shorts, five socks, two pairs of white cotton briefs, a pair of plaid boxers, some blue jeans, a jock strap and a few unidentifiable articles of clothing strewn like so many stepping-stones across the tile. The faint, garbled sound of a television floated down the hallway.

She picked her way through the scattered apparel and glanced into the kitchen on her left. Every cabinet door gaping wide. Every drawer pulled out. Teetering stacks of dirty dishes and more than a few scorched pots littered the countertops. The crusty remains of a breakfast gone awry splattered across the Formica. The odor of burnt toast and bacon hung heavy in the air.

She hurled her keys across the countertop and stormed into the kitchen.

SLAM! BAM! SLAM!—shouted the doors as they felt the full brunt of her fury.

A voice called from the room at the end of the hall, "Is that you, hon?"

SLAM! BAM!—echoed the drawers.

"Honey, if that's you, could you get me another beer while you're up?"

She steeled her shoulders and stormed down the hall toward the living room. She stopped, braced herself and peered around the corner.

Her fiancé Robbie lay splayed on the sofa like a living, breathing, garage-sale afghan. He wore a *'Baby, Take Me to Vegas'* t-shirt and a tattered pair of boxer shorts. A can of Old Milwaukee dangled from one hand as he fished for nourishment from a tube of Jalapeño Pringles with the other. Crumbs of other assorted snacks littered his belly like junk food shrapnel. Three empty beer cans stood as sentinels on the beige carpet accompanied by a legion of crumpled beef jerky wrappers. Three Moon Pies sat unopened on the coffee table.

"Hi, hon," he said without taking his eyes away from the TV. "Did you bring me my beer?"

She crossed her arms across her chest. "Didn't make it to work today, huh?"

"Nah," he replied as he took another swig. "When I got up this morning I thought I might be coming down with a headache, so I figured I'd play it safe and stay home, you know, just in case."

"Just in case?" she echoed.

"And besides," he continued as he stared at the big screen, "Celebrity Poker's on ESPN2. The former cast of *Lost* is taking on the cast of *Arrested Development*." He propped himself up on his elbow and turned to her. "Remember Jeffrey Tambor?"

She pursed her lips. "No."

"And after that comes Japanese Minor League Baseball Bloopers and then the NFL Tricycle Marathon for Cystic Fibrosis. Now *that* should be one hell of a brutal competition."

"Tricycle Marathon. . . Baseball bloopers. . . Celebrity Poker. . ." She looked down the hallway at the piles of scattered sports apparel. "So that's why all of this stuff is out."

"Sure," he said as he turned his head toward her. "What do you think, I'm a slob or something?"

"Actually. . ."

"I'm like an athlete in training."

An athlete? Oh, he used to be. He lettered in three sports in high school back in Mayfield, Kentucky. In college, he was always active in intramural sports. But not now. No, he is no longer an athlete. His fat-to-lean body mass is ample evidence of that. When she first met Robbie he was still very active. They often worked out at the Y and went jogging together. He even enrolled in a beach volleyball league and played every Sunday afternoon. After each match he would come home bathed in sweat and covered in sand.

"*Let's make love,*" he'd say as he pulled her close.

"*No, dear,*" she'd reply as she looked down at her ring finger, gold band conspicuously absent.

"*Well, you're worth waiting for.*"

"*Am I?*"

Yes, at one time, Robbie was trim, buffed, focused. . . and romantic. Then something happened. All of a sudden, he went on autopilot. Was it the beer? The junk food?

Eden had since grown accustomed to working, going to school, and jogging alone. Robbie had grown accustomed to living on the couch. He traded his desire to be fit and successful for an overactive imagination, a big screen television and 156 channels of mind-numbing cable. Sadly, he felt he got the best of the bargain. Now his massive collection of sneakers and sports apparel filled three closets in Eden's two-bedroom apartment. At one time he could justify the expense because he actually participated in a variety of sports. Now he maintained his collection so he could wear the appropriate garments and equipment as he watched sports on TV: cleats for Monday Night Football, Izod golf shirt for the Masters, Zoom Kobes for the NBA all-star game.

She leaned against the doorjamb and scowled. "I thought we agreed that you'd put away your things as soon as you got done with them."

"I will, hon. Soon as—" he waved his hand frantically. "Hush. . . can't you see this guy has a killer hand?"

She turned and walked dejectedly back toward the bathroom. She forced the bile and the anger down where it disappeared somewhere in her midsection. Way to go, she thought. Great self-control. The yoga classes are beginning to pay off.

She pushed the bathroom door open. Wet towels strewn across the floor. Dental floss lay unwound on the vanity like a drunken cowboy's lasso. So, what else is new? And yeah, his razor was lying out next to marshmallow globs of shaving cream. That's OK, she'd seen this before. Nothing a damp washcloth couldn't deal with.

She reached for the faucet when something jumped out of the corner of her eye and caught her attention. She slowly turned her head. She froze and stared at what was the unpardonable sin.

It was up.

The toilet seat was up! And the gaping, bone-white porcelain bowl seemed to mock her, daring her to react.

Arrghhh!!!

She planted her foot on top of the toilet seat and slammed it down with a *crack*, splitting it in two. She snatched up half the seat and stormed back down the hall. She paused at the doorway huffing and puffing.

"What the hell was that noise!?" Robbie asked without looking up from the television. "Please, hon, try to keep it down. Remember, I might be on the verge of getting one hell of a headache." He popped another chip into his mouth. "Besides, this commercial is almost over."

She raised the broken seat like an aborigine with a deadly boomerang and prepared to let it fly.

He turned his head. "Something wrong, hon?"

She caught herself as a gossamer shadow flitted before her mind's eye and whispered, "This isn't you."

"I know," she whispered as she lowered her head and dropped the seat. It hit the white tile with a ringing thud.

He stared at the broken seat. "I asked for a beer. What the hell is that?"

"I have to go," she mumbled.

He propped himself up on his elbow. "Well, since you're going out, could you get me another case of Old Milwaukee and some chips? Then when you get home I could maybe convince you to join me in some serious, mind-boggling sex." He pulled down the elastic waistband of his boxers and thrust his hips forward.

She groaned as she averted her eyes from the sight of his milk-white, flaccid genitals.

"You're so gross."

"Don't be so selfish," he said as he fondled himself. "The least you could do is give me a decent hand job."

"I have to go," she repeated softly, then turned and shuffled down the cluttered hallway.

"And don't forget the beer, okay? Love you, you're the best!"

Tears poured from her eyes as Eden pulled onto Fletcher and pointed her Cherokee toward I-275 and the shimmering skyscrapers in the distance. Her shoulders shook and she pounded the steering wheel with her fist. "This isn't the way it's supposed to be!" she cried.

Then Ginny's voice echoed in her mind. "Step out girl. You got to dive and fly."

"God, if it were only so," she said between sobs. "But I'm afraid I don't have any flight left in me." She wiped her eyes with her sleeve. "I'm just too tired to fly."

The Jeep weaved in and out of the midday traffic and took the downtown exit. Eden turned left and instinctively headed to the Wilson-Peale Gallery.

Art Walk's today, she reminded herself, and Ginny will be working her second job at the gallery. And there will be wine, lots of it. That's what I need, a glass of wine and a compassionate, understanding ear.

She pulled her Cherokee into the Centro Ybor parking garage and drove up the ramp to a space on the second level. She checked herself in the rear view mirror and wiped the tears from her red and puffy eyes. Somewhere above her, the distinct squeal of tires on parking garage pavement echoed through the six-story structure. She locked the Jeep and drifted down the stairs to the sidewalk below.

There was only a handful of people in the gallery but no sign of her friend. Eden approached one of the co-owners. "Hey, Kevin. Where's Ginny?"

"Just sent her down to the deli to pick up another veggie tray for this afternoon. Should be back any minute."

She thanked him then walked over to the buffet table and poured herself a glass of white wine. A late lunch crowd began to fill the room so she moved to an inconspicuous corner and stared absent-mindedly at the five-foot painting before her. An eruption of color and images filled every inch of the canvas. She looked at the small white card next to the painting.

"*Welcome to the Joy of the Lord.* Mixed media. Howard Finster."

She shrugged. Joy? she thought. Yeah, right.

She jumped as a raspy voice tumbled over her shoulder. "White wine. That's a pretty good choice. It's very healthy. Though not nearly as healthy as red. They say that—"

She turned and eyed the thirty-something man in a thin beige turtle-neck and faded blue jeans. A stainless steel spiked dog collar circled his thin neck. His blond, wiry goatee framed a crooked smile and his eyes drooped off to the side as if he had once pulled them down with his fingers as a child and his face froze, just as his mother said it might.

"Excuse me?" she asked.

"White wine. It's good. But it's not the best. Now red, that's a dif-ferent matter. It's the tannin."

She arched her eyebrows and took a step back.

He leaned into her and planted his hand against the wall, hemming her in. "Tannin. In the skin. All those anti-oxidants. It's the neutron bomb against all manner of cancerous and infectious diseases." He held up a nearly full glass of Cabernet. "I'm on my third glass today. I'll never get cancer." He took a sip and continued, "I should know. After all, I'm a Scientist."

"A scientist?" she asked as if she didn't hear correctly.

He smiled a broad smile that revealed he was long overdue for den-tal work. "Glad you asked. Let me tell you all about it."

And as the young man launched into a personal monologue of epic, yet boring, proportions, Eden's frantic eyes darted about the room.

Ginny, where are you?!

CHAPTER 11

BILLY stood on the corner of 16th and 7th waiting for the light to change. Thoughts of Maureen and Chicago ricocheted in his mind. Traffic rumbled by a few inches from his toes.

Every time it seems I'm ready to soar, he thought, something mucks it up. The novels. The women. So what's holding me down?

"Excuse me."

Billy turned to look at the young Asian woman beside him. Korean? He wondered. Japanese? Perhaps.

Flawless caramel skin glistened in the midday sun. Long, straight ebony hair played with her bare shoulders in the gentle breeze. She wore a simple, yet elegant white linen summer dress bedecked with an explosion of blazing blue orchids. A magnificent golden retriever on a well-worn leather leash stood at attention by her side. Her countenance was radiant. Her smile, contagious.

Billy looked into her eyes. Opaque. Gray. Shimmering. Like liquid stone. Is she blind? How odd, he thought. I don't taste a thing. Not a thing.

"Excuse me," she repeated. "Would you please point me toward The Columbia? I've seemed to have gotten turned around."

"Of course I will." He extended an elbow.

She placed her hand through his arm and waited with him for the light to change.

"Isn't this a beautiful day?" she asked. "The sun is shining so brightly and the air smells so delicious."

Billy looked into the cloudless sky. How does she know the sun is shining so brightly?

"I can feel the warmth on my skin."

87

He cast a glance her way. Does she read minds, too? I better fasten my seatbelt; this may be one hell of a ride.

"What's your name?" she asked.

"Billy Shakes. Yours?"

"Sachiko." She patted the dog beside her. "And this is Gabriel, my very best friend."

"Hello, Gabriel," he said as he reached down to pet the retriever. Gabriel wagged his tail and nuzzled Billy's hand.

"I like your voice," she continued. "You sound like a very handsome man."

"I don't know about that," he said with a chuckle. "But I'm probably better looking than your dog."

Sachiko giggled and squeezed his arm. "You make me laugh. You are handsome. I can tell."

The light turned green and Billy led her off the curb. They started to cross the street when something strange began to happen. Although they placed one foot in front of the other, Billy felt like they were walking in place. He imagined he was ten years old again, trying to walk up the down escalator at Macy's. The pedestrians around them sped past, like a video in fast-forward. Did he hit his head when Frank threw him across the lawn? Is this what a concussion feels like? He tried to get his mind around the situation when her voice chimed in. "And what do you do, Mr. Billy Shakes?"

"I'm a writer," he stammered. A businessman in blue whisked by.

"That's interesting. What do you write?"

"Oh, fiction, poetry, some non-fiction. You know, this and that." Two chatty teenaged girls rapidly approached and sped past. Billy's eyes followed their retreating forms. "How about you?"

"Me? I'm an airline pilot."

Billy stopped and turned, "Really?"

"No, silly," she said with a laugh. "But I do love to fly."

"So what do you really do?"

"Oh, this and that," she said with a faint smile.

Billy felt her hand caress the inside of his arm. Her touch was as light as the wind and it gave him goose bumps. It briefly reassured him. He turned to look at her and detected a certain glow, an aura about her. Not physical. Something deeper. Warm. Calming. Mysterious. Is this what Joy feels like? He looked away. People continued to breeze by them in a blur. He stumbled. His senses reeled. He stumbled again and nearly fell. She grasped his arm to steady him. If this is what Joy feels like, I don't think I'm ready for it.

He turned to look at her. Her eyes were now a dangerous, dark and ominous gray. Storm clouds. Whitecaps. Gale-force winds. The sound of her voice changed. Stinging. Penetrating. He suddenly felt like he was staggering along the edge of a rocky ledge. His skin battered by wind and rain. Feet slipping across wet stone. He steeled himself in her grip.

She drew to a halt and with a look of concern, asked, "You okay?"

He caught his breath and stuttered, "It's just that. . . I've never felt this way before."

Sachiko caressed his cheek. Her eyes locked on his. "I know you haven't."

That's when he felt something pierce his side. A razor-sharp blade. Ice cold. Surgical steel. He knew he'd been cut. Not his flesh. His soul. The pain pushed him closer to the brink of the cliff. He gasped and faltered. His knees buckled. She pulled him back from the edge and guided him across the gutter and onto the curb.

"What. . .what happened?" he stammered.

Her soft lips rose in a playful grin. "Well, Mr. Billy Shakes. You've felt the clean, swift cut of Joy."

Billy rocked back and forth. He furrowed his brow, trying to understand.

"And," she continued. "I don't think it will be the last time."

He thought about Maureen and sighed.

Sachiko's face grew stern. "No. Not her. Let her go."

Billy shook his head. "How did you know about—"

"Keep your heart pure and your eyes open. Joy will be there."

"H-how will I find it?"

She squeezed his hand and laughed. "Don't worry, I think joy will find you."

"It won't hurt again, will it?" His voice trembled.

She was silent for a moment. "Perhaps."

Billy shivered at the thought.

"Cherish these scars, my friend. They are very precious and very rare."

At that she leaned forward and kissed him gently on the lips. He looked into her gray eyes again. The storm had subsided. The raging sea was now placid, still as a sheet of glass. There was calm. A soft breeze.

"I can find my way from here." She turned away and Gabriel, her glorious golden retriever, guided her down the bustling sidewalk. She stopped and looked back over her shoulder.

"And remember one thing, Billy," she called out with a smile. "The next time you find yourself up on a cliff, don't hesitate. Jump. Then build your wings on the way down."

A puzzled look crossed his face.

"Ray Bradbury," she said, then turned and disappeared into the lunchtime crowd.

Billy took a long, deep breath and sighed. He looked around to see if anyone was staring at him and was relieved to see that they weren't. He turned to walk the block and a half to the gallery. Joy, he said to himself as he shook his head. You touched it, and it hurt. He massaged his sore ribs. I'm not ready for this. He looked down at his hands and noticed they were still trembling.

"God, now I could really use a drink".

CHAPTER 12

FRANK opened the front door, walked into the den, and unlocked the liquor cabinet. The screech of her tires still reverberated in his ears as he pulled out a bottle of single malt scotch and poured himself a double. He swallowed hard and winced as the whisky burned his throat. He wiped his mouth with his forearm. Hmph. She'll be back.

But there was something in her voice and in her eyes that told him he was wrong. She won't come back. At least not on her own. She'll need some—how could he put it—encouragement. Someone would have to bring her back to her senses. He took another big gulp and collapsed into his brown leather club chair. But who? He sat in silence and nursed his drink. His mind raced, searching for answers. He sure couldn't go get her, he thought. She'd spot him a mile away. Gotta be someone... He sprang forward.

"The Chin!" he said to the empty room. "That's it. Tommy 'The Chin' Paoli could work this out. He knows Chicago like the back of his hand. And he still owes me for helping him out with those *coglioni* and their fucked-up casino grab." He took another sip. "But I gotta come up with a situation. A threat. Something that has the potential to inflict long-term damage." He raised his glass and took another sip as he mulled over the possibilities. He slapped the arm of the chair. "I got it. The Russians!"

Buoyed by this epiphany, Frank got up and strode over to his desk. He fished around in the drawers and pulled out his address book. He leafed through the pages until he found the number for Tommy 'The Chin' Paoli. He picked up the phone and dialed the number of a long-established and infamous social club on Rosebud. Three rings later a high-pitched nasal voice answered, "Yeah, who is it?"

"It's me, Frank, down in Tampa."

"I don't know no Frank in Tampa."

"Listen, I need to talk to The Chin."

"Didn't you hear me? I said I don't know no Frank in Tampa. And neither does The Chin. Now get lost."

"No wait, wait," Frank said as he paced back and forth. "It's me, Frank Valentino. Just tell The Chin that it's Frankie the Valentine. He'll know who I am."

"Just a minute."

Frank recognized the distant sandpaper-voice on the other line, "Who the hell is it?"

C'mon, Mr. Paoli. Take the phone, it's me, Frank!

* * *

In a dimly lit social club on the near-southwest side of Chicago, Eddie 'The Mouse' DeFazio lowered the phone. "I'm sorry Mr. Paoli. It's some guy from Florida. Calls himself Frankie the Valentine. Want to speak to him?"

"Frankie the Valentine? Hmmm. . ." Mr. Paoli drummed his fingers on the small café table. "Oh yeah, yeah, there was that misunderstanding in Florida a couple of years ago. This Frankie the Valentine fellah stepped in and smoothed things over. Kind of rough around the edges, but I think he's a stand-up guy. He's somehow affiliated with Albano, LoScalzo and whoever else is left of the Trafficante Family."

"So he's a made guy?"

"Nah, but he's connected somehow. Here, give me the phone."

The Mouse handed him the receiver then walked over to the bar and pulled out a stool. He sat down and sipped his espresso. The Chin raised the phone to his ear.

"This Frankie the Valentine?"

"Hello, Mr. Paoli," Frank replied with a tone of respect.

Paoli raised an unlit cigar to his lips and took an imaginary draw. "What can I do you for?"

"I got this problem, Mr. Paoli."

The Chin detected a wave of embarrassment in the caller's voice. "We all got problems, Frank. What kinda problem?"

"It's my wife, Mr. Paoli.'

"What, they don't got marriage counselors in Florida?" He burst into laughter, which elicited generous laughs from the other men in the social club. Everyone seemed to laugh when Mr. Paoli laughed.

"No, it's not like that, Mr. Paoli. She's on her way to Chicago."

"So?" The Chin took another imaginary draw on his cigar.

"She's got some information with her. Information that could cause a lot of difficulty for the Family here in Florida. The Russians are after her. And who knows what they'll do to her. They're fuckin' medieval. We gotta get her back."

"The Russian mob you say?" The Chin raised an eyebrow and turned to look at the table of well-groomed, sun-blond men off to his right. "This sounds serious. Hold on a second."

The Chin cupped his hand over the receiver. "Hey, Dimitri!"

A stocky Russian set his half-empty glass down on the table and grinned. "Yeah?"

"D'you know anything about a plan to track down and extract some information from the wife of one of our guys in Tampa?"

"Tampa?" replied the Russian with a deep, guttural laugh. He un-capped a bottle of vodka and topped off his glass. "Mother of God, we own all of fuckin' Florida! What information could we possibly want from any of you Mediterranean grease balls?"

The half-dozen beefy Russians sitting with him burst out in laughter and clinked their glasses.

Mr. Paoli broke into a grin. "Just what I thought. Thanks, Dimitri."

He took his palm off the receiver. "Yeah, Frankie, it sounds real serious," he said stifling a laugh. "We'll get her. I got just the guys who can pull this off. Any idea where she's staying? Chicago's a pret-ty big town, you know."

"I'm not sure where she's staying, Mr. Paoli. But, she'll be at the Film Festival tonight. You got an e-mail address? I'll send you a picture."

"I ain't got no damn e-mail, Frankie. Gimme your number and one of these guys will call you. They know all that computer shit. You can e-mail the pictures to them, *capiche*?" He waved his hand to the little man at the bar. "Hey, Mouse, take this down."

The Chin called the numbers out to The Mouse, who scribbled them down on a napkin.

"Thank you, Mr. Paoli. You don't know how much this means to me."

"No problem, Frankie, glad I could help." The Chin hung up the phone, grinned, and lit his cigar. He blew a generous cloud of white smoke into the air where it disappeared into the ever-present haze above him.

"No disrespect, Mr. Paoli," said The Mouse as he handed The Chin the napkin. "But why did you take this on? The guy was lying to you."

"Yeah," echoed Dimitri from across the room. "I don't get it."

"Listen, Eddie." The Chin put his arm around The Mouse and blew another cloud of smoke to the ceiling. "I owe this guy one. He pulled my ass out of the wringer a year or two ago and this payback is a cinch. I pull this off and I don't owe this Frankie nothin'. The slate is wiped clean."

Eddie the Mouse nodded slowly. "Yeah. I get the picture."

"See," The Chin continued with a wry smile. "I can think of two guys who would jump at the opportunity to work on an 'important' job like this."

"But Mr. Paoli, we got big plans." The Mouse nodded to the table of Russians. "We can't spare any of our guys."

"That's where you're wrong. I know two guys and they're perfect for this job."

"You're gonna waste the talents of two of our guys at a time like this?" The Mouse's voice rose to a whine. "But Mr. Paoli –"

"Yes, Eddie, *especially* at a time like this. See, I got two nephews that are dying to join the organization." He pulled a glass ashtray closer and flicked his cigar. "But the fact is, they're fuckin' morons and I don't want them anywhere near my dealings with our good friends from Commie-Land." He smiled at the table of Russians who returned the smile and raised their glasses.

"I can't use them now—or ever, for that matter," he continued. "But my kid sister's been riding my ass for the last couple of years to do something with these pecker heads she calls sons. This'll be the perfect opportunity to keep them occupied and out of the way."

"That's brilliant," said The Mouse. "Absolutely brilliant."

"I got to hand it to you, Mr. Paoli," said Dimitri. "You're one smart man. It's a wonder you wops ever lost Florida."

And once again, the room exploded in laughter.

* * *

Danny Lucci tossed the carpenter's framing hammer from hand to hand and licked his lips. "You ready Eugene?"

"You kidding? I was born ready."

Danny and Eugene Lucci were down in the basement of their three-flat on Ashland. Danny, 28, was tall and rangy, his brother Eugene, 26, short and dumpy. They shared the same ink-black hair combed back and held in place by dollops of petrochemical goo. They favored double-knit shirts and chino slacks that occasionally matched. But what the brothers lacked in taste, they made up with bravado. And while their active imaginations told them they were well liked and highly respected in the neighborhood, truth was most of their neighbors simply tolerated the two brothers.

Since Danny and Eugene were chronically unemployed, they had a lot of time on their hands. They spent most of their waking hours inventing and playing games. Today the boys sat on brown metal folding chairs at a little card table—the one their mother always brought up for Thanksgiving to "seat the kids." Dust mites and other miniscule debris floated in the stark light of four bulbs set in white porcelain sockets overhead. Danny gripped the hammer. His eyes focused. Muscles tensed. A shiny new carriage bolt sat in the middle of the table. The goal of the game? Eugene would try to snatch the bolt off the table before Danny could smash his hand with the hammer. After an hour of near misses and solid hits, Danny's ring-tone echoed off the basement walls. He pulled his cell phone from the holster.

"Yo."

"This Danny? It's your Uncle Tommy."

He jerked upright. "Hey, Uncle Tommy! How's it hanging?"

A pregnant pause on the other end of the line. "Listen, I got a job for you two."

He covered the phone with his hand and whispered, "It's Uncle Tommy. He's got a job for us!"

"No shit?" said Eugene as he sucked on his swollen and bloody knuckles.

Danny returned to the phone. "So what is it, Uncle Tommy?"

"I can't talk much now. Phones might be tapped." A chorus of titters broke out in the background. "But here's the number of a guy in Florida. He's gonna e-mail you some pictures. Bring them to the club tonight at 5:30. And remember, be discrete, they might be tailing you."

"Tailing us?" Danny glanced from side to side. "Who? Why?"

"Never mind that now," continued Uncle Tommy to more stifled laughter. "Just get on line and get those pictures. I'll see you later on. *Ciao.*"

"You can count on us, Uncle Tommy. *Ciao.*"

Danny leapt to his feet and pumped his fist into the air. "Did you hear that, Gino? Uncle Tommy got us a job!"

"Hot damn," Eugene yelled as he jumped up from his chair. The brothers embraced. Then they danced. Then they began to playfully punch each other. The blows intensified. Before long, Danny had his brother in a headlock.

"You want some more of this?" he asked as he ground his knuckles into Eugene's head.

"Ahhh! Stop! You're ripping my scalp!"

Danny released his brother and pushed him away. "Before we get too excited, we gotta call this guy in Florida."

"Florida?" Eugene asked as he massaged his scalp. "So you're telling me this is gonna be an international job?"

"I think it's beyond international." Danny lowered his voice. "I think it's gonna be transcontinental."

His brother's eyes grew wide. "Then what are we waiting for?"

"Wait," said Danny as he grabbed his brother's shoulders. "How's that left hand of yours?"

Eugene looked down at his bruised and bloody hand. "It hurts like hell. But my right hand is fine." He proudly held it out for his brother to inspect. "See? Good as new."

"Hmm. I see." Danny swung the hammer. Phwack! "Good as dead, you mean."

"Ai-eeee!" Eugene thrust the swelling fingers into his mouth and spun around the room like a whirling dervish.

Danny slapped his thighs and laughed as his brother's dance slowed to a stagger.

Eugene doubled over and hissed, "You crazy sick bastard!"

"That may be," said Danny between howls. "But I'm a crazy sick bastard with a framing hammer." He put his arm around his whimpering brother. "Now stop your sniveling and get upstairs. We got a phone call to make."

"Okay," Eugene whined. "But next time I get to hold the hammer."

"Deal. Next time you get to hold the hammer. Let's shake on it."

At that Danny grabbed his brother's throbbing hand and squeezed it like a wet dishrag.

* * *

At 5:30 sharp, Danny and Eugene swaggered into their Uncle Tommy's social club like they owned the place. There were only a few men in the dimly lit space but Tommy 'The Chin' Paoli stood out like royalty. It wasn't his appearance that caused him to stand out. Sure, he wore a custom-tailored Armani suit, but then, so did the other men. No, Tommy the Chin stood out because of a certain aura that always seemed to surround him. Everyone who met The Chin knew he was a man that deserved the utmost respect. Neglecting to do so guaranteed certain, unpleasant reprisals. Some of those reprisals could induce permanent pain. Some could even be deadly. Unfortunately, Danny and Eugene were severely lacking in aura-detection skills. To them, this was simply their Uncle Tommy— the guy who used to bring them the coolest Christmas presents when they were kids. Scooters, bikes, video game consoles, even the now rusty trampoline sitting in the backyard. But to this day, Danny and Eugene could never figure out how all that good stuff could "fall off the back of a truck" as Uncle Tommy used to put it.

Eugene waved to the men scattered throughout the room. "Good to see you guinea-wops," he said with a familiarity he had not earned.

"Hey, Uncle Tommy! How's it hanging?" Danny yelled as he embraced his uncle. Eugene followed suit and joined in the hug. Uncle

Tommy squirmed to release himself from their combined embrace. He pushed the boys away, smoothed his suit jacket, and straightened his hundred-dollar silk tie. The other men in the club looked down and shook their heads. One capo turned to another and whispered, "Ain't no way these two jerk-offs are Italian. I swear to god they must be Presbyterians."

"Ok, boys, have a seat," Uncle Tommy said pointing to a table.

Danny and Eugene each pulled up a chair and sat down. Uncle Tommy remained standing.

"You bring the pictures?" he asked.

"Got them right here, Uncle Tommy." Eugene slid a crisp manila envelope across the table just like he'd seen them do it in the movies.

"Good." Uncle Tommy pulled out the photographs of Frank's wife.

"Who's the hot babe?" asked Danny.

Uncle Tommy placed his hands on the table, leaned forward and whispered, "She's the wife of a guy in Florida. He's second in command for the—uh—the Trafficante Family. Yeah. The Trafficantes."

The brothers exchanged glances. Danny exhaled and whispered to his brother, "I told you this was going to be big."

"So here's the deal," Uncle Tommy continued. "She has some valuable information that could put us all away."

"All of us?" asked Eugene.

Uncle Tommy paused and cast a nervous eye around the room, then stared at the two boys. "That's right. *All* of us."

Once again, the brothers exchanged glances.

"See boys, there are men out there, evil men, that would give anything to get their hands on that information. The Feds, the Russians, the Colombians, the Chinks, even the—"

"—Bulimics?" Eugene interjected.

"The Bulimics?" asked Danny as he turned and eyed his brother.

"You know, from Bulimia," his brother explained matter-of-factly. "I think it used to be part of the Soviet Bloc."

More stifled laughter echoed throughout the room. "Like I said," the capo repeated, "Fuckin' Presbyterians."

Uncle Tommy heaved an exasperated sigh. "Yes boys, even the Bulimics. They're a new threat and more vicious than all the others combined."

"Jeez," the brothers intoned.

"So here's the deal. I need you to find her and get her back to Florida before the others get to her." He leaned forward and stared at the boys. "It's a rescue attempt of monumental proportions. Just like that old movie, *Saving Private Ryan*."

"Don't you mean *Shaving Ryan's Privates*?" Eugene asked with a confused look.

"Jackass," moaned Danny rolling his eyes. He gave his brother a dope slap. "He's not talking about that porno flick you downloaded last Friday. He's talking about that war movie with Tom Hanks and that other guy with the really big head."

Eugene rubbed the back of his head. "Oh."

Their uncle grabbed their shirts and pulled the boys up onto the table. "Now listen you fucking morons. This is serious." He released his grip and they fell back onto their chairs. "She'll be at the Film Festival tonight. You may have to use some force to get her back home, but no one is to get hurt, especially her, understand?"

The brothers nodded slowly.

"And be discreet. Don't draw any attention from the authorities. *Capiche*?"

"*Capiche*, Uncle Tommy."

"Good. Now get to work, boys," he said as they rose. "Make me and your mother proud."

"Don't worry, Uncle Tommy," Danny said as he slapped his uncle's back. "You couldn't have found two guys more qualified to pull this job off."

"I know that, boys," Uncle Tommy said as he put an arm around each of his nephews and ushered them to the door. "I don't think there's anyone in Chicago that could compare to you two. Now get going, you got a job to do and not much time to do it."

"Goodbye, Uncle Tommy," said Danny.

Their uncle held the door open and the two boys stepped outside. They walked down the sidewalk and Danny gave Eugene another dope slap. "*Shaving Ryan's Privates*," he muttered in disgust.

"Hey, watch it!" Eugene said as he stumbled forward. "That was a good movie. Not Oscar quality, I grant you that. But it had its moments."

"Eugene?"

"Yeah?"

"You're a real fucking idiot."

"At least I'm for real."

The two boys hitched up their pants and sauntered down Taylor to the nearest el station.

"Think about it, Danny. Our first job. What could be easier than kidnapping some helpless broad?"

"Like stealing candy from a baby, Gino".

CHAPTER 13

BILLY approached the century-old, red brick building that housed the Wilson-Peale Gallery and little else. A colorful poster hung on the front door. *Howard Finster Retrospective - Second Floor.* Finster, he thought. Cool.

He entered the building and nodded at the artist taking advantage of the vacant first-floor space. He turned the corner and, wham! He collided with a woman bearing trays of shrimp and cocktail sauce. She stumbled backward and crashed to the floor. Billy fell on top of her, his head buried between her breasts.

"Why, you stupid jackass!" A shrill voice echoed in his ears.

He lifted his head from her chest and met two angry eyes. The voice continued, "Why the hell don't you look—" The woman paused as her eyes roamed over his face, her mouth forming a slight grin. "What I mean is, are you alright?"

"Er, I think so. You?" He propped himself up on his elbows and started to rise.

"Wait." She ran her hands from his shoulders to the small of his back. "Don't be so hasty. You may be hurt." Her hands moved back up to his shoulders, then back down, past his hips and came to rest on his ass.

"I think I'm okay," he said as he struggled to rise.

She continued to stare into his eyes as she pulled his hips into hers. "Just wanted to be sure." She raised her head. Her face nearly touching his.

"Really. I'm okay." He wiggled out of her grasp and climbed to his knees. "Here, let me help you clean this up."

She sat up and regarded the mess before her. "No, no. I'll get it. Looks like you have somewhere to go."

Billy stood and grabbed her hand to help her to her feet. "Oh, my. Look at your blouse. And your jeans."

She glanced down at the bright red cocktail sauce splattered across her like gunshot wounds. She flicked a shrimp off her shoulder and shrugged. "It's okay. But look at your shirt!"

He pulled the damp fabric from his chest. "Don't worry. I have a change of clothes in the car," he said, thinking of the packed suitcase in the trunk. "But let me take care of your clothes." He reached into his back pocket and pulled out his wallet. He handed her two fifties. "Here."

Her eyes locked onto the two crisp bills. "Oh, I really couldn't."

"No, no. I insist. It's the least—"

She snatched the bills from his hand and slid them into her right front pocket. "Okay. If you insist. Thanks."

"And the food, let me pay for the food, too." He pulled out another fifty.

Ginny grinned. "Right front pocket's full. Here—slide it into this one." She thrust her left hip forward. He slid the folded bill into her tight pocket.

"Now let's get this mess cleaned up." He knelt to gather up fistfuls of flaccid shrimp and piled them on the broken platter.

She knelt down across from him, eyes riveted to his. She picked up a handful of shrimp and absentmindedly placed them back on the floor. "We make a good team."

He laughed and said, "We'd make a better team if you got some of those shrimp on the platter."

Her face reddened. "Oh, yeah, of course."

Billy picked up the last of the shrimp then dumped the platter into a nearby trash can. "I'm gonna grab another shirt. See ya 'round . . . er . . . Sorry, I didn't get your name."

"Ginny. Ginny Wheeler." She wiped her cocktail sauce-stained hand on her jeans and extended it.

He took it in his. "Billy."

"Glad we ran into each other today," she said as she held his hand and led him out the door. "Listen, my apartment's only a few minutes away. I'm gonna jump into some new clothes. Don't go anywhere. I'll be right back."

Billy watched her dance down the sidewalk toward a red Toyota then headed to his own car. Feisty girl, he thought. Sure wouldn't want to get on her bad side. He pulled a new shirt out of his suitcase and threw it on. Then he re-entered the building and climbed the worn wooden stairs to join the humming late lunch crowd. Local blues legend Willie 'Dog-Mess' Patterson hopped up on a small platform in the corner and attacked his acoustic slide guitar with abandon. Billy circled the gallery admiring Finster's work, his muscles invigorated by the Mississippi Delta wail that filled the room. He helped himself to some hors d'oeuvres and a glass of wine then found an empty bench off to the side and sat down.

One of the owners whisked by. "Hey, Billy. See anything tasty?"

"Funny, Kev." It was Kevin Womack. Friend since high school. They moved from New York to Florida together, Billy to enter an internship in Jack Kerouac's old home in Orlando, Kevin to attend art school in Sarasota. Billy went on to successfully publish. Kevin? Unfortunately, the only thing Kevin could successfully draw was scathing criticism for his work. So he did what many frustrated artists do: He opened a gallery.

Billy sipped his wine and observed the people around the room. His eyes fell upon a waif-like girl across the room. Smooth ivory skin— mmm—warm, sweet cream. Her finger twirled a strand of raven-black hair that tumbled to her shoulders like a midnight waterfall. Seems vaguely familiar. Did she come to one of his readings? A writer's festival? His eyes moved to the sickly looking young man inching up to her. Is she really with that guy? He marveled at the dog collar fashioned from sharp intertwining one-inch spikes—the kind you would only purchase for a dog you despised. Definitely PETA bait. He recognized him. He was an Art Walk regular. Claimed to be a Scientist. What the hell is that? Billy had met microbiologists, nuclear physicists and nano-technologists. Who the hell calls himself a 'Scientist'?

Billy shook his head and sipped his wine. He knew from experience that the Scientist was enamored with the sound of his own voice. He didn't really converse, he pontificated and expounded. He considered himself an expert in all manner of disciplines and did not hesitate to tell you so— in long, drawn-out and convoluted sentences. He had the unique ability to suck all of the air out of a room, like a shop vac on steroids. Today he appeared to be on the far side of tipsy, swaying back and forth like a cattail in a stiff breeze. His jaw was in constant motion as he leaned in closer— the way people move in on you when they have had too much to drink. Now he was only inches from the young girl's face. Her eyes grew wide and her eyebrows arched high. She seemed totally captivated and completely entranced. I don't get it, Billy thought. Why do so many pretty girls fall for guys like him?

Then he noticed some movement. The girl took a nervous step back and her glazed eyes darted about crowded room. Wait. She's not entranced. She's trapped! The young woman's desperate eyes made contact with his and her pleading expression said it all: Help... me...I...can't...breathe.

He leapt to his feet and strode across the room. "Hey, guy," he said as he slapped the Scientist on the back. "Remember me from last month?"

"Uh. . . sure, dude. . . how've you been?" the gangly man replied with no apparent sign of recollection.

Billy turned and winked at the young girl, then put his hand on the man's bony shoulder.

"Remember what we were talking about the other day? Well, the artist downstairs just asked me about it and I told him I'd send you around. I know he'll be glad to see you."

"Gee, thanks man!" the Scientist replied then turned to the young woman, "Excuse me, darling, but I have to go downstairs now. Another person wants to avail himself of my vast store of knowledge. You rate white here," he said, jumbling his words and pointing to the ground for emphasis. Then he smiled a broad, wet smile and wobbled over to the stairs.

The young girl turned to Billy and beamed. "I don't know how to thank you!"

"Why didn't you just walk away?"

"He had me cornered. I couldn't escape." She looked down and scraped a toe across floor. "And in a way, I felt a little sorry for him. That is, until I felt the oxygen being sucked out of my lungs."

"I know the feeling."

"Besides," she added with a smile, "I was hoping that someone would come to my rescue. 'Course, I didn't expect anyone as handsome as that British actor —"

"I know, I know. What's his name."

"Anyway, thanks."

"'Twas a pleasure, ma'am," Billy said in his very best John Wayne voice. He bowed slightly and tipped an imaginary ten-gallon hat.

The young girl giggled then pretended to swoon. "My hero."

* * *

The Scientist left the gallery and stumbled down the steps to the first floor. He staggered over to an artist unfolding an easel.

"Hey, my man. How's it going?"

"Pretty good, how 'bout yourself?" The Artist pulled a painting from a cardboard box and set it on the easel.

The Scientist took a sip of wine. "All these paintings yours?"

The Artist turned and eyed the Scientist. "No, these belong to Max Ernst. But Max wasn't able to make it today since he's dead and all. So he asked me to help him out."

The Scientist slowly nodded his head. "Ernst? Hmm. I think I've heard of him. He's like that character Finster upstairs. I tell you, neither one of them can paint worth a damn." He approached another easel and stroked his goatee. "But these paintings are actually pretty good."

"Is there something you want?" the Artist asked as he turned and pulled another painting from the box. "I'm really kinda busy."

"Well," the Scientist said to the young man's back, "my friend upstairs suggested I talk to you about some of the things we discussed last month."

"Some of the things you and I discussed?" asked the Artist without turning. "Sorry, I don't recall that conversation."

The Scientist shook his head. "Not what you and I talked about. I mean what I talked about with the man upstairs."

"How would I know what you and God talked about?" The Artist settled the painting and once again turned to face the Scientist.

"I'm a Scientist. I don't believe in God. Why on earth would I be talking to him? I'm talking about the man I just saw upstairs." He pointed a finger. "Upstairs in the gallery." He tossed his head back and drained his glass. "Sheesh."

105

The Artist put his hands on his hips and tilted his head. "Man, what the hell are you talking about?"

"Ok, let's start from the beginning," said the Scientist as he steadied himself. He looked down at his empty glass. "Hey, do you have any wine down here or do I need to go back upstairs?"

"There's some over there." The Artist nodded to a small café table across the room. The Scientist weeble-wobbled over to the table, bumped into it, and knocked over four long stemmed glasses.

"Who moved the damn table?" he muttered.

He poured himself a glass to the brim, then turned and ambled back over to the Artist. "Now, as I was saying. . ."

* * *

An awkward moment of silence filled the air between Billy and Eden when she noticed him staring into her eyes. She interrupted his reverie. "Are you ok?"

Billy started. "I'm sorry. I was just tasting your eyes."

"Excuse me?"

"I said I was tasting your eyes."

She took a step backwards. Oh, boy. Here we go again.

"Man, I guess that must sound weird."

"You guessed right."

"I have this condition - my senses are all mixed up. I taste color. . . I feel sound."

"I see." She tried to sound convincing. "And what exactly do my eyes taste like?"

He stared at the ceiling. "Honey with a hint of. . . apricot, maybe? A vintage French sauterne? No. Something else, an exquisite fino amontillado."

"Fino, what?"

"Sherry. Very expensive."

"And this 'condition'—does it have a name?"

"Synesthesia."

She took another step back. "Is it contagious?"

He shook is head and chuckled. "Don't worry."

"So you really taste color. . ."

" . . . And feel sound," he added.

"I think I understand." She studied his face. She remembered this man. Somehow. From somewhere. Besides, he doesn't seem threatening, and he is kind of cute. Good sense of humor. Quick thinking. Light on his feet. She felt herself being drawn to him. Something warm suffused her inner being. She'd felt it once before. Years ago. The day Robbie Renfro helped her when she locked herself out of her car at the Jazz Festival. He fished a coat hanger from his trunk and popped the lock. He, too, was funny and cute. Just like this guy. Could he be one of the Great Ones? Or—she shuddered. Could this be another Robbie Renfro? Sigh.

Kevin wandered over. "I see you two have met." Then turning to Eden he added, "Watch out for this guy. He's got this incredible pick-up line. Says he 'tastes color.' I didn't believe it at first 'til I came in last week and he's got a Warhol print rolled up like a hoagie. Had to snag it from him before he could take a bite."

She eyed Billy. "For real?"

He shook his head and snickered. "Of course not."

She heaved her shoulders. "Thank goodness, the last thing I need is another weirdo who—"

"It wasn't a Warhol," Billy continued. "It was a Rauschenberg. More wine?"

Her eyes scanned their serious faces, and when they broke into a laugh she smiled. "Touché."

Billy placed his hand on the back of her arm and they began to drift around the room.

"I've always been a fan of Finster," he said as they stood in front of a large panel. Four winged creatures with golden harps circled a colorful mountain. Bible verses were etched across the background like bathroom wall-scrawl.

"I like all the colors," she said. "But these angels give me the heebie-jeebies."

"Why's that?"

"Long story." She pulled him to the next one. "Why does he paint like a ten-year old?"

"It's primitive. Finster had no formal training. See all these little people on the mountain? I read somewhere that he got some paint on the end of his finger and he pushed it against a piece of plywood. The fingerprint resembled a face. All these little faces in his work are just fingerprints, see?"

Eden leaned in for a closer look. "You're right. Fingerprints with little faces painted on them." She touched one and examined the bright red paint on the tip of her finger. A mirror image of the face stared back at her. "I think this painting is still wet."

"Impossible. Finster died years ago," Billy said, still admiring the painting.

"Oh yeah?" She held up her finger. "Take a look at this."

He took her hand and stared at the little face, then turned and inspected the painting. "It sure doesn't look wet."

They turned back to the painting. Small cracks that ran through hardened paint like a hundred varicose veins. She glanced around the room, and when she was sure no one was looking, she said, "You try."

He cautiously reached up and touched a different face. He pulled his hand back and stared at the little face on his finger.

Eden smirked. "Told you."

"I'll be damned," he whispered. "We better get this cleaned up. Give me your napkin." Billy rubbed his finger. "It's not working."

"Here, let me try." She dipped the napkin in her wine and scrubbed her finger. The face continued to stare back at her.

"This is too weird," she said. "What do you think?"

"Painting's dry."

"Definitely dry."

They exchanged nervous glances but dared not touch it again.

Eden stepped away from the painting and changed the subject. "You must really enjoy gallery events like this," she said with forced buoyancy. "With all these colors."

"You're right," he replied. "It's like an elegant buffet."

She slapped his shoulder and giggled. "You're silly."

"Listen," he said. "This *is* Art Walk, isn't' it? What say we take a walk and see some more art."

"Splendid idea," she said with a smile. "I hear they have some very delicious paintings on display."

They skipped down the steps and spied the Scientist helping himself to a glass of wine.

Billy raised a finger to his lips. "Shh, it's our friend with another victim."

The couple tiptoed past the two men and stepped out into the late afternoon sun as the steady drone of irrelevant facts and obtuse opinions wafted on a crisp, light breeze behind them.

* * *

The Scientist ambled back over to the Artist and held up his glass of wine. "Red. It's nuclear. I should know. I'm a Scientist."

"Don't you think you've had enough?" the Artist hinted as he watched rivulets of red trickle from the edge of the Scientist's mouth and over his goatee. The wine dripped off his chin and stained his beige turtleneck.

"Nah, you can never have enough medicine. And this stuff is medicinal," he explained, wiping his mouth with his shirtsleeve. "Now about my friend upstairs."

"What's your friend's name?" The Artist seemed afraid to ask.

The Scientist rubbed the back of his neck. "Um—I'm not sure. I'll go ask him."

At that he wheeled around and zigzagged to the stairs. He raised a foot and missed the first step. "Who moved the damned stairs?" he muttered.

When he reached the top, he took one more step than necessary and stumbled again. He balanced his drink and mumbled something about unexplained architectural movement. He put one shoulder against the wall as if to hold it up, then made his way down the hallway toward the gallery. After five or six feeble steps, the swish-swash of wine seeped from his intestines and into his bladder.

He turned his face and confided to the wall, "Man, I gotta take a whiz." He set his sights on the men's room. With each painful step, he felt his bloated bladder growing heavier. He reached the door with a sigh of relief and pushed. It didn't budge.

A muffled voice said, "Just a minute."

"No problem, dude. I'll just wait here hoping that my bladder won't burst." He crossed his legs and grabbed his crotch. "Hurry," he whispered to the ceiling.

Two excruciating minutes later the door opened and a man appeared, wiping his hands with a paper towel. "All yours, buddy."

The Scientist nodded and scampered into the bathroom. The small room began to spin and he braced himself against the sink. Man, I gotta sit down for a minute. He dropped his drawers and lowered himself onto the toilet. There, that's it, he sighed as he looked up at the flickering light fixture above. The sound of urine hitting water had him crooning, "Oh, what a sweet, sweet sound."

Then he closed his eyes and drifted off into semi-conscious bliss.

Chapter 14

"**D**o you come to Art Walk often?" Eden asked Billy as they strolled arm in arm down 7th.

"I try to make it every month," he replied. "You?"

"I've been a few times. I always wanted to go more often but my, um, 'ex' hated art."

Billy looked at her out of the corner of his eye. Ex? Hmmm. What have we here?

"If the picture wasn't moving he just didn't have any interest in it. Not me. I even took art history and a drawing class last semester."

"You look a little old for college. Er, what I mean is, you don't look like a typical co-ed."

"Nice recovery," she said with a laugh. "Actually, I got a late start. Plus, I'm on the six-year plan. What about you?"

"Writer. I guess it's my calling. I think my parents sensed it too. That's why they named me Billy."

She turned and furrowed her brow. "Huh?"

"William, I mean. William Shakes. As in Shakespeare. But that William churned out great literature. I churn out beach books. That's why I opt for Billy instead of William. How about you? What's your calling, besides attracting the interest of semi-successful authors with rare and unusual conditions?"

Eden paused for a moment. "Good question. I'm not sure. Sometimes I feel there's something more. Something yet to be revealed." She turned her head slightly and stared off into space. "I catch glimpses of it sometimes. Usually in my dreams. No—they're more like nightmares. But sometimes during the day I catch a glimpse of…I'm sorry. That's the wine talking."

"No, no. It's okay. You'll find it someday." He sensed her unease and changed the subject. "You said you took some art classes. Any favorites?"

"I like what I like. How about you?"

"My favorite piece is *Nighthawks* by Hopper. Ever seen it?"

The light changed and they stepped off the curb. "Isn't that the one with Elvis, James Dean and Marilyn Monroe in the diner? My ex had one over the sofa in his apartment before he got evicted. I think it's in some pawn shop on Kennedy now."

"That's a bastardized version. The real one is much more powerful." He hesitated and considered the girl beside him. There was something about her. Was it the way she laughed when he did his John Wayne shtick? The way she touched his arm as they walked through the gallery? Or the way he felt—true confederates—as they tiptoed past the Scientist? He thought about Sachiko and Joy. Could this be it? Joy? A second chance to step out and take another risk? He swallowed hard. "Wanna see it?"

"You have a print?"

"I do, but I'm talking about the real thing. At the Art Institute. In Chicago. Let's go."

Eden stopped in the middle of the street and turned to face him. "Chicago? Now? You can't be serious."

"Why not? Where's your sense of adventure?"

A horn honked as the light turned green. He grabbed her hand and scurried to the curb.

"What do you say?" He gazed into her eyes and shifted from one foot to the other. Oh god, please say yes.

"But you don't even know my name!"

"Remind me."

"Eden Myers."

"Good. Now that we know each other, what do you say?"

She cocked her head to one side and bit her lip. "You're serious, aren't you?"

"As I'm standing here."

Eden turned toward the traffic streaming by. This is nuts, she thought. But then again...

"Well?" Billy repeated as he reached out and touched her shoulder.

"I don't know…It's just that. . . I mean. . . I'll have to stop at my place and pack some things." I can't believe I said that!

"Don't have time, our flight leaves in less than an hour."

"You already bought tickets?"

"It's a long story."

She planted one hand on her hip and poked him in the chest with the other. "Try me."

"I was going to Chicago with a friend but she cancelled at the last minute."

"Oh, was she taken ill?"

"No," he replied with a chuckle. "She was taken by her husband. Right out of my arms and back into the house. C'mon, we have to hurry if we're going to make the flight." He turned and briskly walked away.

"You mean she was married?" Eden called out after him. She scurried to catch up. "Didn't you know about her husband?"

"Of course. He even thought the trip was a great idea. That is, until he realized I wasn't gay after all."

She grabbed his arm and spun him around. "Wait one minute. Why on earth would he think you were gay?"

Billy chuckled. "I'm a poet and writer, so he just assumed I was gay. And since everything was going so well, I didn't challenge it. Then I told him how delicious his wife was, and that's when it hit the fan."

"Ah, the 'condition,'" she said, nodding her head.

"Yep, the 'condition.'" He grabbed her hand and led her forward. She held back. Poet. Writer. It all started to come back to her. She *had* seen him before. Years ago. She was only a high school freshman. He spoke to her creative writing class. She had a crush on him then, too. For about a week. Then she met Todd Levine. He was a junior. But she enjoyed Billy's talk. No wonder she felt so comfortable when they met again at the gallery. Maybe this could work. Wait. What am I saying? I can't do this. She was about to let go of Billy's hand when Ginny's voice echoed in her mind. *Spread your wings, girl.* Once again she felt the warmth course through her. She squeezed his hand and blurted out, "Now I remember. You spoke at my high school once."

"I've spoken at a lot of schools."

"This was around fifteen years ago. Pinelands in Boca Raton."

"My, my, it's a small world."

"It was so inspiring. You quoted Whitman and I came up to you afterwards to tell you how much I loved his chocolates." She giggled. " And you didn't even laugh. You encouraged us to dream big dreams and pursue our passion."

"So what about your dreams?" He stopped and faced her. "You mentioned something about daydreams and nightmares."

She turned away. "There's this shadow. Ginny thinks it's a floater. But I had it checked out at the eye doctor. There's nothing wrong with you, he said. But the specter still comes and goes. When I'm awake, it appears then drifts away. In my nightmares it's drawing me to the edge of an abyss. The closer I get, the more it hurts. I almost feel..." her voice faded off.

He caressed the back of her arm and thought of Sachiko and the cliff. "I think I know what you mean. Like there's something out there to discover."

She turned and nodded. "Yes, yes, that's it."

He searched her eyes. "So let's find it. Together. Come with me to Chicago. It's beautiful in the fall and fifteen years is one hell of a long time. I'm sure we have a lot to catch up on. And besides, I've heard Frango's chocolate at Marshall Fields...er...I mean Macy's, beats Whitman's hands down."

Eden smirked. "Very funny."

He put his arm around her waist and said, "It's settled. Let's go."

She fell in step with him. "But what about clothes?"

"We'll stop by Filene's Basement when we get to town." They turned left on 22nd.

"Um...Okay...But where will we stay?"

"I've got a room booked at the Hotel InterContinental. You're gonna love it."

"It does sound – organic."

"Organic? Ha, that's a new one!" He grabbed her hand and headed to his car. "Come on, we haven't much time."

Once again the specter darted through her peripheral vision. Eden glanced off to her side expecting to see the earth falling away to an emerald valley far below. She breathed a sigh of relief to see a six-inch concrete curb.

When they arrived at his Volkswagen Jetta he opened her door and watched her slide into the leather front seat. The door closed with a clunk behind her.

Eden pulled the seat belt across and fastened it with a click. When was the last time someone opened a car door for her? Not Robbie. No, this Billy Shakes is no Robbie. Her toes curled up in her shoes as she watched him walk around the car.

Billy slid behind the wheel and reached into the glove compartment. "Here's some information about the Film Festival. See if anything sounds interesting."

She opened it as he pulled away from the curb. Several movies intrigued her, but not being a real film buff she didn't want to embarrass herself by suggesting something that might show her ignorance. She laid the booklet on her lap and looked out the window.

"Anything look good?" he asked as they sped toward I-4.

"I'll let you choose the movies."

"No," he said as he pulled onto the interstate. "We'll wait and choose 'em together."

'We'll choose them together.' Hmm. She liked the sound of that. When was the last time Robbie and I ever chose anything together? She stared out the window. A slight but very satisfied smile spread across her lips as the guardrails flickered by.

Billy glanced down at the gauges. "Man, I gotta get some gas." He pulled off at the next exit and drove into a Shell station. "I'll only be a minute."

As he walked into the station to pay for the gas, she pulled out her phone and punched in a number.

A familiar voice came over the line, "Hey."

"Ginny? It's me. Guess what? You're *not* going to believe this. . ."

CHAPTER 15

GINNY Wheeler returned to the gallery wearing a new outfit and balancing two new veggie platters and a bowl of ice-cold shrimp. She punched the door open with her rear end and backed into the room.

"Thanks, Ginny," said Kevin from behind the counter.

"No problem." She set the shrimp and veggies on a table then plopped down into chair, wheezing from the five-block walk. She glanced around the room. "Damn."

"Something wrong?" Kevin asked.

"Nah. Just thought I'd meet someone."

"Good crowd, eh?"

She shrugged then brightened at the sight of the growing lunch-time crowd. Good sign. Crowds mean business. She glanced at her rack of handmade, avant-garde handbags. The one Kevin allowed her to set up during Art Walk to earn some extra income.

Ginny sat up as a woman in a navy blue business suit examined a faux leopard purse. She slid the hot pink boa strap over her shoulder and admired herself in the mirror Ginny borrowed from the hair salon next door.

"That purse is *so* you," Ginny murmured. "And the 120 bucks it'll cost you is *so* definitely mine." She started to tick off a list of items she could buy with the money when a rotund woman waddled up to the rack.

"Gloria, there you are." Her voice was thick and southern, like leftover red-eye gravy. "What in the world are you doing with that ghastly thing around your neck?"

"Don't you like it, Susu?" Gloria replied as she adjusted the strap and continued to pose for the mirror.

"Yes, I love it. About as much as I love hot flashes and physical exercise. Now put that horrid thing away and let's go look at some real art."

Ginny glared. Don't listen to her.

"Real art?" asked Gloria.

"Yes, down the street at Stirling's. Marcus Vining is exhibiting. He's single, remember? And I hear his piece is very impressive."

Gloria shifted the purse to her other shoulder. "You mean pieces. Marcus has produced a lot of work."

Susu rolled her eyes. "Don't be so obtuse. I'm talking about his *piece*." She slid the purse off her friend's shoulder. "Leave that thing here. You don't know where it's been."

"I guess you're right."

"I'm always right." She draped the purse on a hook and pulled her hand back as if she had just released a diseased animal. "Now let's go see Marcus and his piece." She put her arm through her friend's and led her to the door.

Ginny charged across the room. "Why you fat ass piece of shit."

The two women stared at the approaching ball of fire and stepped back. Eyes wide. Mouths gaping.

Ginny slammed Susu against the wall. "And just what the hell is wrong with these bags?"

"Why, I, it's just that—" the large woman stammered as she searched the room for help.

Ginny snatched the purse off the hook and thrust it at the woman called Gloria. "Here, honey. It's definitely you. And today I'll knock 20% off."

"Oh, Ginny," Kevin's singsong voice grabbed her shoulder and spun her around. "Could you come here for a minute?"

She raised her finger in front of the two women and scowled. "Don't move, ladies. I'll be right back." She took two steps and spun back around. "Oh, and I take cash, credit and checks."

The two women nodded nervously.

Ginny squared her shoulders and walked across the gallery. Kevin leaned against the counter, arms folded, toes tapping the floor. She could tell by his raised eyebrow and slight smile that he was ready to 'share' with her.

"Listen, Ginny," he cooed.

Yep, she thought. It's 'sharing time' all right. She lowered her eyes and shoved her hands into her back pockets.

"I don't mind you selling your handbags. But we mustn't abuse the customers." He lifted her chin. "We don't need to have this conversation again, right?"

Ginny nodded twice and almost said, 'Yes, dad', but caught herself. "I'm sorry, Kevin." She dragged her toe across the wooden floor in feigned repentance.

"That's my girl. You know what to do."

She steeled her shoulders and marched back to the quivering women. She forced a smile and said, "Sorry, ladies."

"Hmph." Susu grabbed the bag from her friend and tossed it back on the rack. "C'mon Gloria, let's get out of this sorry excuse for a gallery and take in some real culture."

"Why you son-of-a-bitch—" Ginny raised a clenched fist.

"Oh, Ginny…" Kevin's singsong voice once again grabbed her. She froze, and the two women slipped out the door.

Ginny returned to the bench and dropped down. She slouched forward and put her chin in her hands as Willie "Dog-Mess" Patterson launched into a song about hard times and hard liquor. She heaved her shoulders and sighed. Ramen noodles for another month.

Kevin approached and laid a hand on her shoulder. "Don't worry, there'll be other customers," he said as he gave her a gentle squeeze. "By the way, Eden was here earlier. I told her you had just left to pick up some food. Sure hope everything's ok."

Ginny looked up. "Why do you say that?"

"I think she'd been crying, although she did her best to hide it."

"Robbie," Ginny mumbled. "Do you know where she went?"

He shrugged and looked around the room. "I'm not sure. I'm surprised you didn't run into her as you came up the stairs. She was literally here one minute and gone the next."

"I better call her." She stood and walked behind the sales counter. As she fished in her purse for her phone it started to ring. She flipped it open.

"Ginny! It's me. Guess what? You're not going to believe this—"

"Eden, where the hell are you? Kevin said you looked upset."

"Oh, I was."

"Robbie?"

"Who else? But that was then. This is now."

"What do you mean by that?" Ginny strode across the room and sat back down on the bench.

"I *was* upset when I got to the gallery. I finally decided to leave Robbie."

"It's about time. I've been telling you that for months—"

"I almost clobbered him with a toilet seat."

"You did what?!"

"Don't worry. I didn't. I just hopped in my car and drove off. Then the most amazing thing happened."

"What? What?" Ginny put her elbows on her knees and leaned forward.

"I met this really cute guy—"

"Me, too! We ran into each other at the gallery. He put his head between my breasts. I pulled him close. I felt his bulge."

"What?!"

"His wallet. The bulge in his back pocket. He bought me dinner. Shrimp. And new clothes, too. I think he could be one of the Great Ones."

"Oh, Ginny, I am so thrilled for you."

"And me for you. So where'd you meet him? The personals?"

"No. It was more organic."

Ginny rolled her eyes. "Whatever. Okay, so you met this cute guy-"

"And we're taking a little trip."

"Clearwater?"

"Chicago!"

"What!?" Ginny leapt to her feet and began to pace back and forth.

"It's just like you told me. Do something wild and crazy. So, I am. We're going to the Film Festival. This is so fantastic I can't believe it. I can't wait for you to meet this guy. His name is William Shakes, on account of he's a writer, and he's so cute, and he's so polite, and he opened my door, and he gave me the brochure, and he likes Frango's more than Whitman's, and he's everything Robbie isn't, and—"

"Whoa, whoa, whoa. Hold it right there," Ginny ran her hand through her hair. "You mean to tell me you're going to Chicago with a man you just met?"

"Don't be silly. Of course not."

"That's a relief." She sat back down on the bench and let her shoulders relax.

"At least not really."

Her shoulders stiffened again. "What do you mean, *not really?*"

"It seems we first met each other fifteen years ago. Oh, Ginny, I am so excited."

"Sounds like it. But are you sure about this? Where are you staying?"

"Hotel Intercontinental. He says it's right downtown and—Oops, gotta go, he's coming back. Wish me luck. He could be one of the 'Great Ones,' too. I gotta go." Click.

Ginny heaved her shoulders and stared out the window. "Here's to the 'Great Ones,'" she said with a sigh. "Wherever the hell they are hiding."

Her cell phone rang again and broke her reverie. She flipped it open.

"Hey, Ginny, it's Robbie. I gotta talk to you. It's about Eden. . ."

CHAPTER 16

EDEN'S fiancé Robbie stretched his legs the length of the sofa, scratched his balls, and stared at the TV. He sucked the last drop of beer from his can of Old Milwaukee.

Let's welcome our new contestant. Retired NFL legend—

He yawned and glanced at his bulky black sports watch. What the—? He swung his legs off the sofa and sat up. Dried crumbs and cellophane wrappers cascaded off his t-shirt and onto the beige carpet. Where the hell is Eden? She should've been back a long time ago.

He struggled to his feet and his sleepy legs buckled. The pricking of pins and needles coursed through his ankles and into his calves. He hopped over to his cell phone and dialed her number.

"Hi! Can't come to the phone right now. Please leave a message."

Maybe she's driving back and couldn't get to the phone. He dialed her number again.

"Hi! Can't come—"

He slapped his forehead. That's right. It's Art Walk. She must've gone downtown to hang out with Ginny. He punched in a number. Ginny answered on the second ring.

"Hi, this is Ginny," she said cheerfully.

"Hey, Ginny, it's Robbie. I gotta talk to you. It's about Eden. . ."

"Oh?" She paused for a moment. "And what the hell do you want with her?"

He pulled the phone away from his ear and stared at it. Damn, what's her problem? He raised it back up and asked, "Have you seen her? Is she with you?"

"No," she replied with words caked in ice. "She's not with me."

"I just figured since it was Art Walk she might've gone downtown and—"

"She *was* here, all right. But now she's on her way to Chicago. And it's all because of you."

"Me?!" His voice leapt an octave.

"Yeah, you," she said, her own voice rising. "She's on her way to Chicago with a man who truly appreciates her."

"But—"

"Don't *but* me." The words came quickly. "You had a good thing in that girl and you let her slip away. You had one of the Great Ones and you pissed on her. Now she's met someone who will treat her right."

"Who? I'll kick his—"

"None of your goddamn business. But let me tell you this, he's handsome and he's considerate and he's famous. They'll be living it up in Chicago—staying at the Hotel InterContinental, attending the Film Festival, dining in exotic restaurants." She paused to catch her breath.

"But Ginny—"

"Listen, jackass, she deserves what she just found—and you deserve what you just lost!"

Robbie's voice cracked. "What do you mean lost?"

"You heard me, you stupid fuck."

"But Ginny. . ."

"Now get off my phone, you're using up my minutes."

The line went dead and the numbness in Robbie's toes crept up through his body and into his brain. He couldn't believe she'd do this to him. After all his promises, this is the thanks he got? He tossed his phone on the sofa and shrugged his shoulders. Hmph. Well, she doesn't know what *she's* missing.

He wandered into the kitchen and leaned against the refrigerator. He stared at a snapshot stuck to the door by a zucchini-shaped magnet. Where was that? Daytona? The ocean tumbled in behind them as they sat on the sand. A monstrosity of a sandcastle sat before them. Eden held a small red plastic shovel up for the camera while he used a toy rake to put the finishing touches on their creation. He sighed and turned the picture over. Eden had scribbled *Robbie and me, New Smyrna Beach*. His throat thickened as a lump grew. He wiped a tear from the corner of his eye.

"Three years ago," he whispered. "Damn. Ginny's right. I'm the one who's screwed."

His watery eyes scanned the other photos. Scaling a weathered ladder up coquina walls at the old Spanish fort at Matanzas Inlet. Walking the splintered docks in Cedar Key— the setting sun painting the sky a brilliant conch-pink. Camping out under a shimmering canopy of stars at Bahia Honda. Mugging it up with a few unemployed locals at Cap'n Tony's in Key West. Eden up to her waist in a glistening aqua pool beside a gleeful dolphin at Marineland.

"She really was one in a million," he said to the faded reminders of how things once were. "You gotta fix this."

He opened the refrigerator door and scanned the shelves for another beer. He grabbed a half-empty bottle of Bartles and James hiding behind the mayonnaise. Margarita Cooler.

"Eden's," he whimpered.

He twisted the cap and tossed it toward a wastebasket. It bounced off the wall and landed on the carpet joining a dozen other bottle caps.

I've gotta win her back. But how?

He took a swig and grimaced as the sweet fizz flowed over his tongue.

I'll just have to go to her. That'll show her how committed I am. He snapped his fingers. That's it! I'll go to Chicago! Track her down. Fall to one knee and ask her to marry me. This time I'll even set a date. He broke into a smile and slammed the empty bottle on the counter. Time to do some net surfing. Gotta find some killer deals on airfare and a hotel.

He grabbed his cell phone and turned on Eden's computer. He Googled 'cheap tickets' and found a site that compared all available airfares. Here's one! Dixie Discount Air.

He called the number and a robotic recording explained the airline's low-price policy: No reservations. No agents. No credit cards. Flights booked on a first-come, first-served basis. The voice requested that passengers arrive two-and-a-half hours ahead of the scheduled departure time. He looked at his watch. He had three hours.

He returned to the computer to check on hotels. What did Ginny say? The InterContinental? He found the website: rooms available.

Better make sure she's really there. He picked up his cell phone and dialed the 800 number.

A sunny voice answered, "Hotel InterContinental. How may I help you?"

He sat back in his chair and propped his feet up on the desk. "I'd like to speak to a guest."

"The name, please?"

"Eden Myers."

He heard the faint tappity-tap of a computer keyboard on the other end.

"I'm sorry, no reservation for an Eden Myers."

No? But Ginny said that—He smacked his brow. That's right, the room wouldn't be in her name. It'd be in what's-his-name's name. Okay, on to Plan B.

"I'd like to book a room for the weekend."

"One moment, sir," said the sunny voice. Tappity-tap-tap. "What credit card will you be using to guarantee your reservation, sir?"

He pulled out his wallet and removed a Visa card. "How much?"

She quoted him a price.

"What?! For three nights? That's nuts!"

"I'm sorry, sir, but that price is per night." The sunny voice paused. "Would you still like to make a reservation?"

He frowned and flipped the credit card through his fingers. "All right. I'll take it." He steeled his shoulders and gave the woman his credit card number.

Robbie got up from the computer and jogged into the bedroom. He opened the closet and pulled out a pair of Miami Dolphin sweatpants, an Orlando Magic basketball jersey and a Tampa Bay Lightning warm-up jacket. He changed into his new outfit then grabbed another batch of sports-insignia-embellished clothes and shoved them into his Florida Gators gym bag. He donned his Rays baseball cap and positioned it just right. He sucked in his stomach, thrust his chest out and admired himself in the mirror.

"You the man," he told his reflection. He hitched up his sweatpants and zipped his jacket. "Hide your daughters and wives, Chicago, 'cuz Robbie Renfro's on the move."

CHAPTER 17

OH my god, Ginny thought as she hung up on Robbie. What'd I just do? She folded her phone and tossed it into a nearby chair. I can't believe I told him about Chicago. She planted her hands on her hips and shook her head in disgust. And he's such a jackass he'll probably go after her. She took a deep breath and glanced around the room. 'Dog-mess' was still wailing but Ginny only heard silence. Man, if Robbie shows up it'll screw up everything. I better warn her.

She picked up her phone and frantically dialed Eden's number. C'mon, girl, pick up.

"Hi! Can't come to the phone right now. Please leave a message."

She slammed the phone down on the windowsill. Shit. She must be on the plane already. She paced nervously back and forth. I've got to stop Robbie. She pulled at her necklace and bit her lip. But how? She stopped and stared out the window. Two fighter jets from MacDill sliced through the sky leaving mile-long vapor trails in their wake.

She clapped her hands together. "That's it!" She spun around and shook the shoulders of two elderly women admiring a nearby sculpture. "A fucking pre-emptive strike." The two women stared at her and scampered to the other side of the room.

She turned toward the counter. "Kevin!"

"What is it?" he asked as he walked across the room toward her.

"Something's come up." She picked up her phone and grabbed her purse. "Have to go to Chicago tonight. Emergency."

"Someone sick?" He touched her arm.

"I'm afraid so," she said, thinking of the nauseous feeling in the pit of her stomach from giving Robbie so much information.

He shook his head. "Sorry to hear that. I know things are tight. Do you need any money?"

Ginny froze. She hadn't thought about that. The last she heard, packets of ramen noodles weren't recognized as legitimate currency in the United States.

He caressed the back of her arm. "There's a couple hundred bucks in the bank bag behind the counter. Go ahead and take it."

She threw her arms around his neck and planted a big wet kiss on his forehead then ran over to the counter and stuffed the money into her purse.

"I'll hold down the fort here," he said. "You take care and have a safe trip."

She blew him a kiss. "You're the best." And the door swung shut behind her.

* * *

Bam bam bam bam bam!

The rapid-fire pounding on the restroom door roused the Scientist from his drunken slumber.

Bam bam bam!

"Hey! Anyone in there?" A muffled voice called through the door. "Open up. I gotta five-year-old who has to pee!"

"I'm coming, I'm coming," the Scientist replied. He tried to rise but the toilet seat stuck to his rear end like a giant suction cup.

"Oooh," he moaned as he pried himself off with a *poomph*. He looked over his shoulder at the huge red welt circling his thighs and buttocks. He pulled up his jeans and opened the door.

An angry man glared at the Scientist. "It's about time." Then turning to the boy he added, "Hurry up, Mikey. Go do your business."

As the Scientist limped down the hall to the gallery he heard the plaintive whine of a five-year-old behind him. "But daddy, that ugly man didn't flush."

The Scientist re-entered the gallery and scanned the crowded room. He approached a man removing a painting from the wall and tapped him on the shoulder. "S'cuse me. Have you seen my soul mate?"

Kevin turned. "I don't know. What's her name?"

The Scientist paused and scratched his head. "Jeez, I don't know."

"You don't know your soul mate's name?" Kevin took a step backward and waved a hand in front of his nose to dissipate the alcohol-infused breath.

"It'll come to me in a minute." The Scientist stroked the wisp of hair on his chin and stared up at the ceiling.

"Then what does she look like?"

"She's about this tall." He held his hand about five and a half feet off the ground. "She has black hair and green eyes. I think she's wearing white pants and a blue top."

"You must be talking about my assistant. She's not here. She's going to Chicago this afternoon. Illness in the family."

"Hmm. Illness in the family," the Scientist muttered under his breath. "Now's my chance to impress her. I'll comfort and console her. It's my mission." He thrust out his chest and marched to the door.

"Who should I say was asking about her?" Kevin called after him.

"Just tell her it was me," the Scientist shouted back without turning. He shook the remaining cobwebs from his two-hour nap and tramped down the stairs.

"Did you find out the guy's name?" the Artist called out as he breezed by.

"Can't talk now," he replied over his shoulder. "My soul mate beckons. I'm on a date with destiny."

The Scientist hit the sidewalk and hailed a yellow cab. He slid in the back.

"Where to, partner?" asked the driver with a distinct low-country drawl.

"My apartment." He gave the cabbie his address. "And make it quick. I'm on a mission."

He smiled and tapped his hands on his knees as the cab vaulted away from the curb. He stared out the window and whispered. "Yes, I'm on a mission of love."

Minutes later, a yellow cab screeched to a halt in front of the Scientist's apartment. He hopped out and leaned back into the driver's window. "Wait here. I'll be right out."

He turned and jogged up the sidewalk toward his building.

"Meter's running!" shouted the cabbie.

"I know, I know," he replied with a wave of his hand.

He burst through the front door and ran into his sparsely furnished bedroom. He unclasped the spiked collar and tossed it on the plaid bedspread with a clink then grabbed some clothes from his closet and jammed them into a dark green knapsack. I'm gonna need some serious cash. He reached under the bed and pulled out a stainless steel strongbox. He grabbed a stack of bills and counted them. One thousand, two thousand, three thousand. Should be enough. He shoved them into his pockets and snatched up the bag. Oops, my medicine!

He ran into the kitchen and surveyed his rack of vintage wines. He withdrew two bottles of Bordeaux. Chateau Mouton Rothschilds. A '42 and '43. Excellent years. The perfect complement to his quest. He pulled a pair of jeans from the knapsack and lovingly wrapped the bottles. Anything else? He snapped his fingers. Aha! He opened his junk drawer and pulled out a tape measure. He had to make sure his bag would fit in the carry-on bin. Couldn't risk having these babies break in the cargo hold. He stretched out the tape measure. It'll be close. But it'll fit. He draped the strap over his shoulder and bolted out of the apartment to the waiting cab.

"To the airport," he wheezed as he slid his bag across the back seat and climbed in beside it. "And step on it."

"You got it!" The cabbie craned his neck out the window. "Hold on tight." He jerked the steering wheel left and jammed his foot down on the accelerator. The cab darted out into traffic, nearly running over a senior citizen pedaling an enormous red tricycle.

"And a pleasant day to you too, you old witch," the cabbie said with a laugh as he shook his fist out the window.

The taxi zigzagged in and out of traffic, throwing the Scientist back and forth with each jarring lane change. Angry horns, profane gestures, and screeching brakes filled the air.

"So this mission must be pretty important," said the cabbie as he glanced at the Scientist in his rearview mirror.

"You could say it was a matter of life and death."

The cab driver whistled and arched his eyebrows. "Life and death, huh?"

"Yep, I'm a Scientist." He met the cabby's eyes in the rearview mirror. "And this is a life and death situation."

"So what you got in the bag? Some organs for a transplant or something? I seen that on TV once." He switched lanes, narrowly missing a lumbering cement mixer.

"I'm carrying a heart."

"Damn. Then I better get a move on. Hold on." The cabbie mashed the accelerator and zoomed up the on-ramp to 275.

The Scientist stared out the window.

"Yep," he whispered to himself. "A broken heart."

CHAPTER 18

ROBBIE arrived at Tampa International and parked his Neon in the long-term discount lot. He pulled his bag from the trunk and loped across the asphalt toward the arriving shuttle. He tossed his bag on the luggage rack and plopped down next to a family of five. The kids, all under ten, wore dented Mickey Mouse hats. They giggled, poked and pinched each other, still high on the adrenaline from a day at the Magic Kingdom. The mother and father stared, dazed and unfocused, into space. Robbie imagined that visions of a comfy bed and a well-stocked liquor cabinet danced in their heads.

The shuttle arrived at the main terminal and Robbie hopped off at the first entrance. He jogged into the building and scanned the check-in counters. Long lines of travelers snaked around chrome stanchions and retractable vinyl bands as they shuffled up to the ticket agents. Brightly illumined signs hung above each counter: Delta, Northwest, United. Farther down: American, Southwest, Air Deco. Hmm, no sign of Dixie Discount Air.

A skycap passed by with a flatbed cart piled high with luggage. Robbie grabbed the black man's arm. "Excuse me—could you tell me where I can find Dixie Discount?"

"You flying Dixie?" The skycap pushed his hat back on his head.

"Yeah."

"Heh, heh, heh," he chuckled as his face exploded into a grin.

"Listen, I just want to know where to check in. I haven't much time!"

"Take it easy, cowboy. Just go to that door at the end of the terminal." The skycap pointed to his right. "You'll see a small sign that says Dixie Discount Air. Go through the door and down the stairs. You can't miss it."

"Thank you very little." Robbie turned abruptly and walked away.

"No problem, cowboy," the skycap called after him. "And hey, good luck on your flight." Robbie swaggered down the concourse and the skycap shook his head." You're gonna need it, cowboy, you're gonna need it."

* * *

The Scientist planted one hand against the roof of the cab to steady himself as he bounced from one side to the other. The cabbie's stubby hands clutched the steering wheel, knuckles turning white. They sped down the far-left lane of the highway when the Scientist leaned forward.

"Excuse me, I believe the airport exit is just ahead."

With one quick glance over his shoulder, the cabbie jerked the wheel to the right and the yellow cab screamed across four busy lanes of interstate. Screaming tires and wailing horns filled the air. The Scientist closed his eyes, held his breath and dug his feet into the floorboard bracing for imminent impact. The cab made it across unscathed and hit the exit ramp doing 70.

The cabbie looked into the rearview mirror and laughed. "You can open your eyes now. We're nearly home free."

The Scientist looked behind him to see cars and trucks skidding and fishtailing in their wake. A silver Jaguar with a pickaxe embedded in its trunk plowed into the grass median.

"I thought I was a goner back there," he said as he wiped his brow with his sleeve.

"You kidding? I'm a professional." He tapped the cab license hanging on his dashboard. "That's my picture. I'm certified."

The Scientist looked over the front seat at the laminated license.

"I'm proud to say—" he puffed his chest out and smacked it with his fist —"that in all the years I been in the cab business, almost nobody has died while I've been driving."

The cab slowed to a tortoise-like fifty as they followed the twisting road to the terminal and screeched to a halt, drawing the attention of passengers and skycaps. The cabbie hopped out and ran around to the rear passenger door.

A security guard jogged over and barked, "Hey, you can't park here!"

The Scientist clutched his knapsack, leapt out, and sprinted to the terminal door. The guard did a double take at the fleeing Scientist then glared at the cab driver.

"Okay, buster, I think you owe me an explanation."

The cabbie slammed the door and pushed the startled guard aside. "I ain't parking. Now, outta my way, Barney Fife." He caught up to the Scientist and said, "Leave this to me, good buddy." He ran ahead. "Look out! Medical emergency!" He shoved the door open and burst into the busy terminal, shouting, "Scientist coming through! Life and death heart transplant! Outta the way!"

"I'll take it from here," the Scientist said as he reached the cabbie.

The driver's shoulders heaved as he huffed and puffed. "How'd I do?"

The Scientist reached into his pocket and pulled out a wad of bills. He counted out the cab fare, added a generous tip and handed the cash to the cabbie. "Someone will receive new life because of your heroic efforts."

The cab driver's eyes grew wide as he stared at the pile of money in his hand. He thrust out his chest and said, "All in the line of duty. Have a great flight."

The cabbie hitched up his pants, threw out his chest, and strutted out of the terminal, basking in the appreciative applause of passengers and skycaps. Even the security guard tipped his hat when the cabbie strode past him.

* * *

Robbie skipped down a flight of stairs to the Dixie concourse. He stepped through the door at the bottom and let it close behind him. The room was only as big as a typical Dairy Queen. Toward the front stood a ticket counter serviced by three young attendants – a multi-pierced young man, a Pepto Bismol buzz-cut girl, and a skinhead whose gender was up for debate. An amoeba-like crowd jostled and pushed forward as if trying to catch a glimpse of a horrible accident. Those who weren't on line sat on institutional-grade plastic chairs scattered haphazardly along the walls of the room. The odor of French fries, stale coffee and soiled diapers hung in the stagnant air. A soft drink machine hummed in the corner—Robbie noticed that most of the buttons displayed a flashing red *'please make another selection'* light. A Rubbermaid trashcan overflowing with Styrofoam and plastic stood to his right. A stocky Marine in dress blues bumped into him.

"Excuse me," the Marine said as he balanced the empty cup, paper plate, and crumpled napkins of a lunch eaten on the run.

"No problem." Robbie stepped back to allow the serviceman access to the trashcan.

Then the door behind him flew open and smacked him in the back. He stumbled forward and braced himself against the trashcan. A half-eaten hot dog, crumpled ice cream wrapper, and Pepsi can tumbled from the overflowing can to the floor. A middle-aged Japanese couple entered the room and offered a polite, "S'cuse, please" as they stepped past Robbie and into the crowded room. The Marine looked down at the small pile of trash covering his finely polished shoes and scowled.

"Sorry," Robbie said. "It was an accident. You see, I was standing by the door when that couple opened it and knocked me into the trashcan. Then I—"

"There's ketchup on my shoes," said the Marine.

"Let me get that for you." Robbie knelt and searched the pile of trash for an unused napkin. He found one that looked unblemished and dabbed the Marine's left shoe. He spit on the toe and buff shined it with another fairly clean napkin. He smirked at his reflection in the black patent leather. "There," he said as he struggled back to his feet. "Good as new."

* * *

The Scientist scanned the terminal then approached a flickering bank of video monitors displaying departure schedules. He glanced at his watch – almost 2:30. He looked back up to the screens. His eyes stopped at a 3 p.m. flight to Chicago. Dixie Discount Air. On schedule. His heart quickened and he spotted the information desk. A petite brunette in a navy blue blazer stared at her computer monitor and talked into a headset. "No, sir, you can't take your cat on the plane to sit with you. . . Sir, I don't care how well behaved she is. . ."

"Excuse me," said the Scientist as he folded his hands on the counter.

The woman raised a finger to her lips and mouthed, 'Just a minute.' She returned her gaze to the computer screen and her attention to the man on the phone.

"Sir, no airline will allow a cat to sit on their owner's lap. . . No sir, I've never heard of a seeing-eye cat. . . you'll have to take it up with my supervisor when you get here. . . No, sir, I won't do that with my computer. . . I don't think that is anatomically possible. . . No need to get nasty, sir...Yes, sir. . . whatever you say, sir...have a nice day, sir." She hung up, shook her head and mumbled, "Two years of community college for this?"

"Ahem, could you point me to the Dixie Discount Air ticket counter?"

The girl looked up from her computer screen. "Did you say Dixie?" She raised her hand to her mouth and giggled.

"Please hurry." He pointed up to the bank of video monitors. "The flight leaves in less than a half hour."

"You don't have to worry," she said with another giggle. "Dixie Discount rarely leaves on schedule. You have plenty of time."

"The ticket counter?"

"At the very end of the terminal." She waved her hand to the right. "You'll find the entrance to their. . . um. . . concourse."

"Thanks." He swung his bag over his shoulder, turned, and trekked through the busy terminal to the lonely gray door at the far end.

"My, how I love this job," the young woman said to herself as the Scientist disappeared into the crowd. The phone rang. "Tampa International, how may I help you today? No ma'am, I'm afraid geese..."

The Scientist reached the end of the terminal and entered the dimly lit stairwell. His footsteps echoed off the cinder block walls as he traipsed down the steps and pushed the door at the bottom. It opened a few inches then stopped. He placed both hands on the door and with a mighty shove, pushed it open. He leaned forward and peered into the room. His eyes fell on the young man, clad in an odd variety of sports attire, lying prone at his feet.

"Sorry," the Scientist replied. He stepped over the man and elbowed his way through the throng of impatient passengers toward the ticket counter. A multitude of voices rose in protest.

"Hey buddy, wait your turn!"

"Who do you think you are?"

"Get back in line!"

"Knock it off. I'm a Scientist and I must get on this flight."

He wrestled his way to the front of the line and up to the ticket counter.

"So, what do you want?" asked a tattooed ticket agent with multiple facial piercings.

"Do you give medical discounts?" The Scientist set his knapsack on the counter.

The illustrated man snickered and nudged the agent standing beside him—a young woman with Pepto Bismol-pink hair. "Sorry, professor. No discounts."

"Surely you must give some type of discounts for medical reasons."

The agent scratched his ear with his pen and yawned. "This is Dixie Discount Air. Everybody gets a discount, see?" He looked at the end of his pen and wiped the small dab of yellow goo on his shirt. "You want a ticket or what?"

"Do you take credit cards?"

"Cash."

"How about debit cards?"

"Read my lips." He leaned across the counter and jabbed the pen into the Scientist's chest. "Cash."

A gangly young man with a mop of ink black hair got up from behind a desk and ambled up to the counter. "Is there a problem here, Pierce?"

"Seems this guy don't understand English, boss. I keep telling him cash." He turned and sneered. "But he won't listen."

"I'm a Scientist, and I understand English perfectly. I have to get on this flight."

"I don't care if you're Albert-fucking-Einstein." The man reached over the counter and grabbed the Scientist by the shirt. "If you want a ticket then hand over the dough, got it?"

The Scientist gulped and nodded.

"I'm glad we understand each other. Enjoy your flight." He released the Scientist's shirt and ambled back to his desk.

"How much do I owe you?" The Scientist pulled out his bankroll.

The ticket agent ran a pierced tongue over pierced lips. A thin smile slithered across his face and he quoted an entirely outrageous and inaccurate price. The Scientist sighed and licked his thumb. He peeled off the bills as the ticket agent watched with hungry eyes.

"Thanks," snorted the agent as he shoved half of the bills into his pocket. "Enjoy your flight."

The Scientist picked up his bag and wiggled back through the crowd toward an empty seat. Well, my sweet love, your prince is coming. Prepare to embrace your destiny.

His mind drifted off into deep thoughts of passion as an enraged and very obese woman beat and kicked the soda machine behind him.

* * *

Robbie glared at the scraggly man who stepped over him. He picked himself up off the floor and looked up at the Marine. "Like I said, your shoe is good as new."

The Marine continued to stare at his feet. "There's mustard on my other shoe."

Robbie dabbed it with the tip of his finger and repeated his attempt at a professional shoeshine. He stood back up. "How's that?"

"Thanks." The Marine turned heel and marched back toward the counter.

Robbie slung his backpack over his shoulder and took his place among the throng of people eager to get a cheap ticket to somewhere. When he finally reached the counter, he bought a roundtrip ticket with cash and searched for a seat in a less populated section of the room. A room, he now noticed, with no windows.

While every other airline had waiting areas in concourses that overlooked the runways, Dixie Discount Air had plain, cream-soda-colored cement block walls. As if to make up for the lack of windows and the vistas they provided, the airline mounted large colorful posters of impressive looking jets sitting proudly on shimmering tarmacs.

Robbie admired the poster in front of him. In the foreground, a buxom flight attendant in a form-fitting uniform teased him with the caption: *"Fly Dixie Discount. And Fly Me."*

"Oh, yeah. That's the kind of service I'm talking' about," he said to the poster.

He strolled around the room and admired the attractive flight attendants and sleek jets with Dixie Discount Air painted on the gleaming light-blue fuselage. At least they have state-of-the-art jets. Who cares where we have to wait? But as he looked closer, he noticed that the Dixie Discount Air lettering had been added to the posters. Hmm. Photoshop. A cut-and-paste job. And not a very good one. Even the flight attendants were the obvious work of an amateur computer geek with an overactive imagination and a raging hard-on.

A voice crackled over the intercom. "Now boarding flight 729W857B to Chicago. Please exit through the double doors to your right."

The mob turned and shuffled toward the doors and up the stairs, pitching forward as if stuck with giant cattle prods. Robbie found himself carried along with the throng's forward momentum. At the top of the stairs, they stumbled out onto the tarmac and into the dazzling afternoon sun. He raised a hand to shield his eyes from the brightness and looked around. To their left stood a 747 Delta jet, to their right, a Southwest 727.

A grinning skycap emerged from the stairwell, cupped his hands to his mouth and yelled, "Good afternoon, ladies and gentlemen. Be patient, the shuttle is on the way. Please place your bags over there and I'll load them on the tram when it arrives."

One by one the passengers filed by and dropped their luggage in a pile next to the skycap. One woman asked, "Shouldn't we have our bags ticketed or something?"

The skycap grinned and replied, "What's a matter lady? Can't recognize your own bag?"

"I suppose I can," she answered sheepishly.

"Well, then, there you have it. Now put your bag with the other luggage."

It wasn't long before Robbie noticed a distant tram coming across the tarmac. Heat rose from the pavement making the approaching shuttle shimmy and shake. As the tram made a slow arc toward the terminal, Robbie recognized it as one of the typical open-air multi-car vehicles seen in every amusement park in Florida. Each car had several rows of mustard-yellow plastic benches with the exception of the last car—a flatbed to hold the luggage.

The tram rolled to a stop between the idling jets and the skycap encouraged everyone to board. "But only five to a seat, please," he shouted.

As the tram rumbled across the runways, they had to occasionally stop to let zooming jets pass for take-offs and landings. The ensuing drafts scattered hats, mussed hair, and raised blood pressures. After five or six such crossings, the tram pulled up to an open hangar at the far end of the airport. Dixie Discount Air was painted in bold and uneven red letters on the side of the corrugated metal building. Beside it sat one lonely jet.

Robbie scratched his head as his eyes wandered over the plane. While the jets on the posters sported sparkling blue and white fuselages, the colors before him now seemed washed out and anemic. Cerulean blue had long since faded to dishwater gray. Brilliant white was now the color of abject boredom.

Either this is a really old jet, Robbie thought, or it's a highly experimental camouflage model. Perhaps an ex-military troop transport plane designed to disappear in a cloud-filled sky. He hoped it was the latter, but neither thought was reassuring.

The passengers spilled out of the tram and climbed a rickety metal staircase to the plane's door. Five skycaps hustled out to unload the baggage. They stood in line like an old fashioned fire brigade, pitching bag after bag down the line and tossing them up into a hungry black hole in the belly of the plane. Robbie grabbed his knapsack and followed the crowd, mumbling a brief prayer as he went.

CHAPTER 19

EDEN and Billy boarded their plane and were surprised to find art deco club chairs, sofas, and a variety of designer tables scattered across a sea of blue carpet inlaid with intricate geometric designs. A tanned and trim male flight attendant approached and said, "Welcome to Air Deco, Florida's newest airline." He handed Billy a wine list. "What is your pleasure this afternoon?"

Billy studied the list. "Hmm. The Emilio Lustau looks good."

"Excellent choice," the flight attendant said before backing away.

Billy and Eden settled into a dark blue love seat as the plane sped down the runway and lifted gently off the ground. When they leveled out, the flight attendant reappeared and set two crystal glasses on the table. He poured a splash of sherry into Billy's glass.

"Thank you." Billy handed the glass to Eden. With a look of surprise, she took it and raised it to her lips

"Exquisite," she said with a smile.

The flight attendant finished pouring their glasses then bowed and moved on to the next couple. Eden eyed Billy over the rim of her glass. He returned her gaze and savored the sherry—both in her eyes and in his glass. Her eyes, he thought, were finer. More complex. An excellent vintage.

"So we're staying at the Hotel InterContinental?" Eden asked, breaking his thoughts.

"You're gonna love it. It's right on Michigan Avenue. If the weather's nice we'll be able to walk to just about everything." He paused and took a sip. "Everything, that is, except Lou Mitchell's. For that, we'll have to take a cab."

"Lou Mitchell? Is he a friend of yours?"

"No, it's this great little food joint down near Union Station. A Chicago institution. Breakfast to die for."

"Sounds like you have quite a weekend planned."

Billy swirled the sherry in his glass and stared out the window and into the bright blue ether. "I thought I had things planned."

"So did I," she said as she followed his gaze. "For the last three years. Funny, isn't it? Sometimes life throws you one heck of a curveball."

He turned to her and smiled. "Well, maybe this time we'll hit one out of the park." He picked up the bottle and added, "More sherry?"

She reached for her glass. "Please."

* * *

It was late in the afternoon when their plane banked high above Lake Michigan and began its approach to Midway. Eden looked out the window as they soared over the scarred and tortured industrial sites of long-forgotten and idle industries. They passed over rusting refineries, corroding chemical plants and soot-spewing steel mills. She watched the plane's shadow roam over a rat maze of rail yards and acres of abandoned warehouses. As they flew over the South Side, she thought she heard the howling ghosts of the infamous stockyards. Her eyes grew wide as the plane began its descent over the blue-collar neighborhoods of Bridgeport and Pilsen.

"It seems odd that they would put an airport smack-dab in the middle of town," she said as the plane nearly scraped the TV aerials that sprouted like dandelions from the rooftops.

Soon they touched down at Midway and the plane taxied up to the terminal. A large gate sidled up to the front door. Passengers rose as if on cue and made their way to the front of the plane. The pilot stood smiling at the door and thanked the passengers for choosing Air Deco. Eden and Billy exited the plane and walked through the busy terminal to the train station. Billy had insisted they take the train, and at two bucks and a quarter why not? He purchased two tokens and they boarded an El into town. They found two seats in the middle of the car and sat down as the train lurched forward.

"Most folks prefer O'Hare, but for the life of me I don't know why. It's so far out and it takes forever to get to town. This trip is cheaper, shorter and has much more character."

Eden glanced around the train. She noticed the homeless man across the aisle.

Perhaps this is his home, she thought.

The rumpled man returned her gaze, smiled a toothless smile and tipped his hat as if to say, *"Welcome to my estate. I hope you will find everything to your satisfaction."*

Three rows down a large African-American woman struggled to corral two young boys. They careened up and down the aisle, screams like fingernails on a chalkboard. Catty-corner from them sat a young Hispanic tough—slick black hair pulled back tight into a pony tail, scar on his cheek, left leg bent inward in an unnatural way. Tattooed on his knuckles: *Dead Meat.* Eden noticed he was reading The New Yorker. He looked up and returned her stare.

"W-what are you reading?" Eden stuttered as she felt herself blush. "Anything interesting?"

"Short story," he replied with a sneer and a mouthful of gravel. "Bradbury."

Billy perked up at the name. "I like Bradbury."

The punk gave him a look that said, 'So?' then turned back to his magazine.

Billy turned to Eden and confided, "I just heard a great line from Bradbury. "First you jump off the cliff—"

"Then you build your wings on the way down," the punk added without looking up.

"You know that quote?" Billy asked.

"No," mumbled the young tough as he flipped another page. "But I've jumped." He looked up from his magazine and glared at the couple. "Have you?"

"Is that how you got hurt?" Eden asked glancing at his bent leg.

"Sorta." The punk looked down and rubbed his knee. "I shoulda jumped sooner." He looked back up. "Least that's what the blind chick said. You gotta jump when you gotta jump."

Billy leaned forward, intrigued "What blind chick?"

"Some Chinese girl I met at a bar in Wicker Park. It was raining like all hell. Told her I'd walk her home – she was pretty hot. Thought I might get lucky. Anyway, we're stumbling up North Avenue when the weirdest shit happened. It's like she stabbed me…" The punk's eyes glazed over as his voice trailed off.

"Stabbed?" Billy slid closer. "What happened?"

The young tough snapped to. "What are you, taking a fucking census?"

Billy faded back into his seat.

The el crawled to a stop and the young punk struggled to his feet and limped to the door.

"What an odd man," Eden said.

Billy rubbed his side. "I wonder."

The train lurched forward causing the fat businessman in front of them to belch. Folds of flesh from his pale, pink neck spilled over the starch-white collar of his wrinkled dress shirt. He was reading the Trib and his broad, oval head bounced and swayed like a bobblehead doll in the rear window of a Chevy. He belched again as he turned the page.

"You were right," Eden whispered as she leaned into Billy. "This trip is just full of character."

Their train rumbled down the elevated tracks past grit-brick warehouses and luxury lofts. Some buildings were so close the train seemed to scrape them as it rattled by. At each stop, Eden and Billy looked into the windows and witnessed a kaleidoscope of lives: A red-haired woman washed dishes as she stared blankly out of her kitchen window. An elderly couple in two large easy chairs read and relaxed in their familiarity. A GQ-like model played with a Scott terrier on a sisal carpet. A young couple made passionate love on an antique wrought iron bed. On and on. More lives, more stories.

They arrived at their stop and walked through the crowded station to the turnstiles. They wiggled through then made their way up Michigan Avenue like two minnows swimming against an endless stream of office workers, shoppers and panhandlers. Eden was taken back by the diversity of people— people of every race and nationality. Many smiled and some even said hello as they passed by. She didn't expect this display of hospitality in a big city like Chicago and mentioned the fact to Billy.

"Chicago's not New York," he explained. "It's much more human. It's slower paced and it seems the people here have no real axe to grind. "

"I kinda like that," Eden said.

The sun began to set and the buildings cast dark shadows across their path. Soon they arrived at the InterContinental and entered the plush lobby. It was crowded with people and luggage but there wasn't much of a line at the front desk. Eden sat down in a comfortable club chair while Billy checked in. He returned with the key card and suggested they get some shopping in at Filene's before heading upstairs to their room.

Eden concurred. "After all." She poked him in the ribs. "We did just get reacquainted today so there's no way I am going to bed naked tonight."

"Absolutely. I wouldn't think of such a thing," he replied. "And besides, there's always tomorrow night."

"In your dreams, buddy."

"I'll take it any way I can get it."

The light from the lobby chandeliers sparkled in her eyes. Mmm. . . that sherry.

"Let's go,' he said with a smile. "We need to get you 'not naked.'"

* * *

Eden held a white, cotton nightgown up in front of her and arched in front of a full-length mirror. "What do you think?"

"You're not Amish are you?" Billy asked.

She smoothed the fabric against her hip and turned from side to side. "Do you think I should get something a little more...revealing?"

"No, no, of course not," he stammered. "It's just that. . ."

She met his eyes in the mirror. "Just what?"

"Well, that nightgown looks so simple. So pure."

"Good. That settles it," she said with a nod. "Here, hold on to this."

He took the gown into his arms and followed her to casual wear. There she selected two pairs of comfortable jeans, a white long-sleeve cotton shirt, and a light green pullover and tried them on. Perfect.

They moved on to dresses where she decided on a simple black Donna Karan and a light blue scarf for her shoulders. She added two pairs of sheer stockings and an elegant pair of shoes to match.

"You wait here," she said as she spun away. "I have to pick up some intimate things."

"You sure you don't need any help?"

Eden smirked and shook her head. "Wait here."

He shrugged. "Just thought I'd ask."

Billy laid the pile of clothes on a nearby table. Why don't they have carts in this place? Several other men trailed behind wives, girlfriends, or significant others. All burdened with piles of female attire. Billy chuckled. And who's the weaker sex? He turned to a nearby rack of clothes and picked through the outfits. One caught his eye so he pulled it off and admired it. He turned over the price tag. Jeez!

The original price was crossed out and Filene's deep-discount price was printed below it. But Billy thought it was still a very pricey piece of fabric and thanked the gods for having the good sense to bless him with the simple, inexpensive taste of manhood.

When Eden returned, he held up the outfit and sputtered, "Do you believe these prices?"

"Now *that's* pretty," she replied as she snatched it away from him. "I'm going to try it on."

She walked back to the fitting room and closed the door. Billy restrained himself from picking up any more outfits.

"What do you think of this?" she asked as she emerged from the dressing room. She stretched her arms out and slowly spun around.

"My god," he said. "You look wonderful."

"That may be so," she said with a smile, "but what do I taste like?"

"Sweet cream," he replied. "And chocolate."

"Frango's?"

He nodded. "You bet."

"Great. I'll take it."

Eden returned to the fitting room to change. When she came out, she added the new outfit to the pile of clothes in Billy's arms.

"That about does it for me. What are you going to sleep in?"

"I guess I'll pick up a pair of flannel boxers and a cotton tee-shirt," he replied.

"Are *you* Amish?" she asked with a giggle.

"Back off. I sleep in comfort, not style."

"Obviously."

They walked over to the men's department and Billy picked out a pair of plaid boxers. Eden yanked them out of his hands. "Not flannel! We're getting you silk."

"Oh, we are, are we?" he said as he arched his eyebrows.

"Yes, we are. Where's your sense of adventure?"

She picked out a pair of midnight-blue silk boxers and ran them through her fingers. "These will do just fine."

They added two pairs of Levi's along with two long-sleeve cotton shirts. Then she picked out a pair of dress slacks and a light blue oxford shirt. She helped him select an expensive silk tie.

Good, Billy thought, I hate buying ties.

"Now," she said proudly as they left the checkout line, "we're a couple."

"Yes, we are."

Then she announced, "I'm starved, let's eat."

They stepped out onto Michigan Avenue and breathed in the early evening air. A cool breeze wafted in from Lake Michigan.

Eden slipped her arm through his. "Where to, my handsome tour guide?"

"South, my dear, to Heaven on Seven. It's Cajun and Creole. . ."

"To die for," she interjected.

"Bingo."

They walked arm in arm, their packages swinging and bouncing off the side of their legs. Her arm felt good in his. Like two puzzle pieces. A perfect fit.

"You're a good shopper," she said as they passed window after window of beckoning mannequins.

"And you have good taste."

"My ex hated shopping. One time he actually had the nerve to lie down in the middle of the aisle at Dillard's while I tried on blouses. He said 'Take your time, honey, I'm just going to take a quick nap. Wake me when you find something.' Then he dozed off. Customers had to step over him. I was mortified."

"The ass," Billy said.

"The fool," she added.

"The jerk."

"The idiot."

"The ex."

"Yes," she said with a sigh. "The ex..."

They walked a few blocks in silence when she asked, "How about you? Is there an ex in your life?"

"Besides Maureen?" Billy asked.

"She doesn't count. She was married, remember?"

"Oh, boy, do I." His stomach tightened as he recalled the feeling of Frank's fists clamped around his neck.

"Well?"

"Yes, I guess you could say so. Her name was Jill. I met her during a writer's conference. She was an agent for a small press out of Sarasota. We were together for almost a year and a half. So caring, so sensual, so alive. Except. . ."

"Except what? She sounds delightful!"

"Her eyes were brown."

"So?"

"When I see certain shades of brown I taste bitterness. Like bad medicine. Hers happened to be that particular shade of brown. So you see, it just wasn't going to work out."

"Ah. . . the 'condition.'"

"Yes, the 'condition.'"

"Anything about me taste 'off'?"

"Not yet." He playfully bumped his shoulder against hers. "But then again there are parts of you that I haven't seen yet."

"And likely won't," she said as she squeezed his arm.

Again they walked the next few blocks in silence. Billy savored the moment. He loved the feel of her arm against his. Puzzle pieces indeed.

"Turn right here," he said and they walked to the entrance of Heaven on Seven. "It's not the original," he explained. "That one's down in The Loop and it's only open for lunch. It does a killer business. In fact, it did so well Jimmy opened this one on the Mag Mile and it's always packed as well."

"You know, I don't think I could have lived without those details," she said with a playful smirk.

He turned red. "Sorry. I have this innate need to explain."

"That's okay," she said squeezing his arm. "You're a very attentive tour guide."

They climbed the stairs and were met with a potpourri of wonderful and inviting aromas: cumin, sautéed peppers and onions. Blackened fish. Roasted tomatoes. When they entered the restaurant they encountered a long line so they opted to sit at the bar that overlooked the open kitchen. Preps, sous chefs and cooks moved maniacally in front of stainless steel worktables, blazing gas stoves and a bank of broiling ovens. The smoke, steam and scent that eluded the droning exhaust hoods rose in plumes to the exposed steel beams overhead. A waiter approached and quickly took their order before moving down the bar to the other customers. Billy was surprised to see that all of the kitchen staff appeared to be Central American. Guatemalans? He wondered. Hondurans? All except one. He was tall and thin. Anglo, or perhaps French. Obviously the chef. He moved deftly through the kitchen area, his fluid movements in vivid contrast to the helter skelter of the kitchen. It was obvious he had been in this element for quite awhile.

A server slid two ice-cold bottles of Dixie Beer toward them then returned with bowls of piping-hot shrimp jambalaya and a plate of fresh-out-of-the-oven bread. Billy and Eden dove into their meal and continued to enjoy the performance before them. Eventually, the tall, thin chef turned and approached the bar.

"How's your meal, friends?" he asked as he wiped his sweating brow with a side towel.

Billy recognized him instantly. Another noted author of a book that exposed the inner workings of the high-end restaurant business.

"I know you. Loved your book!"

"And I'm reading it now!" Eden gushed. "In fact, I have it right here." She pulled a small paperback copy out of her purse. "Would you sign it for me?" She dug in her bag and searched for a pen.

"Of course," he said offering his own.

"Could you write: "Dear Eden, Here's to a successful cooking career. Good luck. Your friend. . ."

He signed his name with a flourish. "I have to get back to work. Thanks for coming tonight." He then returned to the men at the blazing stoves, pointing and shouting instructions.

Billy turned to look at Eden. "You're telling me you read books by four-star chefs and are contemplating a cooking career?"

"Does that surprise you?" she asked then raised her bottle to her lips.

"A little bit. You never mentioned it. I just figured a born-and-bred Florida girl like you would settle for macaroni and cheese, grits and fried baloney sandwiches."

Eden coughed into her beer and spun around on her stool. "So because I'm Florida born and like simple nightgowns you assume I'm into mystery meat and macaroni and cheese?"

"Watch it." He poked her with his bottle of beer. "I make a killer batch of mac and cheese."

"Batch? Did you say *batch*?" She tossed her head back with a laugh. "Is that a technical culinary term? Gee, must be new. I never read that in my four-star chef books. I guess I'll have to wait until I graduate to the five-star chefs to learn about terms like '*batches*.'"

"Okay, okay." Billy hunched his shoulders and took a sip of beer. "I'm just saying you surprise me." Then he looked at her out of the corner of his eyes. "I bet you're full of surprises."

"Ha! You're one to talk with your crazy 'condition' and all," she said with a laugh. "And besides, it's not like we've had a lot of time to get to know each other."

He turned on his barstool to look at her. "I'm serious. You don't really know me and yet you flew halfway across the country with me. That would be a mystery to most folk."

She traced her finger up and down the sweating bottle and studied the label. "Maybe I have my own 'condition.'"

"You mean the dreams and visions?"

Eden squirmed then shrugged her shoulders. "Could be. Don't know for sure yet."

"Oh?" Billy arched an eyebrow.

"But I have a feeling I may find out soon."

And looking away, she raised her beer to her lips and smiled.

CHAPTER 20

ROBBIE looked down at his ticket. Seat 22-A. Good, a window seat. *It'll give me a chance to try something I've always wanted to try.*

He shuffled down the narrow aisle when, halfway down, the line came to a halt. Up ahead a young man with stringy blond hair and a red-stained beige turtleneck attempted to wrestle a bulky knapsack into the baggage compartment above his seat. A flight attendant hovered over his shoulder.

"Sir, I don't think your knapsack will fit in the compartment," she offered in a cheerfully singsong voice.

"Yes it will," the young man replied without looking at her. "I measured it."

"I really don't think so," she continued with a broad smile. "Why don't you let me put it with the suitcases below."

He glanced over his shoulder. "I did all the calculations. I'm a Scientist. It'll fit I tell you."

"Sir, if you would just let me. . ."

"I said it'll fit," he said a little louder as he pounded and shoved the canvas bag.

"Sir—"

"I said it will—"

"GIVE ME THE GODDAM BAG YOU STUPID JACKASS!" she roared.

Conversations stopped and all heads snapped toward her. Her eyes scanned the wild-eyed expressions of the silent, gaping passengers. She smiled a broad, sheepish smile.

"I mean. . . please," she added as her voice returned to a lilt.

The Scientist looked at the flight attendant, then out at the passengers, then back to the flight attendant. "Sure," he mumbled. "I guess you can have it." He handed her the bag.

"My pleasure," she said cheerfully. "Thank you for flying Dixie Discount Air."

She sashayed to the back of the plane and opened the rear door. "Hey, Randy!" she barked down to baggage handler. "Put this bag below and make it snappy!"

She drew the knapsack back with both hands and hurled it high into the air. The bag arced and plunged toward the outstretched arms of the man waiting below. He almost caught it.

The line began to move again. Robbie scooted through to his seat and discovered he'd be sitting next to the blonde-haired man with the stained turtleneck. He casually slid his bag into the overhead compartment.

"Mine would've fit," the Scientist mumbled. "But that waitress was rushing me."

"You mean flight attendant," Robbie offered.

"Whatever," he said with a shrug. "Now it's down in the baggage hold with all those other suitcases. They better take good care of it. I have two bottles of vintage Bordeaux in that knapsack and if anything happens to them—" He paused and scowled. "Someone's gonna pay."

"I wouldn't worry about it," Robbie said as he snapped the compartment shut. "After all, they are professionals."

"I guess."

Robbie scooted in past the Scientist to the window seat.

"So, you brought along some wine, huh? I'm a beer man myself." Robbie pulled the seat belt across the small roll of his belly and snapped it shut.

"Yeah, I'm definitely into wines. They even have a special name for people like me."

"What's that?" Robbie asked as he cinched the seat belt tight.

"Oena... no... Ineo... no wait... Wenna... no that's not it..." He stroked his goatee and stared up at the ceiling. "I got it. We're called Expert Wine Drinkers. Yeah, that's it."

Robbie nodded and smiled. "They got a special name for beer drinkers like me."

"What's that?"

Robbie leaned in and confided, "Alcoholics."

The Scientist stared at Robbie for a moment. Then Robbie punched him in the arm. "Alcoholics. Get it?"

"Ha! That's a good one!" He returned Robbie's punch.

The two men rubbed their smarting shoulders as the plane taxied the runway, preparing for takeoff. The pilot pointed the bulbous nose down the tarmac. Engines roared and the plane accelerated. Robbie looked out the window and watched the white lines on the pavement speed by with a zip, zip, zip. Now's my chance, he thought and started to rapidly blink his eyes. The white lines stood still. He stopped and his face lit up in amazement.

"Hey, check this out," he said as he poked his new friend in the ribs. "If you blink your eyes really fast the white lines on the tarmac stand still."

The Scientist leaned over and blinked his eyes. "Man, that is so awesome."

A businessman looked up from his laptop when he overheard Robbie's comment. He closed the computer, stared out the window and began to blink his eyes.

"Holy moly," he said under his breath.

He turned to his colleague in the seat behind him and shared his new discovery. An elderly woman in a white woven shawl overheard them. Soon the whole left side of the plane was leaning toward the windows and blinking their eyes. A woman with an infant on the right side of the plane noticed the commotion and craned her neck to see what she was missing. She leaned across the aisle and tapped the elderly woman on the shoulder. "Hey lady, what are you all you people looking at?"

The woman turned with excitement and said, "It's the lines! The lines on the pavement! If you blink your eyes really fast they stand still!"

The young woman shifted her baby to her other knee and turned to look out the window. She had to lean across a thin African-American man who had just dozed off. He snorted and squirmed under her weight.

"Hey," he said as he shoved the woman back into her seat. "What the blazes do you think you're doing?"

"The lines, she replied. "Look at the lines and blink real fast. They'll stand still."

He turned toward the window and blinked his eyes.

"Well, I'll be," he muttered. "Them lines are standing still!"

"Told you," said the woman.

Soon all the passengers on the right side of the plane joined in on the activity. This piqued the curiosity of the flight attendants and they found themselves stretching over passengers to stare out the windows. It wasn't long before word reached the cockpit and soon the whole flight crew joined in. As the pilot, co-pilot and navigator emitted oohs and ahhs at their newfound discovery, the plane lifted off the ground then dropped back to the pavement with a bounce, jostling the passengers and interrupting the symphony of rapidly blinking eyes. The plane struggled to rise again but came down with a bone-shaking thud. The tires bounced and screeched and the engines whined and screamed. Robbie looked ahead and saw the end of the runway rapidly approaching. He stopped blinking and started sweating. The plane rose, wavered and pitched to the right—the wing nearly scraping the tarmac—then continued its climb. It swerved and dipped several more times before it leveled out and began a steady ascent. Robbie relaxed as the voice of the pilot came over the intercom to apologize. In a buzzed and scratchy voice typical of public address systems, he mumbled something about glare, wind shear and static white lines.

The jet reached cruising altitude and Robbie extended his hand to the Scientist, "Name's Robbie. You?"

"I'm a Scientist," the young man replied with pride.

"A Scientist, eh?" echoed Robbie. "Tell me this, have you ever been. . . mad?"

"Mad?" asked the young man.

"Yeah. Are you a. . . Mad Scientist?" Robbie slapped his knee and burst into laughter.

The Scientist obviously missed the joke this time. He sat and stared at Robbie.

"Man, I kill myself," Robbie wheezed and wiped a tear from his eye.

"As a matter of fact I have been mad at times," the Scientist explained. "But at this moment you could say I was heartbroken."

"Really?" said Robbie, regaining his composure. "That's weird. So am I."

A shapely, redheaded flight attendant approached them and asked, "Would you two fine gentlemen like any refreshments?"

Robbie ogled the young woman. Hmm, she's not like the babes on the posters, but she sure is easy on the eyes.

The flight attendant noticed Robbie staring at her breasts, scowled and repeated, "Refreshments?"

"I'll have a ham on rye, a bag of chips and a beer," Robbie said. "Hold the mayo."

"I'll have the same, but make mine a white wine," the Scientist added.

"I'm sorry," offered the flight attendant. "We no longer offer sandwiches on our flights."

"No sandwiches?" Robbie said. "Then how about a bag of chips and a beer."

"Ditto for me, but with the wine," said the Scientist.

"Sorry, no chips either," said the smiling flight attendant.

"How about a beer for me and a wine for my friend," asked Robbie.

"Sorry."

"Wait a minute." Robbie slapped the armrest. "You're the one who asked us what we wanted for refreshments. What the hell do you have?"

"We only stock hard liquor," she replied. "We found it's the only way our passengers enjoy their flight. So what can I get you two gentlemen?"

Robbie and the Scientist exchanged glances.

"I'll take a scotch on the rocks," said Robbie. "Make it a double."

"I'll have the same," said the Scientist.

A few minutes passed when the flight attendant returned, pushing an aluminum cart full of sloshing, highly alcoholic drinks. She handed two glasses of amber liquid to Robbie and the Scientist.

"That'll be nineteen fifty, please."

Robbie leaned over to the Scientist. "First round is on me." He reached into his wallet and pulled out two tens. "Keep the change."

The flight attendant stared at the crumpled bills. "Gee, can I? You sure you don't need any change? I could go back up to the cockpit. The pilot might have a couple of quarters on him."

"No, don't bother him," Robbie said. "I'm sure he's plenty busy flying this plane across the country and stuff."

She rolled her eyes and sauntered up the aisle handing out what was to be the first of many servings of 'refreshments.'

Robbie and the Scientist sat in silence and sipped their scotches. When they finished, the Scientist waved and ordered another round. The flight attendant approached with two fresh glasses and removed the empties. The Scientist pulled out his wad of cash and peeled off a twenty. "Here, hon, you can. . ."

"I know, I know. Keep the change."

The Scientist winked. "You got it, babe."

"Y'know, my mother was right," she explained as she leaned in. "I should've become a proctologist like my cousin Larry. At least I would have made some decent money dealing with assholes all day." Then she turned and strutted back to the galley.

"Touchy, touchy," Robbie said then nudged the Scientist. "That's one helluva bankroll you got there."

"Trust fund." He shoved the wad back into his jeans pocket. "I come from a long line of successful scientists and inventors."

"No kidding?"

"Yup. My great-grandfather was the guy who figured out how to keep the raisins from sinking to the bottom of Raisin Bran boxes. My grandfather invented the machine that prints the 'Ms' on M&Ms."

"Always wondered how they did that. How *do* they do it?"

"Can't tell. Family secret. Heck, they didn't even tell me. And my dad - you've seen digital clocks, right? The kind that blink when the power goes out?"

"Your old man invented the digital clock?"

"No, he just invented the blinking. Sold the technology to Sony and they use it in their electronic gear."

"Man, no wonder you're so loaded. How 'bout you? Working on anything?"

The Scientist leaned over and whispered, "You've heard of Viagra, right? Well, I'm working on a pill that will make you feel like every time is the first time." He punched Robbie's arm. "Awesome isn't it? Remember your first time?"

Robbie's mind drifted on a wisp to Molly Ricker and the lake in Kentucky. He played JV football and she was a cheerleader. It was late September and they stole out behind the trees with a wool blanket and a bottle of Boone's Farm. Lips locked in a fumbling embrace, sweat building up under their clothes, grass shifting beneath their writhing bodies. Molly moved Robbie's hand to her breast and moaned. Robbie immediately ejaculated in his jeans. He felt the passion that was overwhelming him drain from his body and into the sand. He rolled onto his back and stared up into the sky.

"What's wrong?" Molly raised herself up on her elbow and searched his eyes.

"Promised your dad I'd have you home by eleven."

She mounted him and ground her crotch against his. *"We have plenty of time. I'm just getting started."*

He pushed her off and stood, face hot with embarrassment. *"A promise is a promise."*

The Scientist's voice brought Robbie back to the present. "Remember?"

"Uh, yeah. It rocked!"

"That's why this pill is going to be the greatest. I've already got the shape and the color figured out. I just need to come up with the formula." He leaned back and stroked his chin. "Plus, I need to experience what a first time feels like myself so I can get it right."

Robbie slapped his knee. "Ha! Are you telling me you've never—"

The Scientist sat up straight and scowled. "Not that I haven't had the chance. Been too busy inventing stuff. That's why I need to find my soul mate. She's the missing piece to my project."

The young couple in front of them eased their seats back to the full, reclining position. Robbie nudged the Scientist and whispered. "This ain't going to cut it." Then he winked and said aloud, "So, like I was saying, the doctor said he never encountered a case quite like mine. Sure, it's highly contagious, but he said if I avoid crowds there'd be no cause for alarm. By the way, how's that rash of yours doing?"

The young man in front of Robbie snapped his seat back to the upright position.

"The oozing has slowed but it still itches like crazy," the Scientist said, returning the wink. "As long as I keep my hands to myself, there should be little chance of it spreading. In fact, I better go back to the restroom to check the bandages. Here, hold my drink."

He reached around the seat and shook the shoulder of the young woman in front of him. "Excuse me, lady. Could you please put your seat up? I need to go back to the lavatory to check on my weeping sores."

The woman glared at the hand resting on her shoulder as if it were a large insect. With a yelp she frantically brushed it off and jerked her seat to the upright position.

"I'll be right back," said the Scientist with a smile. He returned a few minutes later to find the seats in front of them empty.

"What happened to the pretty, young couple?" he asked.

"Beats me," Robbie said with a snicker. "They just got up and moved to another part of the plane."

"Too bad. I was hoping to get to know them a little better." The Scientist sat down and took his drink back. "They seemed like such a nice couple."

"So tell me about your loss." Robbie said. "Were you and your girlfriend close?"

"She wasn't just a girlfriend, she was my soul mate." The Scientist paused as a tear welled up in his eye. He wiped it away with his sleeve. "Then the boom fell. One minute she was there." He heaved his glass and knocked back a gulp. "The next minute—gone."

"I know how you feel." Robbie stared into his glass and sighed. "It was the same with my fiancée. One minute she's there, the next minute—gone." He raised his hand to snap his fingers. He was successful on the third try.

"Your *fiancée*?" the Scientist asked. He looked down at his drink and shook his head. "Man, that sure sucks."

"We were this close to setting a date." Robbie held up his hand and stared at the small distance between his extended thumb and forefinger. "This friggin' close."

"That *really* sucks," the Scientist said shaking his head.

"That's not the worst of it," Robbie said holding back a whimper. "This afternoon she went out to pick up some groceries and... and... she never came back." He drained his glass and waved for the flight attendant.

"Maybe she was in a wreck or something," the Scientist offered hopefully.

"Nah," Robbie said as the flight attendant brought two more drinks. "I called her best friend and she told me my fiancée had just left for Chicago."

"No kidding!? My soul mate's boss told me she was on her way to Chicago, too. What are the odds?"

"What are the odds?" Robbie echoed as he stirred the ice with his finger.

"What's your fiancée's name?" asked the Scientist.

"Eden."

"Pretty name. It almost sounds biblical."

"Y'know, I think you may be right. How about your soul mate?"

The Scientist thought for a moment. Name? Man, He didn't even know. He tapped his fingers on his pant leg. He needed a name. Quick.

"Um, er. Beaujolais."

"Interesting name. Is it foreign?"

"No, it's French."

"That's what I thought. What does she look like?"

"She's a portrait of beauty," the Scientist replied as he stared off into space. "Soft, ebony hair tumbling down past her shoulders, rich emerald eyes, pallid crimson lips, and her milk-white skin is as smooth as satin."

Robbie stared off in the same direction and sighed. "She sounds wonderful."

"How about your fiancée. She pretty?" the Scientist asked.

"Oh, man, yes. Long, black, satin hair, sea-green eyes, pale ruby lips and skin as soft and as white as freshly fallen snow."

"She sounds as beautiful as my soul mate." The Scientist's voice trailed off into a whisper.

The two men sighed and sipped their scotches.

"Women," the Scientist continued, his voice taking on a slight slur. "You can't live with them. . ."

"And you can't live with them." Robbie's voice began to take on a slur of its own.

Then the two men stared off into space, to points that converged in a way that neither would find amusing.

The flight attendant approached and shattered their reverie. "Would you like me to freshen up your drinks?"

"Sure," they slurred in unison.

She reached in her cart and produced a bottle of generic scotch. She topped off their drinks and moved down the aisle. The two young men raised their glasses and took a generous sip.

"So you're going to try and find your soul mate?" Robbie's head bobbed toward the Scientist.

"Yep. I've got to find my Beaujolais and bring her home. It's my destiny." He took another sip of his scotch. "You?"

"I'm going to find my fiancée," Robbie replied. "It's my destiny."

The Scientist nodded in empathy. "Destiny. It's all about destiny." He took two more gulps. "Where're you staying?"

"Hotel InterContinental. You?"

"Not sure. I'll figure something out when I get there,"

Robbie thought for a moment then an idea crashed into his scotch-filled mind. "Hell, why don't you stay with me? We can split expenses and save some money. What do you say?"

The Scientist sat up, "I say it's a deal!"

"Here's to destiny." Robbie raised his glass.

"To destiny," the Scientist echoed.

And they sealed their fate with the clink of a glass.

* * *

Maureen pulled her Jag into the first vacant space she spotted in the Tampa International parking garage. She hopped out and jogged across the suspended walkway to the terminal and approached the nearest ticket counter.

"Welcome to Southwest. How may I help you?" a friendly female voice asked.

"I'd like a ticket to Chicago," Maureen said, catching her breath.

"For what day, ma'am?" The young woman's fingers tickled her computer keyboard with a constant rap-tap-tap.

"Now."

The agent's fingers froze in mid-tap. She looked up and swallowed. "Now?"

"Yes. Today. Any time today."

The young woman scanned her computer screen. Tap-tappity-tap. "Unfortunately, all of our flights to Chicago are booked. But we could put you on standby."

Maureen leaned across the counter and pleaded, "But I need to get there now!"

"That's the best I can do, ma'am. We usually have one or two cancellations. Would you like me to put you down on standby?"

Maureen bit her lip and thought for a moment. "Yes, please do that."

The agent tippity-tapped the keyboard. "I have you down for the 6:10 flight. We'll notify you if there's a cancellation."

"Thank you," Maureen said with a sigh as she touched the ticket agent's hand.

"You really need to get there soon, don't you?"

Maureen nodded. "Hm-mmm."

The agent leaned forward. "It's love, isn't it?"

Maureen met the young woman's gaze. "A love bigger than life."

"Have you checked with Delta or Air Deco?"

"I'm afraid I didn't."

The agent glanced at her co-workers as if to make sure they weren't listening then whispered, "Why don't you go ahead and check with them." She patted Maureen's hand. "I'll keep you on standby just in case."

"Thank you so much!" Maureen answered with her own whisper. She grabbed the young girl's hand and cradled it in her own. "Here's to love."

"To love," the agent replied as she stared at Maureen's diamond encrusted wedding band. "Boy, I hope I'm as crazy about *my* husband when I get to be your age."

"If you only knew," she said with a sly grin, then turned and strode confidently toward the Delta ticket counter buoyed by the prospect of new opportunities.

"May I help you?" asked a rosy cheeked, chunky young man. Maureen's gaze drifted from the man's thick as ice cube glasses and down to his bright red tie. One of the clips poked out from beneath his collar. She leaned forward and adjusted it. The man's rosy cheeks turned bright crimson.

163

"Er, thanks," he stuttered.

Maureen smoothed the man's collar and smiled. She detected a familiar scent. Mmm, she thought. Old Spice. Frank's cologne.

"Do you have any openings to Chicago?" she asked.

"For what date, ma'am?" The man started to tap-tap-tap on his computer keyboard.

She rolled her eyes. Here we go again. "Today."

He stopped tapping. "Today?"

"Family emergency," she explained, trolling for sympathy.

"I doubt if I have anything this close to boarding." He stared at the screen. "No, there's nothing available."

Maureen's eyes fell on his nametag. "Tell me, Glen, is that Old Spice you're wearing?"

He glanced up and nodded. "Mmm-mm."

She narrowed her eyes and purred, "I love Old Spice."

His cheeks flushed crimson again. "Why don't I just check again." Tippity tap tap.

Maureen leaned across the counter and drew her finger across the back of the agent's hand. "Well? Did you find anything, Glen?"

The young man gulped and stuttered, "We have an opening on flight 434. It leaves at 2:10. It's a first class seat," he paused and coughed. "It's very expensive."

"That's not a problem." She opened her purse and withdrew an American Express card.

The agent took the card and turned it over. "Who's Frank Valentino?"

"It's my husband's card." He began to ask her for some ID when she pulled out her driver's license and offered it to the young man. He glanced at it, smiled and handed it back.

"Now, about my flight?"

The agent studied his computer screen." It's not a direct flight. You'll have to switch planes in Atlanta."

"That's all right. As long as I get to Chicago tonight."

The agent printed out a ticket and slid it across the counter. "The plane boards in an hour. Gate 11. Have a pleasant flight, Mrs. Valentino."

"Thank you, Glen." She slipped the ticket into her purse. Boy, is Billy going to be surprised.

A frantic woman rushed up to the counter and nudged Maureen aside.

"Sorry, lady," she said gasping for breath. Then she turned to the ticket agent and grabbed his arms. "You gotta help me," she pleaded. "My best friend is in danger. I need a ticket to Chicago and I need it now."

CHAPTER 21

DANNY and Eugene Lucci tramped up the front steps of their apartment building. All the way home they punched and slapped each other as they reveled in this incredible turn of events.

"Just think," Eugene said. "This morning we were just a couple of goombas hanging out on the front stoop, scoping out chicks. Now we're on our way to being a significant part of the Organization."

"We pull this off, Gino, and there's no telling how far we can go. But we gotta buckle down. Gotta plan it right down to the smallest detail."

Eugene unlocked the six locks to their apartment. Danny went into the kitchen and pulled some paper and a black magic marker out of the junk drawer. Eugene picked up the framing hammer from the hall table where Danny had left it that afternoon and followed his brother into the kitchen.

"What's with the hammer?" Danny asked as he spread the paper out on the kitchen table.

"I had an idea."

"Wait a minute. *You* had an idea?"

"It's brilliant." Eugene bounced the hammer in the palm of his hand.

"Don't keep me in suspense."

"A – We go to the Film Festival. B – We find our mark, the pretty girl from Florida."

Danny nodded. "Go on."

"3 – You get her attention and distract her. D – I sneak up and give her one good shot to the head with this baby." He held up the hammer. "4 – You grab her as she collapses. And 5 – We throw her in the car and head to the airport."

Danny leaned across the table. "Sounds good, Gino."

Eugene nodded and smiled a broad and proud smile.

Danny nodded his head slowly. "Yep. Sounds real good. Let me see the hammer."

"Sure."

Danny took the hammer from Eugene and felt its heft.

"Yep, sounds real good," he continued as he tossed it from hand to hand. "Except for one small detail."

"What's that?"

"Let's see, you got the A, B, C, and the 1, 2, 3. But you forgot the *W*?"

Gino furrowed his brow. "The *W*?"

"The *W*, as in *What* the fuck are you thinking?!" Danny leaned across the table and cracked his brother's knuckles with the hammer.

"Jeee-sus!!!" Eugene snatched his hand away. "What'd you go and do that for?"

"You can't split her head open with a hammer, you moron. You heard what Uncle Tommy said. Nobody's supposed to get hurt. . . least of all her! Now stop your whining and get serious. We only got a couple of hours to come up with a plan."

Eugene shook a gnarled and bloody finger at his brother. "I'm telling you, Danny. One of these days. . ."

His brother held up the hammer. "Yeah, Gino, what? One of these days, what?"

"Um, er," Eugene stuttered. "One of these days. . . I'm going to outsmart that hammer."

"I know you will, Gino," Danny replied with a sympathetic look. "I got complete confidence in you. Now let's get to work."

Danny uncapped the marker and drew a map of the block near the theater. "We drive up State Street. Then you and I get out of the car with a burlap sack, here." He drew an X.

Eugene nodded and Danny continued, "It's gotta be neatly folded so it looks like a handbag."

"Why a handbag?"

Danny glanced up at his brother. "Don't want to draw any attention to ourselves. See?"

Eugene rubbed his chin. "Ohh. I get it."

"Then we go over here." He pointed to a corner on the map. "And we wait."

"Hold on a minute—who's gonna carry the bag?"

Danny poked his brother's shoulder with the marker. "You are."

Eugene shook his head vigorously. "I ain't carrying no fuckin' handbag. No way."

"Why not?"

"Cuz I don't wanna look like no fag."

"Listen, moron. This is a film festival. The whole place will be crawling with homos and people who wished they were. They'll all be carrying handbags. Now shut the fuck up and listen. I don't want to lose my inspiration."

Eugene plopped down into a chair and folded his arms across his chest. "I'm listening."

"So, "Danny continued as he drew another X on the map. "Our girl exits the theater here. Then she makes her way to the curb for a taxi, here." He drew a line and another X. "Our driver eases the car up in front of the theater. We slip the bag over her head and shove her into the backseat. We'll tie her up and knock her out with some halothane."

"Hallow-what?"

"Halothane. Knock-out juice. I can get some from Johnny Cher-rone. He dabbles in all that chemical shit. Sells it at the clubs." He leaned forward and asked, "Remember how easy it was for me to get Barbie Longo to give it up?"

Eugene smacked the table and laughed. "You had some help from Johnny?"

Danny smiled like The Grinch. "The miracle of modern chemistry. Anyway, getting back to this." He looked down at the map. "We get her on a plane. If anyone asks about her wooziness, we'll just tell 'em we came off a night of hard partying at the Film Fest. They'll buy it. Then we turn her over to this Frankie the Valentine fellah in Florida and get back on a plane to Chi-town. Uncle Tommy will have no choice but to offer us permanent positions in the Organization." Danny tossed the marker across the table, leaned the chair back on its rear legs and smiled a broad self-satisfied smile. Eugene sat wide-eyed, his mouth gaping in obvious awe of his older brother's mental capacity.

Then he tilted his head. "So who's gonna be the driver?"

Danny smacked the table with his hand. "That, Gino, is the missing piece." He tapped his fingers on the tabletop and stared up at the ceiling. "We need someone with a car. Someone we can trust. Someone who won't identify us if things don't go exactly as planned."

Eugene stared at the tabletop and traced a swollen finger around the pink and aqua boomerangs on the Formica. "What we need is an accomplice."

"Yeah," Danny said to the ceiling. "An accomplice."

Eugene snapped his fingers. "How about old Charlie-Boy?"

Danny glanced at his brother. "You mean Newsstand Charlie-Boy?"

"Yeah, we can trust old Charlie-Boy. He won't identify us if things go bad."

"Charlie-Boy? Yeah he won't identify us...Cuz Charlie-boy is fuckin' *blind*!"

"Exactly!" Eugene held his hands out to his side and beamed. "He couldn't possibly identify us. Charlie-Boy couldn't identify anyone!"

Danny picked up the hammer. "So, tell me this. How is Charlie-Boy gonna drive the get-away car, if he's blind, you moron?"

Eugene quickly hid his hands behind his back. "Oh, yeah. A detail I must've somehow missed."

Danny let the hammer fall back to the floor with a thud and Eugene breathed a sigh of relief. "So Charlie-Boy is out. Who we gonna get?"

Danny pushed his chair back and wandered over to the kitchen window. He rubbed his chin and said, "Who do we know has a car?"

"Hmmm," Eugene echoed as he rubbed his own chin.

Danny turned away from the window and circled the kitchen with deliberate steps. He finally stopped and slammed a fist down on the table. "I got it! What about Vinnie DiChirico? He's a stand-up guy and he's got that big old black Buick!"

"Danny, you're a genius!" Eugene gushed. "We've known Vinnie since grade school. He's perfect!"

Danny yanked a chair out and sat down. "He *is* perfect, isn't he?"

A look of concern crossed Eugene's face. "But is he home from the mental hospital yet?"

"From St. Elizabeth's? Yeah, I seen him driving around the neighborhood last weekend."

"Can we really trust him. . . I mean, that was some incident he caused at Joey Bobo's Deli. Him climbing over the counter insisting he was 225 lbs. of pure provolone cheese. I tell ya, if Joey and his son Petie hadn't wrestled Vinnie to the floor, he would've surely made it to the slicer. God knows what would've happened then."

"Hell, they wouldn't have let him out if he wasn't ok. Besides, it's not like we got a laundry list of people we can trust who also own cars."

"I guess you're right."

"Gino, I'm always right. Go ahead and call Vinnie. Tell him we'll be over in thirty minutes. But first we gotta stop at Bertolli's Bakery to pick up a burlap sack for the kidnapping."

Eugene dialed a number. Someone answered on the third ring.

"Hello," said a heavy female voice.

"Mrs. DiChirico? It's Gino."

"Ah, Gino, my boy. How's your brother Danny? You two staying out of trouble?"

"Of course, Mrs. DiChirico. Is Vinnie home?"

"He's lying down watching TV. Tell me, what do you want with Vinnie?"

"Danny and me are going to the movies tonight and we'd like Vinnie to join us."

"That's so nice of you boys. Vinnie could use a night out." Her voice dropped to a whisper. "But I need to tell you something."

"What, Mrs. DiChirico?"

"When you're out, be sure that you don't mention the word "cheese.""

"Cheese?" Eugene asked.

"Shh. . . Shh," Mrs. DiChirico cautioned as if her son could hear Eugene through the line. "The doctors said it might send him into a relapse. Remember what happened at Joey Bobo's."

"Of course, Mrs. DiChirico, we'll be careful."

"And be sure he takes his medicine. He forgets when he's having a good time."

"We will, Mrs. DiChirico."

"Good, good." Then she cupped the phone and bellowed, "Vinnie! C'mere son."

"What do you want, ma?!" a voice called out from somewhere in the distance.

"Gino's on the phone. You want to go to the movies with him and Danny?"

"Hold on, ma. I'll be right there."

Mrs. DiChirico returned to the phone. "He's coming, Gino. And remember. . ." her voice dropped back down to barely a whisper. "Don't mention the word *cheese*."

"Got it."

Another voice came on the line. "Yo, Gino! How's it hangin'?!"

"What'd I tell you about using that language in the house?" Eugene heard Vinnie's mom in the background.

"Sorry, Ma. So what's up, Gino? Ma said you guys are going to the movies."

"Yeah, you wanna go?"

"Sure."

"We'll be over in thirty minutes."

CHAPTER 22

G INNY pointed her red '92 Toyota Corolla toward the interstate. The little car sputtered and crawled up the nearly horizontal incline of the entrance ramp. She beat the steering wheel with her fist and jerked her head forward and back. "C'mon little guy, you can do it!"

The hapless little car hesitated for a moment then lurched forward as if responding to her encouragement. A plume of blue-white smoke belched from the rusty tailpipe and the car shuddered like a washing machine full of sneakers. The speedometer wavered at 45.

Ginny stroked the dashboard. "That's it, little buddy, keep it up." The little car nervously merged into a roiling stream of traffic. The speedometer leveled out at 60 and Ginny beamed. "I knew you had it in you!"

It was a little after 2:30 when Ginny drove into the airport's discount parking area. She pulled into the first empty space and hopped out of her car. She caught her breath and gasped at the sight of the little green Dodge Neon next to hers. Robbie's? Can't be. She cupped her hands and peered into the window. Her eyes fell on the picture of Eden Scotch-taped to the dashboard. Well, well, well, she whispered. She straightened up and sashayed toward the shuttle stop. Normally, the sound of key scraping steel would give any reasonable person the willies. But to this girl with the swaying hips, the fingernails-on-blackboard squeal sounded like a symphony.

A shuttle bus ground to a halt in front of the stop and the door flew open.

"Which airline?" asked the driver as Ginny threw herself into the nearest seat.

"Doesn't matter, just take me to the first one. And step on it."

"I've got four other stops to make, lady."

Ginny reached into her purse and pulled out a crisp ten-dollar bill. She thrust it under the driver's nose and smiled. "Not anymore."

He plucked the ten from her hand. "Come to think of it, I already drove by those four shuttle stops." He stepped on the gas and the shuttle made a beeline to the terminal. Ginny leaned forward and stuck her chin out, thinking that might help the bus arrive a little faster. "OK, Eden," she whispered. "Help is on the way."

When the shuttle arrived at the terminal Ginny leapt out the door and ran inside to the first counter. Southwest Airlines. Good, only one other person on line. She took her place behind a woman with sun-bronze skin and wild, mahogany hair. Ginny leaned over the woman's shoulder and overheard the conversation.

". . . I'm sorry. Why don't you try Delta?" said the petite ticket agent.

I hope she's not trying to get to Chicago, Ginny thought. The woman turned toward the Delta counter and Ginny stepped up to the agent. "I need a ticket to Chicago."

"Sorry, I'm going on break now." The agent gestured to the man emerging from the door behind her. "Maurice will be glad to help you."

Ginny grabbed the woman's lapels and pulled her across the counter. "Fuck, Maurice. I need a ticket to Chicago. Now."

The agent gulped. "I'm sorry. We're full. Why don't you try- "

"I know, I know. Try Delta." Ginny released the woman then spun on her heels and jogged across the terminal to the Delta counter. The beautiful bronze woman was tucking a gold credit card back into her purse.

"You gotta help me," she said to the agent. "My best friend is in danger. I need a ticket to Chicago and I need it now."

"I'm sorry, ma'am. Just sold the last ticket."

"But you don't understand. I *have* to get to Chicago. I – I- have a friend. She's in danger."

The bronze woman looked up, "Danger?"

"Mm-mmm," Ginny nodded her head and forced her lips to quiver.

Maureen grabbed the agent's hand. "Listen, Glen, you found *me* a seat. I'm sure you could find one for my friend—" she paused and looked at the distraught girl beside her.

"Ginny."

"I know you can find my friend Ginny a seat." Her fingernails caressed the man's hand. "Surely you can bump someone."

The young man gulped and turned his attention to the computer screen. "This Henderson fellow probably doesn't *need* to get there this afternoon," the agent mumbled under his breath. He tapped the keys again and grinned. "Oh, lookie here. I do have one more seat."

"Fantastic! How much?" Ginny pulled out her wallet.

The agent quoted her a price.

"What?!" She stumbled backward. "You can't be serious."

"It's a first class seat. And it *is* the day of the flight –"

"I don't have that kind of money," Ginny wailed. "Can't you cut me some kind of deal?"

"I'm sorry, ma'am."

Ginny looked away and bit her lip. "What am I going to do?" she whispered.

The bronze woman opened her wallet and pulled out the gold credit card. "Here, Glen, put her ticket on this."

Ginny turned, eyes wide. "But—"

"Don't worry." She handed the card to the agent. "It's my husband's card. There's a lot more where this came from."

Ginny leaned over and planted a big, wet kiss on woman's cheek. "You're the best. Thanks—"

"Maureen."

The agent slid the ticket across the counter. Ginny snatched it up and Maureen put her arm through hers. "C'mon, Ginny, we have some time. Let's grab a drink. Sounds like you have a story that's just dying to be told."

Ginny squeezed Maureen's hand and smiled. "Sounds like you do, too."

A blue and white neon sign above the airport lounge beckoned the two women. They sidled up to the bar and Maureen ordered a white zin. Ginny, Pabst.

"It's *sorta* dangerous," Ginny replied as she raised her bottle. "But not really. See, my best friend just met someone. Love at first sight. One of the Great Ones."

175

"Great Ones?" Maureen asked turning on her barstool. "Like in *A Bronx Tale?*"

Ginny bolted upright. "You a fan of mob movies, too?"

"I'm very fond of movies," she replied. Then her countenance darkened as if a storm cloud drifted between them. "But I'm no fan of the mob."

"Oh," said Ginny, a little taken aback by the change. "Anyway, he asked her to join him on a weekend trip to Chicago. She was so pumped."

"Doesn't sound like she's in much danger to me." Maureen took a sip.

"But then I went and did something incredibly stupid. I told her fiancé where she was going and the jackass hopped on a plane to chase her down." She looked away and bit her lip. "If I don't get to the Hotel InterContinental to stop him, he'll screw everything up. God, I hope I can get a hotel room."

Maureen laughed and said, "You already have one."

Ginny set her bottle down and turned. "What?"

"Stay with me. I already have a reservation there and could use some company." She patted Ginny's wrist. "I have a feeling we'll each need some moral support."

"That's fantastic!" Ginny grabbed Maureen's hand. "How 'bout you? What brings you to Chicago?"

"I was supposed to go on a romantic weekend trip, too. Then my husband found out about it and all hell broke loose. I know my boyfriend made the trip alone so I snuck out of the house." She sipped her wine and her eyes narrowed. "I'm determined to find him."

A heavyset man in an ill-fitting suit tapped Ginny on the shoulder and slurred, "I'm going to Chicago, if you ladies can't find your boyfriends, maybe the three of us could—"

The two women glared at him until he turned red and returned to his drink.

Ginny turned back to Maureen and asked, "You're cheating on your husband?"

She shrugged a shoulder. "Technically? I suppose so. But he has at least six girlfriends that I'm aware of. I've wanted to leave him but I have no real friends or family here. Besides, my husband is, what you say, 'connected,' so it could be risky. But when I met this new man I decided to go for it."

"You think he's one of the Great Ones?"

"Yeah." Maureen sighed. "I'm sure of it."

"You don't have to tell me about slime-ball husbands. I've had my share." She tossed her head back and took a big swig. "At least my last one won't be able to participate in the procreative process—no progeny from his loins. No, siree. Biologically impossible."

"I'm sorry," Maureen asked with a look of concern. "Was he in an accident?"

Ginny chuckled. She thought about the night before his arraignment. He pleaded with her for one last go-round before his impending incarceration. She obliged by blindfolding him and tying him up to the bed. He always did have that kinky streak. She then proceeded to 'service' him. To this day she was amazed at how much havoc a hot iron and dental floss could wreak on a man's private parts. She shuddered at the thought then turned to her new friend. "Yeah. A horrible accident."

Maureen paused then smiled a knowing smile. "Accidents *do* happen."

"They sure do. What about your cheating husband?" Ginny asked. "Surely you gotta get *some* revenge."

"I'll get my revenge when he finds his bed empty and discovers a mailbox bursting with credit card statements." She pulled the American Express card from her purse and kissed it. "Thanks for helping me spend his money."

Ginny laughed. "My pleasure!" She reached into a bowl of peanuts and popped a handful into her mouth. "So," she said between chomps. "Tell me about this new guy."

"I met him at the Film Fest," Maureen replied dreamily. "He's a writer. His name is Billy Shakes."

Ginny lurched forward and spewed a fine mist of peanuts and Pabst Blue Ribbon across the counter top. The businessman brushed the spittle off his sleeve and moved down two seats.

Maureen gently patted her back. "Are you all right?"

Ginny wiped her mouth and nose with a cocktail napkin. "Wrong pipe," she managed to squeak out. "I'll be all right." She balled the napkin up and tossed it across the bar. Shit, she thought. Not only do I have to keep Robbie away from Eden, now I've got to keep Maureen away from Billy. She stared off into space and picked up her bottle. How in the hell am I gonna pull this off?

Then she tossed her head back and drained her beer.

CHAPTER 23

I T was just past six when Danny and Eugene entered Mrs. Bertolli's Bakery. They walked the three blocks to her store bouncing ideas back and forth. They had to think of a way to ask Mrs. Bertolli for a burlap bag without arousing her suspicion—because Mrs. Bertolli's suspicion had a hair-trigger. Legend had it that no one had ever been able pass anything over on Mrs. Josephine Lucrenza Bertolli. Many believed she was blessed with some kind of sixth sense. Some even went so far as to say she had a hotline to everyone's guardian angel, and the angels informed her if things weren't on the up and up. Every single child in the neighborhood suffered a spanking at the hands of their parents based on a single phone call from Mrs. Bertolli. Danny and Eugene themselves endured no less than two-dozen beatings as a result of her 'inside information.'

When they were just a few steps from the shop, Danny and Eugene had formulated a plan. They approached the bakery with confidence and pushed the front door open.

"Hello, Mrs. Bertolli," Danny said with a smile as the little brass bell above him jingled. Mrs. Bertolli was hard at work behind the display case placing loaves of fresh-baked bread into large wire baskets hanging from the ceiling. Danny and Eugene paused and breathed deeply. Only two things in this world could stop two strapping Italian boys dead in their tracks and the wonderful aroma of freshly baked bread was one of them. Mrs. Bertolli turned around at the tinkling of the bell.

"Good evening, boys," she sang as her chubby pink face exploded into a broad and infectious smile.

"Evening, Mrs. Bertolli," the boys chimed in unison.

"My, you two have grown! Come here and let me get a good look at you."

She scooted around the counter and gave the boys a prolonged hug. As they melted into her fleshy arms and ample bosom, they felt overwhelmed and claustrophobic. She pulled away with a giggle, leaving splotches of flour dust and yeast on the boys' clothes. They brushed themselves off as Mrs. Bertolli waddled back behind the counter.

"Now what would you boys like tonight?"

Danny pointed to the baskets above the counter. "We'll take a dozen loaves of bread."

"And two-dozen cannolis," added Eugene.

"Coming right up." She began to stack the items on the counter.

"And ten carrot cakes."

"And a couple bags of those polenta cookies."

"And a dozen of those Venetian almond cakes."

"And eight loaves of focaccia. No not those, the ones with the red peppers."

Mrs. Bertolli mussed and fussed as she piled the requested baked goods on the counter.

"This is quite a selection," she said as she wiped her sweaty brow with her forearm. "Not often do I get an order like this." She furrowed her brow and eyed the boys.

Danny apprehensively looked around the room. Were the angels talking to her?

"They're for the meeting, He said. "At the club. . . yeah, a big meeting at the club. The Sons of Italy."

Mrs. Bertolli planted her hands on her broad hips and tilted her head. She wrinkled her nose and stared at the two brothers. Did they detect a faint frown?

Danny and Eugene held their breath while beads of sweat formed on their brows. They strained their ears for angelic voices. Eugene thought he heard the sound of a distant harp.

Mrs. Bertolli's eyes darted from one brother to the other. Then she said, "I think I have a box big enough in the back. It might hold all of this."

Danny exhaled. "How about a big burlap bag? The bigger the better."

"Good idea! I have some clean ones in the storage room. Let me run back and get one." Mrs. Bertolli turned and disappeared into the back room.

"So far, so good," whispered Danny with a sigh of relief.

Mrs. Bertolli returned and filled the bag with baked goods then hoisted it over the counter with a snort.

"Thanks, Mrs. Bertolli," said Danny.

"Thank you, boys" she said with a broad smile. "And have a good meeting."

"You're the best, Mrs. Bertolli," Danny said as he tossed the bag over his shoulder and pulled the front door open. He took one step outside, and then popped his head back in. "Oh, Gino," he said in a singsong voice.

"What?"

"Don't forget to pay Mrs. Bertolli."

* * *

The Scientist and Robbie stared out the window as their plane began its descent. The Scientist grabbed the elbow of a passing flight attendant. "Where are we?"

"Why Chicago, of course."

"Doesn't look like Chicago to me," he said as he glanced back out the window. "Where's all the big buildings and stuff?"

"Well, it isn't exactly Chicago. At least not technically," she explained with a smile. "But we're in the general vicinity."

The Scientist frowned. "How general?"

"Rockford."

"Man, that's like 100 miles from Chicago!"

"More like 90. Say, do you two boys want another drink for the road?"

The jet crawled to a halt a good half-mile from the terminal and the passengers staggered down a platform of rickety metal steps. They stood in a circle as someone tossed their bags from an open door to the ground below. When all the luggage was unloaded, a porter encouraged the crowd to sort through the pile for their bags. Robbie draped his carryon bag over his shoulder and waited as the Scientist searched through the jumbled pile of luggage. He picked up one bag and tossed it aside. Then he picked up another. And another. He finally looked up and spotted his green knapsack in the hands of a pimply-faced student wearing a Florida School for the Deaf and Blind sweatshirt. He marched over and grabbed the strap.

"S'cuse me, buddy," the Scientist said. "I believe this bag is mine."

"Are you sure?" The boy clutched the bag close to his chest as blank eyes stared past the Scientist's shoulder.

"It's got my name on it you jackass. What are you, blind?"

"As a matter of fact. . ."

The Scientist snatched the bag from the boy and walked back over to Robbie. "Got it. Let's go."

Robbie stared at the dark, red liquid oozing from the bottom. "Hey, dude, I think your bag is leaking."

"What the. . ." The Scientist turned the bag over and examined it. "My medicine! The bottles must have broken." He squinted his eyes, glanced around, and seethed, "Somebody's gonna pay for this."

He marched over to a heavyset, broad-shouldered man by the stairway. He leaned against the rusty railing and cast a thick, pot-bellied shadow across the tarmac. A half-smoked, unlit cigar hung from his bulbous lips and a small rust-brown drop of spittle hung precariously from the corner of his mouth. He was engaged in conversation with his partner, a thin African-American man with graying hair and gold teeth.

"Hey. Buddy," the Scientist barked as he approached the two men.

"You talkin' to me?" asked the big man nonchalantly as he turned his attention from the black man to the Scientist.

"Yeah," the Scientist poked the man's chest. "I'm talking to you."

"My name ain't Buddy," the burly man explained as he pulled the damp cigar from his mouth. The drop of spittle dangled for a moment then fell onto his sweat-stained uniform. He wiped it off with the back of his hand then pointed to his name tag. "It's Mickey."

The Scientist ignored the man's gesture and shook his knapsack in front of the man's face. "Take a look at this!"

"Hmmm, Looks like your bag is leaking." He turned to his partner. "What do you think, Clarence?"

The black man scratched the back of his head and nodded. "Mickey, I think you're right."

"Damn right it's leaking!" said the Scientist. "Do you know what I have in this bag?"

"Lemme see." Mickey took the bag from the Scientist and examined the stain. He sniffed the dark splotch then looked up into the sky and furrowed his brow. "Mmm," he murmured. He sniffed it again then dabbed the splotch with a nicotine-stained finger and touched it to his tongue. He smacked his lips and rolled his eyes up into his head as if searching some vast library for information.

"If I'm not mistaken, little man," he said. "That there is a '42... no, make that a '43 Rothschild Bordeaux. Chateau Mouton. Which, I might add, was a very good year." He tossed the bag to his partner. "What do you think, Clarence?"

The black man sniffed the stain and dabbed it with his finger. He studied it for a moment then touched his finger to his tongue and closed his eyes.

"Yep, that's a '43 all right. And it *was* a good year, although not as good as the '45 Pauillac. Now *that* was a fine vintage."

"Damn right!" The Scientist stomped his foot on the Tarmac and wrenched his bag from the black man's arms. "It *is* a '43! Why I should—" He froze and looked at the two men. "Hey, wait a minute. . ."

"If I was you," said the large man helpfully. "I'd take better care of my wine."

"Cuz that's some damn serious money you got leaking on the pavement," Clarence added.

The Scientist, taken aback, could only mutter, "Yeah, I guess you're right." He lowered his head and skulked back to his friend.

"Don't worry," Robbie said as he slapped him on the shoulder. "I'm sure you can pick up some more wine in Chicago."

A rust-red tram pulled up and the crowd of people clamored aboard.

"My medicine," the Scientist moaned. He stared at his stained and dripping knapsack and shook his head. He climbed onto the tram and took a seat next to Robbie. "My precious medicine."

Robbie put his arm around the Scientist and hugged him as only someone who'd had four scotches could.

The tram dropped them off at the terminal where a skycap informed them that they'd be taking a shuttle bus to Chicago.

"A shuttle bus. Thank god," Robbie said to the Scientist. "I'm sick of these Disney-World-reject trams."

The skycap led them out the front door and toward a luxury coach idling softly at the curb. The late afternoon sun glinted off the metallic blue paint and spit-polished chrome. Someone pointed out the TV monitors hanging in front of the high-backed seats. The group let out a chorus of oohs and aahs.

Robbie nudged the Scientist and said, "That's what I'm talking about."

The Scientist returned the nudge. "You got that right."

Suddenly, the rushing sound of airbrakes pierced the air and a billow of black smoke belched from the exhaust and into their nostrils. Disappointment rose as the bus pulled away from the curb revealing a faded yellow Blue Bird school bus parked beside it. Dixie Discount Limousine Service was stenciled on the side. 'Limousine' was misspelled. The group's oohs and ahhs were replaced by groans, moans and more than a few curses.

The skycap bowed ceremoniously and made an elaborate sweeping motion toward the bus. "Dixie Discount Limousine at your service," he said with an air of pride.

The crowd slinked past the bowing skycap toward the bus. Two more skycaps appeared with an aluminum stepladder. One took the luggage from each passenger and handed it to the other who had scrambled up the ladder. He, in turn, stacked the bags on a makeshift metal rack on top of the bus. The scene reminded Robbie of the buses he saw in National Geographic TV specials. Third World contraptions jam packed with people and roof top luggage racks overflowing with items of every description. Every bus seemed identical, regardless of the country. He scowled and wondered if there was a dealership somewhere that specialized in this primitive form of motorized transportation.

When the skycap had all of the bags stored in the rack, he secured them with an assortment of ropes and bungee cords. By the time he finished, the mound of luggage appeared to be enveloped by an enormous rubber hair net.

"That oughta hold it!" he shouted as he stretched the last bungee cord and fastened it tight.

"It better, Ernie," yelled the other. "Remember what happened last Wednesday."

Ernie replied with a whistle, "Oh boy, do I!"

"That semi-truck driver was pretty pissed. Not to mention the National Guard convoy involved in the pile up."

"Not to worry, Lamont," Ernie said with a smile as he climbed down the ladder. "This time I used twice the bungee cords."

"Man, you're the best. I don't care what your mother says about you."

The two skycaps sauntered back to the terminal. Ernie carried the ladder and Lamont slapped him on the back.

"Yep, a military convoy and a semi tractor-trailer," Lamont said with a laugh. "That's got to be some kind of record!"

"Aw, it was nothing." Ernie replied. "Good thing my niece, Tennille, is married to the Vice President of Dixie. I might have gotten myself canned."

"Here's to job security," Lamont said as he took the ladder from Ernie.

"Job security and beautiful nieces."

"Amen, my brother." Ernie opened the double doors and the two men disappeared into the terminal.

Robbie looked at the Scientist and raised his eyebrows. They took their place at the end of the line as the bus's door creaked open to reveal an elderly man dressed in an ill-fitting uniform. He limped down the stairs and stood by the door, greeting each passenger with a broad, toothless smile. When Robbie and the Scientist reached the door the driver extended a frail and shaking hand.

"Hello, boys. Name's Morty. Welcome to Dixie Discount—"

"Yeah, yeah, yeah," said the Scientist as he ignored the old man's outstretched hand and climbed the steps into the bus.

Robbie gingerly shook the elderly man's skeletal hand. He noticed Morty's glasses. Hubble-telescope thick. Enormous gray eyes stared back at him.

"Oh, boy," he said under his breath as he returned the old man's smile.

The Scientist settled into a seat directly behind the driver. He patted the empty space next to him as Robbie climbed up the stairs. Morty followed close behind, slid into the driver's seat and closed the bus's door shut with a 'whomph.' He turned the key in the ignition and the engine coughed and sputtered to life. Morty eased the rattling bus away from the curb and down the airport road to the interstate.

As the shuttle bus pulled onto I-90 Robbie leaned forward and tapped the driver's shoulder. "So, how long you been driving for Dixie?"

Morty looked up in the large mirror above the front windshield and smiled at Robbie. "Young man, I've been driving for Dixie for as long as I can remember."

"And how long has that been?"

"I don't remember. Ha!"

Morty ground some gears as the old bus struggled to hit 55 miles per hour. They coasted down the entrance ramp and merged into the much faster traffic. Horns blared and drivers swerved as the big yellow bus forced itself onto the busy interstate.

Robbie tapped Morty on the shoulder again. "Hey, old timer, shouldn't you signal or something before pulling this big baby into traffic? I want to get to Chicago in one piece."

"Don't you worry about a thing, young man," he replied as the bus lumbered across four lanes of heavy traffic to the HOV lane. "I been making this trip for as long as I can remember."

Robbie almost asked him how long that had been, but wisely refrained.

"And besides," Morty continued with a big grin. "They got brakes."

CHAPTER 24

BILLY and Eden left Heaven on Seven and strolled back up Michigan Avenue to their hotel.

"So," Eden said, "you taste color. You also mentioned something about sound? Do you taste that, too?"

"No, I don't taste sound. I *feel* it," Billy replied.

"So do I! When I hear a certain song it's like I'm transported back in time. I feel the same emotions, I feel the same—"

"I'm not talking about memories. I'm talking about real, physical sensations. Classical violins for instance. They transport me to a warm, tropical spring. A jazz sax? A gentle massage—I can actually feel someone's fingers kneading my shoulders. A wailing blues guitar is invigorating; my heart begins to pump like I just jogged a mile. Each genre produces a different feeling. Each instrument, a different sensual nuance. And I pretty much enjoy them all. That is, except. . ."

"Except what?"

"Don't get me started on the high, lonesome whine of some country music. My lord, just put my head in a vise and turn the crank. The pain is unbearable. I wind up screaming and cursing at the top of my lungs."

"That's so funny!"

"You think so? An old girlfriend, Brenda Whitehouse, took me to a Willie Nelson concert. Third row, center. It was absolute torture. After each song, I screamed and let loose a string of horribly disgusting and profane words. Let me tell you, Mr. Nelson was not at all amused. And neither were those around us. I got my ass whooped eight times that night. Sometimes even the men joined in."

"You make me laugh," she said as they entered the bustling hotel lobby and took the elevator to the 18th floor. Billy slid his key card

187

in the door of a room overlooking Michigan Avenue. Eden set her bags down near the walnut armoire and wandered over to the window. The hotel room didn't have the standard-issue table and two chairs. Instead, it had a long, richly upholstered window seat and a small coffee table.

"My goodness. The view is stunning!"

She looked below. Dozens of yellow cabs, like worker bees, jostled for space on an asphalt honeycomb. The surrounding buildings rose story after story, gray and heavy, groaning under their own weight. Waterfalls of steel and glass cascaded silently into the pavement below. She looked up into the early evening sky. White-gray clouds tumbled and tossed in a dark deep blue sea. Billy approached and slipped his arm around her waist. She leaned her head on his shoulder and sighed.

"It's a wonderful sight, isn't it?" he asked.

"The city itself seems to be alive."

"It is, and we're about to become a part of it, aren't we?"

They stood silently for a few moments. Eden placed her hand on Billy's and caressed it. He pulled her closer and she nuzzled his shoulder.

"You'd better go and freshen up." He gave her a gentle squeeze. "We need to head over to the Film Festival."

Eden pulled a pair of slacks and a blouse out of the bag and slipped into the bathroom. Billy donned his new clothes then wandered back to the window and watched the city transform itself from a world-weary business persona to one of adventure and possibilities. He sensed a sigh of relief rising up from the slate gray pavement as neon lights illuminated the bustling sidewalks below. A kaleidoscope of color reflected off windows and windshields along the avenue. He savored the palette before him as a cavalcade of colors washed over his taste buds. He felt giddy and weightless as his senses were overwhelmed. The people below seemed to walk with a lightness in their step as they cast off the burdens of the day. Even the taxis and buses seemed to float down the avenue. An air of wonder and expectation filled the air. He was buttoning the last button on his shirt when Eden emerged from the bathroom.

"How do I look?" Eden turned slowly in front of the vanity mirror.

"Delicious."

"Don't get any bright ideas," she said with a laugh then joined him at the window.

"Something's in the air," Eden thought for a moment and hesitated. "I can feel it."

He turned to her. "What do you feel?"

"I'm not sure," she whispered, still staring out on the city. A familiar shadow flitted across the neon-bathed storefronts and beckoned to her. "Something. . ." her voice trailed off.

"Oh, my," she said glancing at her watch. "It's almost seven." She spun away from him and walked toward the door then stopped. "Look," she said pointing to the phone. "The red light's blinking. You've got a message."

He picked up the receiver and punched a few numbers. He broke into a broad grin and shook his head as he listened.

"Everything all right?" she asked.

He replaced the phone. "It's my mother. Wishing me a good time. She and Mrs. Donaghee are watching a Bob Hope-Bing Crosby road movie tonight." He tossed his jacket over his shoulder. "And she says 'hello' to that wonderfully beautiful girl with me."

She put her hands on her hips. "How does your mother know I'm here with you?"

"Long story." He walked to the door and opened it. "Let's go."

He scanned the Festival brochure as they walked down the hallway. "Let's see, there's the new Jim Jarmusch film at the Harris Theater and a Hal Hartley film is playing at the Landmark. What do you think?"

"It's up to you, they both sound great."

"And look, there's a David Mamet film at the Chicago Theatre and he's going to speak."

"*The* David Mamet?"

Billy tapped the program. "That's what it says."

"As in *Glengarry*—"

"*Glen Ross.*"

Eden grabbed Billy's arm and turned him toward her. She put her hands on her hips, cocked them to one side and said, "Won't you please—"

"—go to lunch!" Billy added with his best Kevin Spacey accent.

They stared at each other for a second then burst into laughter and continued down the hallway.

"*Glengarry Glen Ross.* What a classic!" Billy said.

"And how about *The Spanish Prisoner?*" Eden added.

"Or *House of Games?* And who could forget his play *Sexual Perversity in Chicago?*"

Eden halted, grabbed his arm and glared. "Sexual—what?!"

"Um. Never mind."

She smiled and punched his arm. "Now you put that right out of your mind, mister."

"Okay, okay," he replied rubbing his shoulder, "Then how about *We're No Angels.*"

"Much better," she said as she put her arm though his and led him down the hall. "Though I've never heard of that one."

They reached the elevators and Billy pushed the lobby button. "Hmm, *Glengarry, House of Games, Spanish Prisoner...*I thought you weren't a movie buff."

"I like what I like," she said stepping into the elevator.

Billy looked at her out of the corner of his eye and pushed the lobby button. "So, getting back to tonight's schedule, do any of these interest you?"

"If Mamet is leading the discussion, then I say we head over to the Chicago Theatre."

"The Chicago Theatre it is."

The elevator doors closed and they began their descent into a world of wonder and possibilities.

CHAPTER 25

ORTY pulled the big yellow bus off I-90 and onto I-294 toward O'Hare. He took the I-190 exit and followed the highway into the airport. The brakes whined and wheezed as the bus eased to a stop in front of a pale blue, rust-metal warehouse. A faded Dixie Discount Air sign was bolted to the front of the corrugated building. Patches of foot-high weeds sprouted up between the discarded tires, wooden crates and rusty steel drums that littered the small yard around the structure.

Morty threw an arm over the back of his seat and turned to face his passengers. "This is the end of the line. It was a pleasure serving you today."

"Hey, wait a minute," someone shouted from the back. "How are we gonna get downtown?"

"That's easy," Morty replied with a helpful smile. "The El station is only a block away. But if you prefer a cab, why, O'Hare couldn't be more than a half-mile from here. 'Course, if I were you," he confided as he glanced around the deserted neighborhood, "I'd take the El."

Morty honked the horn and the garage door opened with a groan. Two men with ladders emerged and propped them against the bus. They untangled the mass of ropes and bungee cords and tossed the bags to the pavement.

Robbie and the Scientist pulled their knapsacks out from underneath their seats and scrambled out the door.

"Train or a taxi?" asked Robbie as he looked up and down the vacant street.

"Definitely the train," replied the Scientist.

"Yeah, who wants to walk a half-mile?" Robbie threw his bag over his shoulder.

The Scientist stared at Robbie's warm-up jacket. "But I thought you were an athlete?"

"I am, but why walk when you can ride?"

"Good point," the Scientist said with a nod. "Besides, trains are safer than taxis."

"How do you know that?"

"Cuz' I'm a—"

Robbie cut him off. "I know, I know. You're a scientist."

The Scientist thrust out his chest and beamed. "That I am."

"C'mon, let's go before it gets too late," Robbie said as he began to strut down the road to the El Station.

The Scientist picked up his bag. "Right behind you."

The two men took the Blue Line into Chicago and disembarked at Washington. They followed the flow of the crowd up to the street and found themselves surrounded by people who obviously would rather be somewhere else—like home. The exodus from The Loop had begun in earnest and the two young men moved to the side to keep from being carried along by the rush of the ebbing tide.

"Where to now?" The Scientist craned his neck and looked up and down the bustling street.

"Let me check." Robbie pulled out an *Idiot's Guide to Chicago* and opened it to a map. He looked at the street signs above them, then down at the map, then back up to the street signs. He felt he was being watched then noticed a punk with a red bandana leaning against a doorway. The punk tossed a rolled-up New Yorker into a nearby trashcan and limped over to the two men. "S'cuse me. Looks like you two could use a little help."

"I think we're lost," the Scientist explained.

"Allow me."

Robbie handed him the map and noticed the *Dead Meat* tattoo on the man's knuckles. He swallowed hard. "Interesting tats."

"These? Used to work at the stockyards," he explained with a smile. "Part of the dress code."

"Dead meat. Makes sense."

"So, where you guys headed?" asked the punk as he studied the map.

"Hotel InterContinental," Robbie replied.

The man stepped back and eyed the two young men. "That's quite a place. I'll tell you what. I like you two. I'd hate to see you taken advantage of. There's sharks on the streets tonight and it'd kill me to see two nice visitors like you fall victim to their devices. So here's what I'm gonna do." He handed the guidebook back. "I'm gonna make sure you arrive safe and sound at your destination."

"Really?" Robbie asked.

"That is so very cool," added the Scientist.

"But," said the punk. "I'm afraid I can't give that information out for free." He stared at the sidewalk and rubbed the back of his neck. "What with my mother being in the hospital and all."

"I understand," Robbie said. "I'm just glad you're willing to help us out."

"And you say you'll guarantee a safe arrival?" asked the Scientist. "We're kind of in a hurry."

The man removed his bandanna and crossed his heart. "On my grandmother's grave."

"It's a deal," Robbie said with a smile. "So how much, five?"

"Ten."

"Ten?" echoed the Scientist.

"On account of my mother and all."

"Yeah." Robbie turned to the Scientist. "It's for his sick mother."

"I guess ten bucks is worth it." He pulled a wad of money from his pocket and peeled off a ten. "Here you go."

"Thanks." The man snatched the bill out of the Scientist's outstretched hand then stepped into the street and waved his bandanna. A green and white cab skidded to the curb and the young tough leaned into the open window. "Take my good friends to the Hotel InterContinental." Then he opened the back door and bowed. "Gentlemen," he said with a wave of his hand.

Robbie and the Scientist traded disgusted looks then slid into the back of the cab. The punk closed the door behind them and smiled like the Cheshire cat.

"Enjoy your stay!" he yelled as the cab pulled away from the curb.

"Boy, are we idiots," mumbled Robbie as he looked out the rear window. The punk shoved the ten-spot into his pocket and waved.

"Speak for yourself," the Scientist said with a look of disgust.

"So you two from out of town?" asked the cab driver with a nearly indecipherable Middle Eastern accent.

"We're from Florida."

"First time in Chicago?"

The two men nodded.

"Then you must see our Boulevard. It's a real treat!"

"Thanks but no thanks," Robbie said as he shoved the guidebook into his bag. "We need to get to the hotel."

"The Boulevard is on the way," the cabbie said making a U-turn. "You're gonna love it."

And with that, he headed south to the University of Chicago, all the while pointing out points of interest as the meter clicked and whirled.

* * *

An hour and a half later, the Scientist was handing the cabbie a wad of cash as he thanked him for getting them to the hotel safely. The cab drove away and Robbie said, "I had no idea The Loop was so damn far from Michigan Avenue."

"Me neither." The Scientist shoved his money back in his pocket. "Thank god we had a good cabbie. Some of those neighborhoods we passed through on the Boulevard looked pretty rough."

"You got that right," Robbie said as he swung his knapsack over his shoulder. "Let's check in and then we'll grab a bite to eat."

They entered the lobby and the Scientist noticed a cozy bar off to their right. "That's a sight for sore eyes," he said pointing to the warm, inviting light spilling through the open doors.

"I hope they serve food," Robbie said. "I'm starved."

"Who cares?" said the Scientist. "I bet they have one heck of a wine list. Here." He handed Robbie his knapsack. "Go check us in then meet me back in here."

The Scientist sauntered into the bar and plopped down into a dark brown leather club chair. He put his feet up on the small table in front of him and caught the eye of a waitress. She wandered over and pulled a pad and pen out of her apron.

"What do you recommend, young lady?" he asked with a wave of his hand.

She glared at the sneakers resting on the cocktail table. "I recommend you get your dirty feet off my furniture before I kick you in the face."

He followed her train of vision and quickly removed his shoes from the table. "Sorry."

She grinned and asked, "Now, what can I get you?"

* * *

Robbie joined the line at the front desk. He couldn't help but stare at the soft, bare, bronze shoulders of the woman in front of him. Robbie leaned over and breathed deeply. Mmm. Pineapple and coconut.

"Is this your credit card?" the desk clerk asked the woman.

"It's my husband's."

Rats. Married. Just my luck.

"Will that be all, Mrs. Valentino?"

The woman nodded.

"Enjoy your stay."

The woman turned and bumped into Robbie. He gave her his sexiest smile, which she ignored.

"Pardon me," she said as she stepped around him toward another woman facing the elevators.

"No, pardon *me*," he called after her.

The desk clerk jolted Robbie out of his dreamland. "Can I help you, sir?"

Robbie turned. "I gotta reservation."

* * *

Eden and Billy stepped out of the elevator and into the crowded hotel lobby.

"Mamet it is," Billy said. "On to the Chicago Theatre."

As they walked toward the front door, Eden glanced over to the registration desk then tugged on Billy's arm.

"Will you look at that get up," she said pointing to a young man clothed in a wide variety of mismatched sporting apparel. She shook her head. "From the back, he looks just like my Robbie!"

"I'm sure there's at least one in every city," Billy said as he held the front door open.

"You're probably right," she said with a laugh.

* * *

Robbie finished checking in then ambled into the hotel bar. The Scientist looked up from his drink.

"Have a seat. Take a load off."

Robbie dropped the two bags then pulled up another club chair and plopped down. He flipped a key card to the Scientist. "Man, you wouldn't believe the beautiful women that are staying at this hotel."

"Wouldn't I?" asked the Scientist as he nodded to the waitress across the room. "I think that flight attendant has the hots for me."

"Waitress."

"Same difference."

"But what about your soul mate?"

"I didn't say I wanted *her.*" He pointed his glass to the waitress. "She's not my type." He leaned forward and confided. "I think she's into S & M."

Robbie eyed the waitress. "What makes you say that?"

"Cuz the first thing she wanted to do was stand on my face."

"Damn." Robbie shook his head. "That's pretty hardcore."

The Scientist raised his drink. "That's why she's not for me."

Robbie signaled for the waitress. The Scientist raised his glass to his lips and whispered, "Be careful."

"What's your pleasure?" The waitress asked.

"And just what do you mean by that?" Robbie glanced at her feet.

The waitress regarded Robbie and his eclectic sports attire. "What happened? You involved in some kind of explosion at the Nike plant?"

Robbie scrunched his eyebrows. "Huh?"

She looked over to the Scientist and asked, "Is he with you?"

"Sure is."

She rolled her eyes. "Figures."

"I'll have a Bud Light," Robbie said. The waitress made a brief notation on her pad then walked over to the bar. "And keep your feet off my friend," he shouted after her.

Three bottles of beer and three glasses of wine later, the two young men were feeling relaxed and philosophical.

"What'll happen if you don't catch up with Eden?" asked the Scientist. He sipped his Cabernet and leaned back in his chair.

"Oh, I don't know," Robbie replied as he set his empty bottle down and waved for the waitress. "Like they say: 'There's more than one way to skin a fish in the ocean.'"

"I'll drink to that." The Scientist raised his nearly empty glass. "Course, I'll drink to just about anything." The waitress approached their table and Robbie asked for another round.

"You guys aren't driving, are you?"

"Nah," Robbie replied. "We're staying upstairs." He pointed a wobbly finger above his head.

"All right. One more round. But promise me one thing," she added.

"Anything for my little face-stomper," Robbie said seductively.

"Face-stomper? What's up with that?"

"You know what I mean," Robbie said with a chuckle then looked at the Scientist and winked.

"Whatever. Just promise me you won't even drive the elevator up. Get someone else to do that, okay."

"You got it, babe," Robbie said as he leaned back in his chair.

She returned with their round and Robbie raised his bottle in a toast. "Here's to our soul mates. Each and every one."

"To all of them!" echoed the Scientist and clinked his glass against the beer bottle. They threw their heads back and chugged their drinks.

Robbie rose from his chair. "C'mon," he said. "We better head upstairs and freshen up. We don't want to look like complete jackasses for our soul mates."

CHAPTER 26

ANNY and Eugene trudged up Taylor Street. They took turns carrying the burlap bag full of baked goods, although Eugene felt that, for some reason, his turns lasted longer than his brother's. When they arrived at Vinnie's building, they climbed the three flights of steps up to his apartment. Ancient oak stairs moaned and creaked with each footstep and the odor of grilled sausages, sautéed onions, and thick Italian gravy hung in the air. It was suppertime and every building on the block emanated the rich and savory aromas of southern Italy. The boys' mouths began to water and by the time they got to the third floor they were nearly ravenous. They walked down the hall to apartment 3-C and rang the bell. Mrs. DiChirico answered the door and invited the boys in.

"Have you eaten yet?" she asked as she led them through the living room and into the kitchen.

Danny and Eugene knew that no matter what time they showed up at Vinnie's, Mrs. DiChirico would ask them if they had eaten yet. She always had something delicious simmering on the stove or baking in the oven. The boys followed Mrs. DiChirico as if she had them on a leash. Two well-used stainless steel stockpots stood steaming on the white porcelain stove. One pot for the pasta, one for the sauce. Vinnie stood over the sauce stirring with a large wooden spoon.

"Hey, Vinnie," Eugene said as he nudged his brother in the ribs. "You're a regular Martha Stewart."

"Is that the best you can do, Gino?" Vinnie replied. "Cuz that hurt me real bad." Then turning to his mother, "Ma, I gotta go lay down. My ego hurts."

"Never mind Eugene, son. Keep stirring." Mrs. DiChirico opened a gigantic box of linguini and eased the golden strands into the rapidly boiling water. She picked up another large wooden spoon and began to stir.

"Danny," she said as she wiped the steam from her face with a small white towel. "Be a good boy and get some plates from the cupboard. And Eugene, could you get out the silverware?"

Temptingly delicious sounds filled the cramped kitchen: The rapidly boiling pot of pasta, the glub-glubbing of the simmering sauce, the clinking of plates and the jingle-jangle of silverware. Mrs. DiChirico poured the pasta through a colander in the sink and a cloud of steam rose with a whoosh, filling the entire room.

"We brought you some bread, Mrs. D," said Eugene.

"Just put it on the counter."

The three boys sat down as Vinnie's mom piled mounds of steaming pasta on each plate. Generous ladles of Italian gravy soon followed. Chunks of sweet sausage and enormous pork meatballs swam and bobbed in the thick, red sauce.

"Mrs. D?" asked Eugene. "Could you please pass me the chee—"

Eugene felt a swift, stinging kick to his shin. His eyes met Mrs. DiChirico's scowl.

"I mean," he swallowed hard. "Could you please pass me the Parmesan?"

Mrs. DiChirico handed the Parmesan to Eugene. "So you boys are going to the movies tonight? I hope to god you're not going to that new Mafia movie."

"What's wrong with Mafia movies, ma?" asked Vinnie with a mouth full of pasta and sauce.

"Don't talk with your mouth full," she said as she smacked his hand. "Those movies paint such a poor picture of our people."

"And speakin' of *our* people," Danny nudged Eugene under the table. "Where is Mr. D tonight? On the road again?"

"Yes," she replied with a sigh. "There's a shower curtain ring convention up in Milwaukee. He'll be gone for a couple of days."

"So Mr. D's still in the shower curtain ring business?" Eugene stifled a laugh.

"Thirty-two years now," said Mrs. DiChirico proudly. "I'm hoping Vinnie here will follow in his father's footsteps." She patted his hand.

The three boys exchanged glances. They all knew the closest that Johnny "Bang-Bang" DiChirico ever got to shower curtain rings was in his own bathroom.

"I gotta tell you, Mrs. D," Danny finally said between gulps, "you make the best gravy in Chicago."

"Thank you, Danny," she beamed. "More bread?"

When the boys had their fill, they went back to Vinnie's room. Danny closed the door as Eugene and Vinnie sat on the bed.

"So what movie we gonna see?" asked Vinnie.

"Actually," Danny replied in a hushed voice. "We ain't going to see a movie."

"But I thought you said we were going to the movies?"

"We're goin' to the movies all right. We just ain't gonna actually *see* one."

"Huh?" Vinnie looked from Danny to Eugene.

"See," Danny said as he leaned back against a chest of drawers. "We are going to the movies but we're actually doin' a job for our Uncle Tommy."

"No shit?! We're doing a job for your Uncle Tommy?!" Vinnie yelped.

"Shh. . . shh. . . keep it down. We don't want your mom to hear. Are you in or not?"

"You bet your ass I'm in!" Vinnie rubbed his hands together and smacked his lips. "What kind of job are we doin'?"

Danny glanced left, then right. He leaned into Vinnie and confided, "Uncle Tommy said it's of historic, maybe even biblical proportions."

Vinnie's eyes grew wide. "No shit?"

"There's this lady we gotta kidnap and bring back to Florida," Danny continued as he pulled the folded photograph out of his pocket and handed it to Vinnie. "Look."

He stared at the photo. "She sure is pretty."

"Pretty or not," said Danny, "she's going to Florida."

Vinnie nodded and continued to admire the woman in the photograph.

"Everybody's after her," added Eugene. "The Russians, the Colombians, everybody."

Vinnie turned to Eugene and ran a hand through his thick black hair. "Everybody?"

"Even the Bulimics," Eugene whispered.

"The Bulimics?" Vinnie asked looking back to the picture.

"From Bulimia," Eugene replied and shuddered at the thought. "They're vicious."

Vinnie nodded slowly and murmured, "So I've heard."

"She's got information that could put us all away," Danny said. "So we need to get her back to the Trafficante Family before it's too late."

Vinnie let out a low whistle and asked, "What do we have to do?"

Danny moved in closer and crouched down on one knee.

"OK. Here's the plan. . ."

CHAPTER 27

MAUREEN and Ginny's flight touched down at O'Hare just a little after six thirty. They raced through miles of terminal and down a long escalator to the taxi stand. They bypassed all the yellow, green and white cabs and ran toward a waiting line of black limousines idling at the curb. Maureen opted for a Mercedes. Ginny followed close behind.

"Do you take American Express?" Maureen asked the chauffeur, a Clive Owen look-alike.

"Yes, ma'am, we do," he replied as he bowed and opened the door.

"Good." Maureen slid into the soft black leather seat. Ginny followed.

The driver climbed behind the wheel and opened the glass partition. "Where to, ma'am?"

"The Hotel InterContinental."

"Excellent choice, ma'am." He pushed the partition closed with a 'whoosh' and pulled the luxury car away from the curb.

"Now we're getting somewhere," Maureen said as they sped toward the towering buildings silhouetted against the early evening sky. She pulled out her cell phone and dialed a familiar number. A gruff Italian voice came over the line. "Yeah? What is it?"

"Frank?" Maureen winked at Ginny.

"Yeah?"

"Bite me."

* * *

By the time Maureen and Ginny arrived at the Hotel InterContinental, it was well past seven. They approached the front desk and Maureen asked for her room.

"I'm sorry, ma'am," the desk clerk said politely. "But we're full."

"Full? But I had a reservation."

The clerk looked down at his watch. "It's after six. We only hold rooms until six."

"Even with a credit card?"

"Sorry. There must've been an error."

"Surely there must be something available."

"It's Friday evening ma'am. It doesn't take long to fill all of our rooms."

"You have nothing?"

He checked his computer. "We do have one room. A penthouse suite. I'm sure madam could find less expensive accommodations elsewhere. Perhaps you should try—"

Maureen reached into her purse, pulled out her husband's American Express card and slid it across the counter. "I'll take it."

Maureen unlocked the door to their suite and caught her breath. She was accustomed to luxury on a grand scale in her own home, but Frank had never treated her to anything quite like this. She turned to Ginny. "Can you believe this?"

"Are you kidding? This is incredible!" Ginny replied as she stepped across the threshold.

"C'mon, let's check it out." Maureen laughed as she danced and spun across the living room, through the dining area, past the den and into the master bedroom. She threw herself onto the four-poster bed and sank into the billowy mattress. She let out a squeal of delight as she hugged five enormous pillows and rolled back and forth.

"Oh my word, I could sleep here forever!"

After the initial excitement, she composed herself and lay back on the bed. Ginny slowly entered the room, still seemingly in shock at this wonderful turn of events. Maureen put her hands behind her head and stared at the ceiling.

"Okay, Ginny, first things first." She leaned across the bed, picked up the phone and pushed the button for the front desk.

A taut and anal-precise voice answered. "Mrs. Valentino! What can I do for you?"

"Would you please connect me to Billy—I mean, Mr. William Shakes' room?"

"My pleasure, Mrs. Valentino."

Maureen sat up on the edge of the bed as the phone in Billy's room rang—and rang—and rang.

"Shit," she said as she replaced the receiver. "He must be out for the evening." She picked the phone back up and called the front desk. "I'd like to leave a message for Mr. Shakes."

"My pleasure, Mrs. Valentino."

Ginny leaned against the door. Thank god Billy's not in. She had to do something. She couldn't let Maureen find him. She had to think.

While Maureen dictated her message to the front desk, Ginny walked across the room to the large window overlooking Michigan Avenue. Her eyes feasted on the glowing lights of the shops on the Magnificent Mile. Saks, Bloomies, Elizabeth Arden. . . they were all here and their siren songs beckoned. She snapped her fingers. I got it! A shopping spree. Girl's night out.

She turned back to Maureen. "Since Billy's probably out for the night, we shouldn't let the next few hours go to waste."

Maureen joined her at the window. "What do you have in mind?"

"Look at all of those shops. And they're still open." She smiled a devilish grin. "Do you think there's much left on that credit card?"

Maureen returned her look with a devilish grin of her own. "American Express has no limit."

Ginny nudged Maureen with her elbow. "Then what are we waiting for?"

Maureen spun around, grabbed her purse off the nightstand and marched to the front door. "I'm sure we'll be back before Billy gets in."

"Absolutely." Ginny paused and added, "But we should freshen up a bit, don't you think? You go first."

As Maureen closed the bathroom door Ginny snatched up the phone and called the front desk. She asked for Robbie's room number and scribbled it down on the notepad by the phone. Then she pulled out the yellow pages and turned to the E's. Her finger traced down the long list of escort services and came to rest on Dahlia's Fantasy Escort Service. She dialed the number and a friendly, grandmotherly voice answered.

"Dahlia's Fantasy Escorts, where your fantasy is our finesse."

"I need an escort tonight. All night. Maybe longer. For a guy friend."

"That would be our pleasure. And what is his fantasy tonight?"

Ginny went on to request a leggy, buxom blonde who would dress up in as wide a variety of sports-insignia-laden apparel as possible. The more variety, the better.

"I see, a sports fetish," the grandmotherly voice said.

"To put it lightly."

"It's Chicago. We get lots of those. You should see it when the auto show hits town."

"Yeah, yeah, I can imagine." Ginny glanced at the bathroom door. "But I'm in a hurry." She gave the woman a description of Robbie and his phone number then told her to have the escort call him this evening and ask to meet him in the hotel bar. Then she opened Maureen's purse and pulled out Frank's American Express card and read the number aloud. She hung up and was just replacing the credit card when the bathroom door opened.

"I'll only be a minute," Ginny said as she stood up and breezed by Maureen.

She emerged in a few moments and the two women left the room, hastening down the hall to the elevators. When they stepped out of the lobby and onto the busy sidewalk they stopped to breathe in the cool fall evening air.

"It smells so luxurious and rich," Maureen said as she hugged herself.

"Even the breeze feels expensive," sighed Ginny.

The two women turned right, locked arms and marched with confidence up the Magnificent Mile.

"First, we'll hit the shops on Michigan. Bloomies, Saks, Ann Taylor," Maureen said. "Then we'll move to the boutiques on Oak Street. Who knows? Some may still be open."

Ginny envisioned herself on pure white carpet, surrounded by walls of full-length mirrors and racks of designer gowns.

"Would madam like another glass of champagne while I fetch the Jean Paul Gaultier we discussed?"

"Please. And could you bring out the Dior as well?"

"It would be my pleasure, madam."

The women crossed the street at the Water Tower and Ginny squeezed Maureen's arm. "Remind me to thank your husband Frank, someday," she said with a laugh.

* * *

Robbie and the Scientist opened the front door to their room and tumbled in.

"I call first dibs on the shower." The Scientist set his bag next to the nearest double bed and stepped into the bathroom.

"Go ahead." Robbie tossed his suitcase on the other bed and the phone rang. "Hello?"

"Robbie Renfro, please," a soft and sultry voice said.

"Um, speaking."

"Hello, handsome. This is Destiny. You don't know me but I saw you a little while ago."

Robbie sat on the edge of the bed. "Where? In the bar? The hotel bar?"

"Um—yeah. The bar. I couldn't take my eyes off of you..."

Robbie swallowed hard.

"And now," she breathed. "I can't take my hands off myself." She let out a sensuous moan.

"H-h-how did you get my room number?"

"Never mind that. We have to meet, Robbie. Tonight. I can't wait much longer. I need to see you. Touch you. Taste you. Can you meet me in the bar in, say, half an hour?"

Robbie gulped and stared at the wall above the bed. "H-how will I know you?"

"I'll be wearing a Chicago Bulls jacket and a White Sox ball cap. See, I'm into sports."

Robbie gulped. "For real?"

"Especially gymnastics. I'm incredibly limber." She paused then cooed, "I can't wait to show you."

Robbie nearly slid off the bed and onto the floor. He caught himself and sat back up. "I'm into sports, too," he managed to stammer.

"That's what really turned me on. You had soul mate written all over your hot, delicious body. See you soon."

The phone clicked silent and Robbie sat for a moment, his breath heavy and measured. He pulled off his ball cap and wiped the sweat from his forehead.

"Hurry up in there!" he shouted toward the bathroom. "I gotta get ready for my date with Destiny!"

CHAPTER 28

ANNY, Eugene and Vinnie bounced down the front stoop of the apartment building and up the sidewalk to Vinnie's car. Eugene began to chant the Mission Impossible theme song.

"Ba ba ba-da, ba ba ba-da. . ."

"Gino, what are you doing?" asked Danny.

"I'm singin' the Mission Impossible theme song."

"I can see that. But, why?"

"Cuz we're on a mission. You can't be on a mission without a theme song."

"He's right, you know," Vinnie chimed in. "A mission is just bound to fail if you don't have a theme song."

Danny rolled his eyes and looked up into the evening sky as Eugene once again burst out in song. "Ba ba ba-da, ba ba ba-da."

Vinnie joined in and provided the high notes, "Da – di – la, Da – di – la, Da – di – la."

"C'mon, Danny, don't jinx us," Vinnie said between verses. "Sing the 'ba ba bas' with your brother."

Danny shrugged his shoulders and reluctantly joined his brother. He started off quietly, and then found himself caught up in the momentum. Soon all three boys were singing as if they were auditioning for American Idol. Somewhere above them an angry voice called out, "Could you boys put a lid on it!"

Danny grabbed Vinnie and his brother by the shoulders to stop them. He looked up and searched the building beside them. He shielded his eyes from the streetlight overhead and called out, "You gotta problem?"

"Yeah, smart ass. You're the problem."

Danny scanned the building until his eyes fell on a round head hanging out of an open window five floors up. "You talking to me old man?"

"Yeah, I'm talking to you, wise-guy."

"I can't hear you so good. Why don't you drag your fat ass down here and talk to me?"

"'Cuz if you make me come down there, I'll hit you so hard it'll kill you and those other assholes with you."

At that, Danny bent over and picked up a stone from the small garden in front of the building. He flipped it in his hand then looked back up to the open window.

"Hey, old man, I got your asshole right here." He cocked his arm then hurled the stone toward the window. The old man didn't see it coming. The stone struck the center of his forehead and he reeled back with a howl. The head disappeared from the window and Danny brushed his hands together in triumph.

"No one messes with the Lucci brothers," he proclaimed. "Especially during a musical interlude."

The round head reappeared at the window and shouted, "Why you little piece of—"

"What? You want some more old man?" He stooped to pick up another stone.

The head turned and shouted to someone back in the apartment, "Frances! Get me my gun!"

Before the boys could react, they were staring up at what appeared to be the barrel of a chrome revolver. Flash. Pop. A bullet slammed into the pavement by Eugene's foot. Flash. Pop. Another bullet pierced a parking meter, spilling a week's worth of quarters into the gutter. The boys spun on their heels and sprinted down the sidewalk as bullets pinged off bricks and cement. They turned a corner and drew to a halt. Eugene fell against the brick building, panting and heaving. Danny and Vinnie bent over, hands on knees, trying to catch their breath.

"What's his fuckin' problem?" asked Eugene between gasps.

"Got me," Danny wheezed. "Guy's a damn psycho." He searched the ground around him. "Get me another rock. I'll show the bastard what-for."

"Forget that." Vinnie coughed and straightened back up. "Let's get out of here. My car's just down the street." He turned and limped down the sidewalk.

"Wait up," Danny called after him. He spat on the sidewalk and grabbed his brother's arm. "C'mon, Gino."

They arrived at Vinnie's big-as-a-tank Buick and Danny opened the back door. "Get in."

Gino started to climb in then stopped. He straightened up and faced his brother. "Why do I gotta sit in the back?"

"Cuz, I said so." He motioned to the door. "Now get in."

"That ain't fair."

"C'mon, you guys," shouted Vinnie from the other side of the car. "Quit playing around and get in. We got a job to do."

Danny sighed. "Okay, Gino, we'll do it fair and square. Pick a number between one and ten."

Eugene thought for a moment. "Four."

"Wrong. It's six. Now get in the car." Danny grabbed his brother's arm and pushed him toward the open door.

"Hey, wait one minute." Eugene wrenched his brother's hand off his arm. "How do I know you were really thinking about six and not four?"

"Cuz I wasn't."

Eugene jabbed his brother in the chest. "You think I look that stupid?"

"Okay, Gino. You're such a big shot. Why don't you pick a number and let me guess it."

Eugene rolled his eyes up into his head and searched for a number. "Okay, I got one," he said with a grin.

"Eight."

Eugene's smile melted to a frown.

"I said *eight*," Danny repeated.

"I heard you, I heard you," Eugene said with a violent shrug of his shoulders. "Go ahead and get in the front. I'll sit in the back."

The black Buick cruised down State Street toward the Chicago Theatre. When they crossed the Chicago River they could see a thousand lights sparkling on the grand old theater's marquee just a few blocks ahead. The traffic slowed to a crawl at Wacker.

"All right, everyone know what to do?" Danny asked as he pulled a black ski mask over his head.

"Roger," Eugene called out from the back seat. He pulled his own ski mask over his head. Vinnie followed suit.

"Good. We'll follow State Street past the theater to scope out the situation."

The car inched along, the boys scanning the faces on the crowded sidewalk.

"Look at all these people," Eugene whispered. "We'll never find her in this mess."

"Keep your eyes peeled, boys. We'll find her," Danny said confidently.

The black Buick continued to crawl along the curb when suddenly Danny reached over and punched Vinnie's shoulder. "Look over there!" He glanced down at the photo on his lap and looked up again. "It's her, I tell you. It's her! Slow down a little more, Vinnie."

"If I go any slower I'll be going backwards."

"I'll be damned," said Eugene. "I think you're right." A city bus rumbled down the street and they lost sight of her for a moment. She reappeared through a dissipating cloud of diesel exhaust.

"Are you guys sure?" asked Vinnie as he stole a few glances her way. "Her back's turned. How can you be sure it's her?"

"Look at that build. The hair. That skin. It's her all right." Danny rubbed his hands together. "Okay Vinnie, we gotta go around the block so we can pull the car right up in front of the theater. Turn right up here on Madison."

Vinnie eased the car around the corner and circled the block.

Danny licked his lips. "There's the theater up on the right."

Vinnie tightened his grip on the steering wheel. Danny shook his leg in anticipation. Eugene leaned over the seat and said, "Man, this is getting intense."

Heartbeats quickened, adrenaline flowed, beads of sweat collected under black wool ski masks. Eugene nervously tapped the back of the car seat and quietly launched into the Mission Impossible theme song, "Ba, ba, ba-da, ba, ba, ba-da. . ."

Vinnie responded with a whisper. "Di-da-li. . ."

"We're gonna make you proud, Uncle Tommy," Danny said under his breath.

Vinnie kept the car in the far right lane, as close to the sidewalk as he could get. At times, the slowly rolling tires scraped the curb with a screech that reminded Eugene of the sound his pet cat would make when he tied its legs together and pushed the poor, helpless animal across the kitchen floor with a broom.

"There she is, right by the curb," Danny whispered. "Everyone ready?" He grabbed the door handle. "Go! Go! Go!"

The two brothers leapt from the car and dashed up behind the unsuspecting woman. Eugene wrestled the burlap bag over her head as Danny grabbed her around the waist and hustled her back to the car. Eugene leapt into the back seat and grabbed the plastic ties while Danny shoved the writhing, squealing girl in beside him. He jumped in and slammed the door. "Hit it!"

Vinnie threw the car in gear and peeled away from the curb. Because he stopped in front of the theater, he was able to back up traffic. Now an open lane lay ahead of him for at least a block. The Buick fishtailed up State Street leaving behind hundreds of wide-eyed witnesses—witnesses who couldn't understand why anyone would want to kidnap Luci Wong, Taiwan's newest martial arts actress who had come to the festival to promote her latest film, *A Tiger's Vengeance*.

Eugene struggled to get the plastic cuffs on the woman's flailing arms while Danny wrangled the rope around her thrashing legs.

"I can't get the cuffs on!" shouted Eugene.

"Hold still goddamit!" Danny added.

Vinnie wrestled a small plastic bottle open with his teeth. He poured the contents into a washcloth and tossed over the seat. "Here, use this!"

Danny grabbed the washcloth while his brother lifted the burlap sack up over their captive's face. The brothers froze at the sight of two jet-black Asian eyes glaring back at them. Vinnie glanced into the rear view mirror. "Oh, shit."

With a scream that would rival the howl of a banshee, Ms. Wong exploded in a violent flurry of punches and kicks. Teeth cracked, facial bones broke and nose cartilage shattered. Vinnie tried to keep the car on the road as he reached back and pummeled whatever he could reach.

"Gino! She's killing us!" Danny managed to yell before a pointed elbow cracked three ribs.

"We need our secret weapon!" Eugene cried as two small but tenacious hands grabbed his ears and repeatedly smashed his head against the window.

"What secret weapon?!" squealed Danny. A stiletto heel found his groin. "Arggh! My 'nads. The bitch speared my 'nads!"

"Cheese!" Eugene howled. "Cheese!"

The word entered Vinnie's ears and implanted itself in some deep dark crevice of his brain. His entire body jerked and trembled. Rabid doglike foam spewed from his mouth and oozed down his chin. He released his grip on the steering wheel and leapt into the back seat. He became a human Tasmanian Devil—a whirlwind of punches and curses. The entire back seat rattled and rumbled beneath a blur of fury and wrath. The Buick continued to roll up the street before it veered to the right, climbed the curb and crashed into a light pole. A growing crowd surrounded the car as the cacophony within faded to an eerie silence. Everyone took one cautious step forward then stopped as the back door slowly creaked open. A shapely pair of legs swung out onto the pavement. Luci Wong emerged from the auto and smoothed her dress. She shook back her mahogany-brown hair and stepped up onto the curb. Behind her, three moaning men clawed their way across the back seat and tumbled into the street. A collective gasp rose from the crowd as they gazed at the bloody, bruised and swollen heap before them. One film buff stared at the door handle embedded in Eugene's right ear. He fished for a kernel from the bottom of his popcorn box, shook his head and whispered, "Man, that's gotta hurt."

Eden and Billy pushed their way through the crowd to get a better look. She stared at the mangled bodies and hugged Billy's arm.

"This is insane," she whispered. "Didn't you say Chicago was a 'human' city? I'd expect something like this in New York. But here?"

"Don't worry," he said out of the corner of his mouth. "This has got to be a set-up. A publicity stunt."

"Publicity stunt?" she asked doubtfully. "Sure looks real to me."

"It has to. That's why they spend the big bucks. Think about it. Luci Wong is in town to promote her new movie. She shows up at the Film Fest and gets kidnapped. Then she beats the shit out of her kidnappers. It has publicity stunt written all over it. I mean, who in their right mind would even think about kidnapping a triple black belt martial arts movie star?"

"I see what you mean."

"C'mon, the movie's going to start in a few minutes." Billy put his arm around Eden and they walked back to the theater entrance.

A trio of tabloid cameramen and a half-dozen freelance paparazzi hovered over the carnage and illuminated the scene with a continuous lightning storm of flashbulbs. Luci Wong posed and smiled briefly for the cameras then strolled through a crowd that parted like the Red Sea before her.

CHAPTER 29

R OBBIE and the Scientist strolled back into the hotel bar and stopped. Their eyes scanned the dimly lit room for any sign of Robbie's Destiny.

"Why'd you bring me along?" asked the Scientist.

"Cuz, she might have a friend. You never know."

"But I already have a soul mate." The Scientist leaned into Robbie and shook his finger for emphasis. "And so do you."

"Shh," Robbie said as he slowly surveyed the room. "This girl sounded hot. And besides, you can never have too many soul mates."

A familiar waitress approached the two men. "You two again?" she asked as she rolled her eyes. "You gonna sit somewhere or are you gonna stand here blocking the door?"

"We'll sit over there," Robbie said motioning to a small table off to the left. "Bring me a Bud Light and a red wine for my friend."

The waitress returned with their drinks. "Start another tab?"

"Uh-huh. Charge it to our room," Robbie replied as they settled down to wait.

The waitress returned and set the drinks down. "And remember, keep your feet off my table." Then she turned back to the entrance to greet another couple.

The Scientist and Robbie had each taken generous sips when the Scientist froze. He glanced over Robbie's shoulder and slowly set his glass on the table.

"What's wrong?" Robbie asked.

"Over there." The Scientist nodded and pointed his chin. "At the bar. The very end."

Robbie turned to look but the Scientist grabbed his arm. "Wait, don't be so conspicuous. I think it's her. She just came in. You need to check this out. But slowly." He released Robbie's arm. "Slowly."

Robbie turned his head toward the bar. In the corner, by the beer taps, stood a young woman in her late twenties or early thirties. Silk-blonde hair tucked up into a White Sox ball cap. She removed her Chicago Bulls warm-up jacket and draped it over the back of her barstool, then slid her perfectly formed rear end onto the seat. She arched her back and ran her hands across skintight black leotards that showed off her long lean legs. Robbie blinked his eyes and marveled at the prodigious breasts straining at her tight Blackhawks jersey - one that was cut off just below her delicious pair. The bartender slid her a Bud Light tallboy and she turned her attention to the TV screen above her. Championship Bocci on ESPN2. Robbie placed his own Bud Light on the table and stared at the magnificent apparition.

"It's okay if your eyes bug out," said the Scientist with a laugh. "But at least keep your tongue in your mouth."

The woman turned and glanced around the room. Her eyes fell on Robbie and his eclectic attire. She winked and offered a smile that seemed to say, "Hey handsome, why don't you step up to the plate and drive me home?"

"That's my Destiny," Robbie whispered to the Scientist. "Is she something or what?"

"Soul mate?" he replied raising his eyebrows.

"Bingo."

Robbie stood, smoothed his own jersey, straightened his Jaguars cap and began to make his way over to the bar.

"Hey, wait." The Scientist grabbed Robbie's sleeve. "What about Eden?"

Robbie turned. "Who?'

"Eden. You know, your *other* soul mate."

Robbie thought for a moment. "Screw her." Then he nodded to the girl at the bar and added, "This babe is hot."

The Scientist watched his friend walk over and introduce himself to the life-size Barbie doll at the bar. She ran a hand over his jersey then broke into a wide and welcoming grin. Robbie pulled up a stool and ordered two more Bud Lights. He raised his bottle and glanced over to the Scientist with a smile, then turned his attention back to his Destiny.

The Scientist sighed as he watched the couple huddle together. The waitress approached. "Can I get you anything else?"

The Scientist leaned back, threw his feet on the table and managed a smile. "Well, young lady. As a matter of fact you can." He glanced back to the bar. Robbie had his arm around the girl as she nuzzled his neck. The waitress followed the Scientist's gaze over to the bar, then turned back around. "Are you hitting on me?"

"Hitting's a strong word," said the Scientist with a gleam in his eye.

"Oh yeah? I don't think it is." She hauled back and smacked his feet off the table.

"Hey!" he cried rubbing his foot. "What'd you go and do that for?"

She kicked the table aside and the Scientist flinched, spilling his drink on his lap. He shrunk down into the chair as she leaned over and put her nose an inch from his face. "Didn't I tell you to keep your feet off my table?" she said, jabbing her finger into his chest. The Scientist cringed and covered his face with his arms. He eyed her though a gap as she turned and sashayed back to the bar. When she disappeared into the back he pulled himself up from the chair and rubbed his sore breastbone.

"Geez. What's her problem?!" He glanced back over to the bar to see the woman draped over Robbie. "I guess I'll hit the sheets and wait to see what tomorrow brings." He ambled into the lobby and set his sights on the elevators. A pair of doors opened with a chime and the Scientist entered. An elderly couple called out from the lobby, "Hold the elevator!" They joined the Scientist in the car. "Eleven, please."

The Scientist pushed the button and watched the numbered lights above him blink as the elevator began its ascent.

The woman turned to the old man and said, "What an unexpected surprise, meeting you at the theater tonight, James. That was such an incredible play." She squeezed his arm. "And thanks for inviting me back to your room. What shall we do tomorrow?"

"Perhaps we should visit the Art Institute after breakfast."

"Marvelous."

The elevator dinged and the couple stepped out onto their floor. As the doors closed the Scientist said to no one in particular, "Hmm.

The Art Institute. Sounds interesting. Maybe I'll head over there my-self. Seems like everyone in this town is finding their soul mates."

* * *

It was nearly ten when Maureen and Ginny emerged from the backseat of a yellow cab with armfuls of bags and boxes. The driver threw open the trunk and unloaded more bags onto the sidewalk. A bellman appeared with a buffed bronze cart and stacked their cargo. Maureen handed the cab driver a $100 bill.

"I'm sorry, ma'am. I only drove you a few blocks. I don't carry enough cash to—"

Maureen smiled. "Keep the change." She turned to the stunned bellman and flicked a button on his chest. "To the penthouse, my good man."

The bellman beamed and grabbed the cart. "My pleasure!"

The elevator opened and the bellman followed the women down the hall to their suite and opened the door.

"Just put them over there," Maureen said with a wave of her hand. The bellman carefully unloaded the packages and stood at at-tention. She grinned and handed him a $100 bill. "Thank you, my good man."

"No, ma'am, thank you!"

The door closed behind the bellman and Ginny plopped down on the sofa and threw her feet up on the coffee table. "I'm beat. I never realized how tiring it is to spend so much money."

"Yes, shopping sure can take a lot out of you." Maureen picked up the phone and asked the front desk for any messages. "No? Thanks." She replaced the receiver and sighed. "Oh, well. I guess I'll have to contact Billy in the morning." She looked at Ginny. "You hungry?"

"Starved."

Maureen picked up the room service menu and joined her new friend on the sofa.

"Let's see," she said as her eyes surveyed the delectable offerings. "That looks good. Oh, and so does that. Oooh, that too." She looked up. "What are you hungry for?"

"At this point, I'll eat just about anything."

Maureen picked up the phone. "Room service? I'd like to order two spinach-arugula salads with the blood oranges and goat cheese." She glanced at Ginny with raised eyebrows as if to ask, "Okay with you?"

Ginny beamed and whispered, "Oh, yeah!"

Maureen scanned the menu and continued. "And two bowls of the lobster bisque...And let's see, the Beef Wellington with roasted new potatoes...Oh, and could you roast those with a touch of garlic and Parmesan?. . . Wonderful!. . . Dessert? Yes, the biscotti al'anise sounds marvelous. Oh, and please send up a bottle—"

Ginny waved two fingers in front of Maureen.

"No, make that two bottles of your finest Cabernet...Perfect."

She cupped a hand over the phone and turned to Ginny. "Did I forget anything?"

"Champagne?" Ginny offered with a smile.

Maureen nodded and returned to the receiver. "And your most expensive bottle of champagne....I see...." She cupped the phone again and turned to Ginny. "Dom Perignon or Cristal?"

Ginny mouthed, "Either one!"

Maureen giggled and returned to the phone. "We'll take a bottle of both."

Ginny clapped her hands.

"And would you please send a bottle of your finest brandy to my friend Mr. Billy Shakes? With a note that says..."

CHAPTER 30

BILLY pushed the keycard into the slot and opened the door to their room.

"What a glorious evening," Eden said as she glided across the carpet and threw herself on the bed. "Mamet was great. And so was the publicity stunt. I can't wait for tomorrow."

"Hey, look at this." Billy pointed to the table by the window. Glittering lights from the surrounding buildings illuminated a bottle of brandy resting on the table. Courvoisier. VSOP. Next to the bottle sat two crystal snifters and a card. He read it out loud, *"Compliments of a friend."*

Eden rolled over and propped herself up on her elbows. "How sweet."

"Hmm. Wonder who that could be?" he asked as he opened the bottle. "Want a glass?"

"I'd like to take a shower first." Eden slid off the bed and pulled her new nightgown out of a shopping bag. "But you go ahead—I'll only be a minute."

Billy opened the bottle of Courvoisier and poured a splash into the brandy glass. He sat on the edge of the bed and swirled the rich, thick elixir to release its aroma. A thin film clung to the side of the crystal like a sheer curtain. He took a sip. It was warm and smooth, thick and earthy. Billy let it linger on his tongue. He swallowed and it went down easy. He was careful not to look at the brandy in his glass; the amber hue might turn his taste bitter. He heard Eden turn on the shower and the sound of the streaming water relaxed him. Billy sighed and walked over to the window. Far below the dancing lights of a hundred cars illuminated the avenue. A new sensation. Peppermint. Peppermint and brandy. Hmm. Mint-julepy. Not bad.

He turned as Eden emerged from the bathroom dressed for bed. The nightgown was as simple and pure as it was in Filene's, but in the shimmering moonlight her lissome figure transformed it into an elegant gown. She joined him at the banquette by the window and he poured her some brandy. They touched glasses in a silent toast and took a sip. He slipped his arm around her waist and caressed her side as they looked out on the city. She tilted her head and nuzzled his shoulder.

After a few blissful moments Billy turned and said, "I'd better get ready for bed, too."

"Must you go?" she asked with plaintive eyes.

"Don't worry, I'll be right back," he said with a laugh.

He set his glass down on the windowsill and walked over to the shopping bags. He grabbed his new boxers and tee shirt and stepped into the damp bath. Steam hung thick in the air and covered the mirror with a fine mist. He detected a faint scent in the air. Lilacs?

He climbed into the shower. The fine spray moved over him. . . like she had.

After drying off, he donned the boxers and joined Eden on the banquette. She sat curled up at one end, sipping her brandy, entranced by the view.

He poured himself another glass and sat at the opposite end of the window seat. The nightgown had slipped off her left shoulder revealing a smooth curve. His eyes traced the gentle arc of her back to the nape of her neck, then drifted over her cheek and down to her lips. Unadorned with lipstick, they were still a delicious pink. He knew smiles and laughter came easily to those lips. The hue tasted of strawberries. He felt something stirring deep within. Words blossomed in his mind:

> Thrown together in circumstance,
> Friendship borne on the wings of chance.
> What do I make of this winsome girl
> Who tips the axis of my world?

His shoulders rose with a gentle sigh as he turned toward the window. The sun had long since set and lights shone bright through the windows of neighboring buildings, an illuminated checkerboard. He wondered what stories were unfolding behind each of the glowing squares.

"What do you think is happening over there?" Eden asked as if reading his thoughts. "In that office window, the one with the bluish light."

Billy stroked his chin. "Hmm. I see an intern. A graphic designer. It's his last year at Columbia. He hopes the internship will grow into a full-time, six-figure position. It won't and deep down he knows it. The company will discard him after his internship. They always do." He sipped his brandy and continued, "Everyone has left for the day. He's in his supervisor's office rigging the computer. Now every e-mail he sends will have a link to a hardcore porn site. Something involving underage candy stripers, woodworking tools and camels. His boss will do some jail time."

"You're so bad." She slapped his foot and raised her glass to her lips.

"What about that window, the one above the sign?" he asked pointing to the granite building on the corner.

"Hmm, I see a stressed-out account executive. He's been unhappily married for 12 years. His secretary is 33, attractive and available. She adores him, but he doesn't pick up on her signals. It frustrates the heck out of her. Six months later her fondness turns to bitterness. In two weeks, she'll come to despise him. By the end of the month, she'll quit. Meanwhile, he'll continue to return to his prairie bungalow in Oak Park wondering why life doesn't toss him a slow, soft pitch — one he can hit out of the park."

Billy laughed. "Well over there I see. . ."

On and on, late into the night. More stories. More brandy. More laughter.

Eden finally rose and said, "If I don't get some sleep, I'm going to be absolutely worthless tomorrow."

"Eden, my dear." He raised his glass in her honor. "You will never be worthless."

She smiled a sheepish and sleepy smile. "You coming to bed?"

"I'll be with you shortly," he replied. "I just want to finish my brandy."

She kissed him softly on the brow then lingered, staring into his eyes. "Good night, my handsome tour guide," she whispered.

"Good night, my mystery girl."

She wandered over to the bed and noticed the blinking light on the nightstand. "Looks like you have another message."

"Probably my mother, again," he said with a shrug. "Just making sure I'm behaving like a gentleman."

"Are you?" She brushed her hair back with her hand.

"What do you think?"

She smiled. "A perfect gentleman."

Billy perked up and grinned. "So does that mean I've earned the right to…"

"Don't even think about it, Romeo."

"Didn't hurt to ask."

She pulled back the comforter and slid between the soft linen sheets. Billy sighed then turned back to the window and sipped his brandy. The full moon rose over the towering buildings and cast yellow-white streams of light through the window. He turned his head and followed the moonbeams as they caressed the pale, smooth skin of Eden's face. The taste of warm, sweet cream rolled over his tongue.

"My lord, she looks like an angel."

Eden's eyelids flickered then closed as she fell deep into slumber. Once again, he marveled at her long and elegant eyelashes – soft as angel kisses. Her shimmering hair rolled and swirled over the soft white pillow. Her lips were slightly apart. Was that a faint smile? His eyes roamed over her. Petite, but perfectly formed breasts rose and fell with each gentle breath. He detected a sweet smell. Delicate and winsome. Incense? It seemed to hover in the room like a lovelorn ghost. He leaned back on the window seat and drank it all in.

Eden stirred and slowly turned onto her side away from him. Billy caught his breath and leaned forward. Broad, pearl-white wings peeked out from beneath the sheets. She clenched the covers and pulled them to her breast, leaving her back exposed. Supple and soft, the wings stretched from her head to her toe. Feathers gently fluttered as she hugged and cuddled her pillow.

Billy looked down at the brown liquid in his glass. Is this brandy, or absinthe? He set his glass down on the windowsill and rubbed his eyes. Was he awake? He shook his head. Yes, he was awake. This was no dream. A hallucination? A step into an alternate reality similar to the one he experienced with Sachiko? He felt a dull ache in his side then looked down and noticed his hands were shaking. He'd learned to cope with his synesthesia. At least it was constant. But this? Popping up intermittently? He took another sip. Whatever *it* was. He knew he couldn't fix it. He just had to roll with it. He finished his drink and walked to the other side of the bed. The wings fluttered again. He pulled back the comforter and slid in beside her, taking special care not to wake her. When he settled himself, he rested his hand on the gentle curve of her side. He sighed and admired this angel bathed in moonlight. He moved closer until he could feel her breath. It was warm and sweet. He leaned in and kissed her softly on her lips. Mmm. Strawberries. His hand followed the graceful contour from her hip to her shoulder and back again. She sighed at his caress and her wings gently stirred. He closed his eyes and drifted away as the taste of sweet cream and strawberries lingered on his tongue.

CHAPTER 31

BILLY woke to the early morning sun streaming through sheer white curtains. He rose from the warm bed and stretched as he ambled over to the window. It was only eight, and even on a Saturday the city was already alive with activity. He turned to look at his still-sleeping friend. She was curled up in the soft cotton linens. A chorus line of morning sunbeams danced around her.

He noticed that the shimmering wings that graced her shoulders the night before were gone. He slowly shook his head. Too much to drink, he guessed. But she'll still be an angel to him. Eden stirred and opened her still-sleepy eyes. She sat up and noticed small white feathers scattered across the bed. She picked one up and examined it.

"My pillow must be leaking." She twisted the feather between her thumb and finger then cast a sly glance toward him.

"I'll tell the front desk when we leave," he said with a smile. "I'm sure they'll send up another."

She rose from the bed and shuffled into the bathroom. The door closed and Billy heard her turn on the shower. Again, the streaming sound relaxed him as it had the night before. Small white billows of steam began to seep out from under the door. His mind drifted and he tried to imagine what his angel looked like in the shower. He saw sparkling drops of water, like liquid diamonds, cascading off her smooth and supple back. Is she running her hands through long, silken hair? He longed to join her. To hold her in his arms. To feel her naked body against his. To kiss her hard and deep. He reached for the doorknob and turned it. It wasn't locked. He slowly eased the door open, hesitated, then backed away. He wasn't invited. Let it go. He heard the water stop and in a few moments the door opened and she came out wrapped in a white terrycloth bath towel.

229

"Your turn," she said sitting down at the vanity. "I'll finish up here."

Billy walked up behind her and laid his hands on her shoulders. "Sleep well?"

"Very well." She said sliding a brush through her hair. "Except. . ."

He felt a shudder run through her shoulders.

"Nightmares?"

"Uh- huh." She looked in the mirror as if to gauge his reaction. His eyes met hers in the reflection as he caressed her shoulders.

"The shadow. I saw it again."

"Go on."

"Six wings. Many eyes. Bright as diamonds. The image used to frighten me. But last night it was different." She drew the brush through her hair. "I felt myself floating." She paused, her brush suspended in mid-stroke. "High above the clouds. I saw the sun dance. I heard the stars sing." She shifted in her seat and laid the brush on the vanity. "Then I heard the voice. A voice borne on the wind. It whispered, *It's time.*"

Billy leaned forward and studied her eyes. "Time for what?"

She glanced at Billy's reflection in the mirror. Her sleepy eyes now seemed full of mischief. She shook her head. "It's silly. Never mind all that. How about you? Did you sleep well?"

"No, I made a few mistakes."

She slapped his arm. "You're so weird."

"And you're so beautiful."

He kissed the back of her neck and walked into the bathroom. The warm water felt good as he lathered shampoo in his hair. She was here. I can feel her presence. Soft skin. Silken hair. Then his mind latched onto her curious statement about time. Time for what?

Billy stepped out of the shower, dried himself off then slipped into his clothes. Eden was already dressed and waiting at the door.

Let's go," she said. "We have a day of adventures before us. Besides, I'm famished."

They took the elevator down to the lobby and found themselves on the sidewalk hailing a cab. She put her arm around his waist and it felt right. A yellow cab zipped past, made a quick u-turn and pulled up to the curb.

"Where to?" the cab driver asked in a distinctly Pakistani accent.

"Lou Mitchell's—" Billy said as he climbed in.

"—by way of Wells and Adams," Eden added.

Billy raised an eyebrow. "Since when did you learn your way around the city?"

"Glanced at Fodor's while you were in the shower." She leaned in closer and added, "Now Mr. Pakistani-accent knows we're not rookies and will think twice about taking us on a roundabout route."

"Learn that in Fodor's, too?"

She smiled and nodded. "I'm a quick learner."

It was nearly nine o'clock when they got out of the cab at Lou's. Billy pulled open the door and counted thirteen people ahead of them. A harried hostess worked her way down the line greeting the waiting guests and offering each woman a small box of Milk Duds.

"What's up with this?" Eden asked as she stared at the yellow box of candy in her hand.

"It's a tradition at Lou's," Billy explained. "All the ladies get a free box of Milk Duds while they wait."

"I love Milk Duds! And look." She pointed to the counter. "A whole basketful! Let's get some more."

He pulled her back. "Wait a minute. We can't take more Milk Duds."

She planted her hands on her hips and asked, "Am I a lady?"

Billy's eyes roamed over her body. "Last time I looked."

"And the Milk Duds are for who?"

"The ladies."

"So let's get some more."

"Um, I don't think we should."

She grabbed his shoulders, her eyes accusing his. "You said this was the day for wild and crazy adventures, right?"

Billy considered the basket of candy. "Milk Duds?"

"Hey, you gotta crawl before you can fly."

"I think you mean walk. Crawl before you can walk."

"Walk. Crawl. Whatever." She poked him in the ribs. "The important thing is, we gotta fly."

She grabbed his hand and led him over to the basket of Milk Duds. When she was sure no one was looking, she scooped up dozens of boxes and shoved them into her purse.

"That should do," she said as she struggled to latch the clasp.

Moments later, the hostess seated them at a table where they feasted on double-yolk omelets, spicy home fries and sweet hickory-smoked bacon. Busboys and waitresses scooted behind them with an occasional "Excuse me." The room buzzed with conversations that competed with the clamor of banging plates, shouting waitresses, and the steady hum of human interaction.

"Y'know," Billy said as he buttered a piece of thick, copper-brown toast, "I don't think I've ever met anyone by the name of Eden before."

"It's Hebrew," she explained. "It means paradise."

"So, you're paradise." He nibbled his toast and reflected for a moment. "But since we've never made love, I guess I wouldn't know if you are paradise or not."

Eden giggled and said, "I think you're wrong there. I believe we did make love once or twice."

He raised an eyebrow. "Oh, really? When?"

"Yesterday."

"It seems to have slipped my mind. Remind me."

"When you slipped your arm inside of mine as we strolled down Michigan Avenue. I think we made love then. And last night, as we sat on the banquette, sipping brandy and telling those crazy stories." She paused. "Yes, I think we made love then as well."

Billy considered her with a puzzled look.

"True," she went on to explain, "We've never had sex, but I'm positive we've made love."

He pointed his fork at her. "You certainly are an interesting woman."

"A mystery girl, as you say." Then she picked up her cup of coffee and gazed at him playfully over the rim.

* * *

Billy and Eden left Lou's diner with two steaming-hot cups of coffee to go. Billy stepped to the curb to hail another cab and they got in. The taxi smelled of garlic, newsprint and shoe leather. Eden cracked a window.

Billy leaned over the front seat. "To the Art Institute, my friend, via. . ."

"Damn," the driver whispered under his breath. "Another stinkin' local. Why can't I get some tourists and make some serious money?!"

The cab lurched away from the curb and drove east on Jackson. They crossed the river and passed beneath the heavy shadow of what used to be called the Sears Tower.

"So you two lovebirds eat at Lou's often?" the cabbie asked over his shoulder.

"Lovebirds?" Billy whispered to Eden. "Where'd that come from?"

"Got me," she whispered in reply.

"I heard it in an old movie last night," explained the driver. "Very American, eh?"

Eden looked at the cabbie in his rear view mirror. "What makes you think we're lovebirds?"

"Oh, I can tell," said the cabbie with grin. He was missing several front teeth but his smile was genuine. "It's a gift. I picked it up from my gran-mama Sophie. Yep, I can tell lovebirds when I see them." He held up a finger and shook it for emphasis. "And you two are lovebirds."

"Lovebirds," Billy echoed as he chuckled and shook his head. "That's a new one."

"He may be right you know." Eden reached over and squeezed Billy's hand. "After all, we *did* make love last night, didn't we?"

Billy looked at her out of the corner of his eye.

She briefly met his gaze then stared straight ahead. He continued to watch her and through her smile he could hear her whisper. "Yes, Billy, we certainly did."

The cab pulled up to the Art Institute. Billy paid the fare with a generous tip.

"My best customer today," the cabbie said as he tucked the money into his shirt pocket. "May all your children be Americans!"

The cab squealed and bolted away from the curb and Eden turned to face the two stone lions standing like sentinels in front of the Art Institute. She grabbed Billy's hand. "C'mon. Who knows what adventure awaits us in these hallowed halls."

CHAPTER 32

ILLY and Eden purchased two tickets and took their place at the end of a winding line. Billy had read that a recent spate of terrorist threats forced the museum and other tourist attractions to install metal detectors and x-ray machines. Several armed guards stood at attention, arms tightly crossed over their chests, scanning the crowd.

"Damn terrorists," Billy said. "They've certainly mucked up everything."

He remembered his recent trip to D.C. It was very different from his visit back in '95. Now every venue had barriers, and as a result, very long lines. Even the open spaces were cordoned off. No more cutting across lawns to reach your destination. Blockades. Checkpoints. Lines upon lines. What a pain in the ass. New York City was even worse.

When they reached the metal detector, Billy passed through unscathed. Eden laid her handbag on the conveyor belt and also passed through the detector without incident. When her handbag entered the x-ray machine the conveyor belt jolted to a stop. The young woman in a baggy blue uniform stared at the monitor in front of her. She called another guard over, pointed to the screen and whispered something in his ear. He looked up and nodded toward Eden and Billy. Two more security guards converged and stared at the monitor. One grunted. The other shook his head.

What has my mystery girl done now? Billy wondered. Then he remembered the Milk Duds. Dozens and dozens of the little yellow boxes. Nah, can't be. Or could it?

A voice with the air of authority sliced through the din. "I'm afraid we can't let you enter the Museum. Come with me, please."

235

Suddenly, all activity in the lobby ceased.

Billy and Eden quickly obeyed and followed the security guard to a small table off to the side. Several hundred eyes followed them. Murmuring conjecture and muted accusations rumbled through the crowd.

"They don't look like terrorists, Bernie," an elderly woman whispered to her husband as Eden and Billy passed.

"You never know," he said.

"But she's so petite and he's so handsome."

"Those are the worst kind."

Eden and Billy stepped up to the table, and the guard opened her purse. Dozens of boxes of Milk Duds tumbled across the tabletop.

The guard scowled at the couple. "What's the meaning of this?"

Eden and Billy looked at each other, then down at the pile of boxed candy, and then back at the burly guard.

"Well, I—" Eden stuttered.

"You see, Officer, she has medical condition," Billy said.

"A medical condition?" He raised a bushy eyebrow.

"Sure," Billy continued, thinking quickly. "She's a contra-diabetic. She doesn't get enough sugar so she has to carry around these Milk Duds in case she has an episode. Doctor's orders."

"What kind of episode?" The guard rubbed the back of his thick neck and frowned.

"Oh, it's ugly," Billy said with a grimace. "You don't want to be around when it happens." He waved his hand over the pile of little boxes. "Thus the Milk Duds."

"The Milk Duds," Eden echoed.

The guard picked up a box to examine it. He held it to his ear and shook it. Something click-clacked against cardboard. He opened the box and two small chocolates tumbled onto the table. He picked one up and nibbled it.

"She needs the sugar. Doctor's orders." Billy continued. "That's what makes her kisses so sweet. Go ahead, Eden. Give him a kiss."

Eden looked at Billy out of the corner of her eye and her expression said it all – what in the world are you doing?!

He gave her a gentle nudge. "Kiss him. Just like you kissed me this morning."

She leaned across the table and gently kissed the security guard on the lips.

He fell back as if jolted by an electric shock and blurted out, "Jesus, Mary and Joseph! That's the sweetest kiss these old lips have ever tasted. Damn unbelievable!"

Billy smiled and nodded. "Told you."

The guard re-gathered his composure and donned his grim and serious demeanor.

"Still, I'm afraid I am going to have to clear this with my boss. It's standard policy." He turned and shouted, "Hey, Sarge, come over here for a second."

A stocky man sauntered over and asked in a thick Irish brogue, "What seems to be the problem here, Tony?"

"It's this young lady, Seamus. She wants to take her purse into the museum."

He eyed Eden with suspicion and turned to the other guard. "Does she have any weapons?"

"No."

"Then what's the problem?"

"Look at this." Tony pointed to Milk Duds.

Seamus stared at the pile of yellow boxes. "What the hell is this, young lady?" He pushed his cap back. "Some kind of joke?"

"She has a medical condition," offered Tony.

"A medical condition," Billy added.

"A condition," Eden repeated.

The Irishman looked at Eden, then down to the boxes on the table, then up to the other guard. "Well…I don't know."

"It's true," Tony explained nodding his head, "She's some kinda contrabetic or something. That's why her kisses are so sweet." He turned to Eden and waved his hand. "Go ahead, young lady, show him."

Eden shrugged then leaned across the table. She gave the Irishman a soft peck on the lips.

"Lord have mercy!" He steadied himself against the table and his cheeks turned fire ant red. "That is one sweet kiss!"

"What'd I tell you, boss?" Tony slapped his superior on the back.

"Well," Seamus said with a faint smile. "Since it's a medical condition, I guess you can take your bag in."

The two guards scooped up the Milk Duds and shoved them back in the purse. "Sorry for all the trouble," the Irishman offered. Tony broadcast an 'I told you so' smile.

"Not a problem," Eden said as she retrieved her purse. "Everyone makes mistakes." She turned and glared at Billy. "Don't we?" He returned her look with his best 'What me?' expression. The couple turned away and walked through the stunned and speechless crowd toward the museum entrance.

"Eden, I was only trying to—" Billy stammered.

"I know what you were up to," she said. "But you took it one step too far."

"But did you see the look on the Irishman's face when you kissed him? Hilarious! And besides, we're supposed to be on an adventure today. You know, push the edge of the envelope and all that."

"You're right," she said grabbing his hand and pulling him forward. "Let's go."

He pulled her back. "Wait a minute. I thought I was the one leading this adventure."

She spun around and looked into his eyes. "That was yesterday."

He raised his eyebrows.

She smiled and said, "And trust me, you ain't seen nothin' yet."

"Then here's to our conditions and the adventures they might bring."

"To our conditions and adventures," she echoed.

They raised imaginary glasses in a toast then followed the map to Gallery 262.

* * *

Fifteen blocks away, Danny, Eugene and Vinnie pushed open the door to Uncle Tommy's social club. As they stumbled in, all eyes seemed to turn on them. Eddie the Mouse dropped his espresso cup back onto his saucer. Two guys in the corner muttered a "What the...?" Uncle Tommy smashed his cigar out in an ashtray and rose.

"What the hell happened to you?"

Danny looked down at the sling that held his right arm, then over to Gino's leg cast, and then to Vinnie's neck brace.

"Y'know that job we was supposed to do last night?" he asked through swollen lips.

"The piece-of-cake kidnapping job, right?"

"Yeah. 'Cept it wasn't such a piece of cake."

"More like getting a piece of Jackie Chan," said Eugene.

"Jackie Chan and Bruce Lee combined," added Vinnie.

"You're telling me that little broad did this to you?" Uncle Tommy asked as he thrust his hands out to his side.

"Hey, it coulda been worse, Uncle Tommy," Danny said in a plaintive voice. "She woulda killed us if my brother Eugene, here, hadn't yelled 'cheese.'"

Danny heard a growl just to his left as Vinnie tore off his neck brace and hurled it across the room. Eugene hung his head and mumbled, "Oh, shit."

And that's the last thing he, Danny, or any of the men present that morning, remembered.

CHAPTER 33

THE museum teemed with a weekend crowd as Billy and Eden wandered through the galleries admiring the diverse collections. And there it was, just ahead, *Nighthawks*, full of simplicity and depth. They approached slowly and reverently, as if they were entering an ancient, sacred shrine.

"What do you think?"

She stood silently for a moment as her eyes lingered on the masterwork.

"Why, it's magnificent. And so melancholy," she said softly. "The people in the diner seem to be biding their time. Waiting for something to happen."

"See the cash register in the storefront behind them. You think a heist is in the works? They're just waiting for the right time?"

"Perhaps, but they're definitely waiting, for something, or someone, to emerge from those shadows."

"Are we talking about the painting? Or about you?"

She turned, face flushed. "You think I'm a little crazy don't you?'

"Because you have dreams and visions? Ha, like I'm the one to judge."

"So tell me," she said, changing the subject. "What do the colors in this painting taste like?"

"That dark shadow there," he pointed to the area just below the diner window—licorice. Black licorice. The yellow walls—iced tea, with a hint of raspberries. And the green..." his voice trailed off. That's it. This is where I've tasted the color of her eyes before! That soft, luscious, yet iridescent green.

"And what about that shadow over there?"

Her voice brought his mind back to the painting.

"The one in the window up in the corner? Hmm. That would be—"

"No not that one. The one in the doorway. The one moving to the left."

"Huh?" He took a step toward the painting. "Moving?" He turned back around. "To what left?"

Eden ignored him. A faint smile crept across her face and she slowly turned her head, eyes sparkling, as if watching a child dance across the room. "Maybe I'm just seeing things. Never mind." She turned to face the gallery. "Y'know," she said as she touched a finger to her lips, and furrowed her brow. "I think the Hopper would look much better over there," she said pointing to the south wall. "Between those two paintings."

"What're you talking about?"

"Over there. Just picture it. The stark loneliness of this piece would be the perfect foil to the color and exuberance of the other two paintings."

"Don't tell me you want to move it?"

She put her hands on her hips. "So, are you done taking risks?"

"No."

"Then trust me on this one."

Billy ran his hand through his hair and looked across the room. "But these are priceless works of art. National treasures. We just can't walk in here and…"

She turned to walk away. "Just as I thought."

"No wait," he said as he grabbed her shoulder and spun her around. He stared into her eyes. Eyes that were now a dangerous, dark and ominous gray. Where had he seen *this* before? Whatever it was, the spell was working and he found himself being drawn into her mischief. "You know, I think you're right."

Eden broke into a smile and her eyes returned to a sparkling green. "So. . . let's move it."

"Okay, let's."

They marched up to the painting, carefully lifted it off its hooks, and carried it across the crowded room. Some people stopped to stare, their attention drawing the interest of others. Soon everyone in the gallery watched in awe as Eden and Billy crossed the room with the Hopper painting.

"It'll look better over here," Eden explained to the questioning looks.

Some people pointed and gasped. Others whistled in astonishment. A few cheered them on for their chutzpah. A security guard in the next gallery must have heard the commotion.

"What the hell?" he yelled as he marched into the gallery and confronted the couple. "All right, hold it right there!"

Billy eyed the pint-sized guard and thought he'd be much more intimidating if his uniform wasn't a size too big. The guard planted his hands on his hips and glared up into Billy's eyes. He stood a good eight inches shorter than Billy, but what he lacked in stature he seemed to attempt to make up in volume.

"Just what in the goddam-hell do you think you're doing?!" he barked.

The crowd drew close and hovered around the trio.

"My friend here thought the painting would look much better on that wall over there," Billy explained as he pointed to the wall across the room.

"Who the goddam-hell gave you authority to do that?!"

Billy started to answer but the angry guard cut him off.

"Of all the—You think you can just waltz in here and move things around? Why that's the most goddam ridiculous thing I've ever heard. Why I oughta—" His eyes locked on Eden's. Billy watched her sparkling green eyes turn back to a dark and ominous gray. The guard froze like a deer in someone's headlights. Then he cocked his head to one side. "What wall?"

"That one," answered Eden, nodding to the south wall.

He removed his cap and ran his fingers through comb-over hair. He stared at the far wall for a minute or two. "Hmmm."

"Well?" Eden asked.

"Y'know," he said nodding slowly, "I think you just might have something there. Here—let me give you a hand."

He spread his arms and began to part the gathering crowd. "Gangway!" he ordered. "Move aside! That's it! Comin' through!"

Billy leaned over and whispered, "I don't know how you do it."

"Do what?" she asked without looking at him. A faint smile crossed her lips as the trio worked their way through the throng of people toward the south wall.

"Here," the guard offered, "let's take this Warhol down and we'll hang the Hopper in its place."

Soon others chimed in, offering comments and making suggestions.

"Why don't you put the Albright over here?" a middle-aged woman proposed.

"I think this Ernst would look fab over on that wall, particularly in that light," offered a college-aged student with a British accent.

"This Lichtenstein should really be in the gallery next door," suggested a young mother cradling a small child.

Before Billy knew it, the whole gallery had come alive with motion. Young people and old began removing and re-hanging art. Paintings and sculptures found new places. Suggestions, opinions and laughter collided and embraced.

Someone produced a hammer and a small crowbar from a nearby janitor's closet.

Great! Now hooks could be moved.

A ladder appeared from somewhere and was passed around.

Excellent! Now we can reach that mobile.

A strapping teenage boy climbed up the ladder, unhooked the mobile and handed it down to another teenager.

"That'll look much better near the winding staircase," a voice called out. The mobile clinked and tinked as the two teenagers wove through the crowd and toward the stairs.

"Someone give me a hand with this Hepworth," a man in an electric wheelchair said as he nudged the heavy sculpture across the marble floor with his feet.

A covey of suggestions and laughter took flight and filled the air. Energy and mirth supplanted the staid and stuffy tenor indigenous to museums. The spirited crowd became a model of creativity and efficiency.

"This is so communal," shouted a bearded man with a gray ponytail. "Just like Fresno in the old days."

"And fun!" squealed an elderly woman as she banged her walker on the marble floor.

"And hopelessly insane," added a priest as he grabbed the hand of a nun and danced across the gallery floor while twirling a Lucas Samaras bird box.

Billy nudged Eden and laughed. "Now look what you've gone and started."

"Just blame it on my 'condition,'" she said, her eyes beaming. "Here, help me with this O'Keefe."

The security guard carried a Rothko across the room, barking orders and directing traffic. As new people poured into the gallery, they joined the flurry of activity.

"Where did they find that cordless drill?"

"Hey, pass me that crowbar."

"Someone got a Phillips head?"

A sleek bronze sculpture slipped out of sweaty hands and crashed to the floor. "No harm done. Just a small chip in the marble floor."

"You done with the ladder?"

"Who's got the hammer?"

* * *

Two galleries down, Johnny the Guard stood at attention in his corner and wondered at the people rushing past him. He followed the crowd, drawn to the clash and clatter up ahead. He cinched up his pants and swaggered around the corner into the gallery. His jaw dropped open and he froze in his tracks. He yanked a chrome whistle from his shirt pocket. The shrill noise brought everyone to a staggering halt.

"What's the meaning of this?!" he shouted to nobody in particular.

Everyone stopped in mid-movement. A hush fell over the room. He hung his thumbs on his belt and strutted through the surreal tableau. He stopped in front of a freckle-faced boy in a Cub Scout uniform. The child tried to hide a Rauschenberg behind his back. "I. . . I..." he stuttered.

The guard patted the boy's shoulder then slowly shook his head and clicked his tongue. Tsk, tsk, tsk. He turned and addressed the dumbstruck crowd. "In all my 20 years in this venerable institution," he said, "I have never, *ever* seen anything like this. Who in the world gave you the authority to rearrange this gallery?"

A young Asian-American woman nodded to the little security guard holding the Rothko. "Well, *he* said it was OK."

245

Johnny the Guard spun around. "Is that true, Gracey?"

Gracey stared back and gulped. He let the Rothko fall from his hands and the frame cracked as it hit the marble floor.

Johnny the Guard turned his head and spat on the floor. "I'm appalled! What a disgrace."

Gracey stammered, "But J-Johnny, it wasn't my idea!"

Johnny reared up and bellowed, "Whose lamebrain idea was it?!"

All fingers pointed to Eden and Billy. "It was *their* idea."

Eden and Billy glanced at each other and shrugged.

"I'm gonna have to call for backup," said Johnny the Guard. "Nobody move."

He pulled a matte black walkie-talkie off his belt and pushed a button on the side. The radio crackled with static.

"Hey, Judy. It's me, Johnny. Listen, I got a Code 11 here...That's right, you heard me, a Code 11...Flagrant Realignment of Priceless Museum Pieces.... I'm gonna need some backup...Yeah, send 'em all...It's a real mob scene...Could get ugly...I don't want a riot on my hands..."

He clipped the walkie-talkie back on his belt and steeled his shoulders.

"OK everyone. Slowly—very slowly—put the artwork down."

The crowd obeyed as Johnny the Guard removed his gun from its holster and continued, "That's right, no sudden moves. Now everyone put your hands on your head where I can see them. Slowly now. . . slowly. That's it. Everybody stay calm and no one's gonna get hurt, OK?"

Eden turned to Billy. "Since when do museum security guards carry guns?"

"Ever since those Taliban nutcases threatened to blow up all of America's great museums, I guess."

A few moments later two dozen additional guards stormed into the room with guns drawn and veins bulging in red necks. They faced down the cowering crowd. One veteran turned to a younger guard beside him and said in a low gruff voice, "This, my man, is what we live and train for. It's show time."

Billy turned and whispered to Eden out of the corner of his mouth, "We need to make a break for it."

"Are you crazy?" she whispered back.

"Just look at these guys. They're rent-a-cops. Police academy rejects. They smell blood. They want revenge and now they got guns. Who knows what carnage they are capable of?"

Her eyes scanned the fuming men in dark blue uniforms. "I see what you mean."

"OK, here's the plan. On the count of three, I'll create a diversion and we'll make our break down that hallway." He nodded behind him.

"All right," she whispered.

"One," Billy slowly said.

"One," she echoed softly and squeezed his arm.

"Two."

"Two..."

"Three! Oh my god!" Billy shouted as he pointed to a small Salvador Dali painting. "Is it my imagination or does that farm silo look just like a GIANT PENIS!"

As everyone spun around to look at the painting, Billy grabbed Eden's hand and they bolted from the gallery and down the hall.

Behind them, mass confusion and chaos—a raging torrent of shouts, curses and more than a few gunshots. Soon the guards led the crowd in hot pursuit. Their profanity-laced admonitions urged the fleeing couple to halt. But since Eden and Billy had a good head start, they ignored them. Several guards leveled their weapons and blasted away. Some guards aimed high. Some aimed low. Most didn't aim. Billy and Eden heard bullets ricocheting off marble and stone, piercing canvas and board, chipping bronze and steel, creating new sensations for Billy. The crack of gunfire burned his skin and the pinging of bullets off marble whipped his flesh. It energized him and drove him forward. Like a school of malnourished piranha, the guards were caught up in the frenzy of the moment. Several hundred art patrons—Billy and Eden's former allies—followed in their wake. The crowd shook their fists and lustfully joined in the pursuit. Someone shouted, "Give us Barabbas! Give us Barabbas!"

Billy and Eden ducked their heads as bullets and curses zipped by overhead. They ran from gallery to gallery passing startled tourists and art students. They sprinted past a young man with long greasy hair and a scraggly goatee. He had his arm propped up against the wall, corralling a young woman in a jeans dress and flip-flops.

"White wine is good," they heard him tell her, "but red is better. I should know. I'm a Scientist."

Eden and Billy looked at each other. No, it couldn't be.

Overhead, a Calder mobile spun wildly as bullets zinged and pinged off its metal arms.

"This is insane," Billy panted.

"And just think," Eden huffed, "yesterday we were nearly strangers."

"Ah. . . Yesterday. . ." he said between pants.

"Yesterday. . ." she echoed as they turned a corner.

"Quick," Billy said as they passed a stairwell. "Up these stairs. That'll slow them down."

"But where does this lead to?" she asked.

"Up. . . I think."

They slammed through the door and bounded up the stairs, skipping every other step. Several floors below, they heard the guards tumble into the stairwell.

"Which way did they go?!" one of them shouted. Billy glanced over the railing. The guards had hesitated in their confusion.

"Good, it'll buy us a little more time," Billy said as he pulled her forward.

"We have to split up," someone shouted from below. An argument broke out as they disagreed about who should go up and who should go down. Their indecision bought Eden and Billy even more time. The couple increased their lead as they vaulted up the stairs. The footsteps, shouting and gunshots echoed far below as they reached a metal door at the top of the stairs. Billy pushed the safety bar and they burst out into the dazzling sunlight. An alarm bell erupted overhead, announcing their presence. The couple stopped for a moment to catch their breath, covering their ears from the incessant clanging of the bell over the doorway. In between gasps and heaves, they looked around to get their bearings. They were on the roof.

The breather gave Billy a chance to ponder and assess their situation. What was he thinking?! People do this in the movies all the time. And he hated it. They always go up. Up the stairs. Up the ladder.

Up the escalator. . . Up, up, up. What idiots! And now he was one of them. So now what?! Keep calm. Think. He had to think.

"What do we do now, my handsome tour guide?" Eden asked between gasps.

"I have a plan," Billy replied as his eyes swept the rooftop. "Follow me."

He grabbed her hand and they sprang across the roof, leaping over vent pipes, skylights and galvanized air ducts. Their shoes crunched the loose, white gravel on tar and sent pebbles flying from their heels. When they neared the far end of the roof their pursuers spilled out of the stairwell, guns blaring into the bright blue sky. Billy and Eden leapt up onto the granite ledge and looked down.

They were nearly 100 feet from the ground.

CHAPTER 34

AUREEN awoke the next morning to the dazzling rays of sunlight filtering through sheer white curtains. She rubbed her forehead, yawned, and stretched her stiff limbs. She raised her throbbing head off of her pillow and glanced over at the pile of dishes littering the small table across the room.

"Ohh," she moaned.

Then she noticed the empty bottles of wine and nearly empty bottles of champagne on the table beside her bed.

"Ohh," she repeated as she rolled her eyes.

She propped herself up on her elbow and looked at the attractive woman lying in peaceful slumber next to her. Ginny stirred, then pulled the covers tight and rolled over on her side. Maureen patted the woman's shoulder and turned her attention to the flickering TV.

"This is CNN News and I'm Bob Baskins."

Jeez, Bob, keep it down, will ya? She groaned again and slowly sat up. Ohhh, this is no good. She gently laid her head back down and stared up at the ceiling. Violet polka dots whirled and swirled against the white plaster. She took a few deep breaths and let out a heavy sigh. Her whole body ached – even her hair hurt. She turned to the clock on the nightstand. 11:30?! Damn! She nudged Ginny who woke with a snort.

"What? What?" She pried her eyes open.

"Get up, it's late!"

"Ten more minutes."

"No. Now." Maureen sat up and gingerly swung her legs off the side of the bed. "I'll get us some coffee."

Ginny stretched, rubbed her eyes and let out a plaintive moan of her own. "Ohhhhh. My god what have we done to ourselves?" She pulled the covers over her head and turned away.

Maureen wandered over to the coffee maker and prepared a pot that soon filled the room with a delicious aroma. She drifted into the bathroom and splashed cold water on her face. She looked at herself in the mirror.

"You look like shit," she said to her reflection.

Splish, splash.

"Girl, you still look like shit."

Splash.

"Oh, it's no use." She dried her face and ambled back into the bedroom where the aroma of fresh brewed Colombian filled the air. She poured two steaming cups of coffee and wandered back over to the bed.

"Here you go," she said as she perched on the edge of the bed.

Ginny sat up and took the cup. "Smells good. Thanks."

Maureen cradled her cup in her hands and took a sip. Ahh. So much better. Another sip. Then another. Her mind began to clear and the ache subsided. "I better try Billy again." She picked up the phone and dialed the front desk.

"Good morning, Mrs. Valentine."

"William Shakes, please."

She stared blankly at the television as Billy's phone rang. And rang. And rang.

The voice on the television filled the void.

". . . yesterday's Dow was 18 points higher than. . ."

Maureen shook her leg. Come on Billy—

". . . that's right Bob, and we can expect this week's market to hit. . ."

—answer the damned phone!

". . . we interrupt this program to bring you this special report from Chicago..."

Chicago? She sat up straight and tried to focus her eyes. Ginny followed her gaze.

"We're live at the Art Institute in Chicago. A hostage situation or suicide attempt is unfolding before our eyes. What have you heard, Dennis?"

The two women stared at the flickering screen.

"Well, Camille, it appears that. . ."

Maureen slowly replaced the receiver. She blinked her eyes and leaned forward as a shaky camera zoomed in on the faces of the two figures perched high on the edge of the roof of the Art Institute. Her eyes moved from the man, to the woman, then back to the man.

"Billy?" Maureen whispered.

"Eden?" Ginny said leaning forward.

Then two coffee cups fell to the floor and tumbled across the Persian carpet at their feet.

* * *

Nicole slowly opened her eyes and blinked. Bright white institutional lights stung her eyes and amplified the pounding in her head. She winced and struggled to sit up. A hand gently touched her shoulder and eased her back down to the pile of pillows.

"Easy, young lady, easy. You're a very lucky girl." A kindly woman in white smiled. "There, there. Sip this." She held a paper cup up to Nicole's parched and swollen lips.

"But I..." Nicole rasped as she tried to push the cup away.

"Don't talk." The paper cup touched her lips. "Just sip."

Nicole parted her lips. The cool liquid felt good as it rolled over her sticky tongue and down her dry throat.

"You've been in a terrible accident." A gruff yet seemingly friendly voice rolled in from somewhere beyond the kind woman in white. "Like the nurse said, you're one helluva lucky girl."

Nicole slowly rolled her eyes to the right and focused on a shadowy form. She squinted and made out a dark suit and white shirt. Thin black tie on a barrel chest. Up behind the form hung a TV set. Noise, muted and garbled, tumbled down from the speaker. Slow motion applause? Hail on a tin roof? The whop-whop of a helicopter rotor?

"But I do have to ask you a few questions. I won't be long."

Nicole struggled to prop herself up on her elbows. Every bone and sinew seemed to cry out in pain. She collapsed back onto her pillow.

The form stepped forward and touched her shoulder. "I can come back later."

"No, no," she managed to reply through her swollen lips. "Let's get this over now."

"I'm Sgt. Johnson. Hillsborough County Sheriff's Department." He pulled a ragged note pad and a pen from his coat pocket. "I'm sorry about your accident; you're lucky to be alive. Damned lucky. But I need to get some answers." He clicked the pen and placed it against the pad. "You have the right to remain silent…"

Nicole closed her eyes and swallowed hard as the voice above her droned on. She drifted away for a minute. Hours? Days? She awoke, sighed and slowly opened her eyes again. "I understand," she whispered.

"That submachine gun," the gruff voice continued. "What's a young lady like you doing with hardware like that? The pot, hell, I can understand that. Toked a few in my day." He placed his foot on the bed frame and leaned forward. "But the gun? Tell me about that gun."

Gun? What gun? Nicole asked herself. Then she remembered the Nazi pervert. The horrific crash. Shards of glass. Illegal immigrants darting down the embankment. The taste of metal on her tongue. Oh, yeah. *That* gun.

"To tell you the truth," the officer continued. "We have reason to believe this weapon was used in a string of recent murders across the county. In fact, some guy was gunned down inside a neo-Nazi shop by the docks yesterday. Broad daylight, too. We're running ballistics now, but this caliber weapon could very well be linked to the deaths of three black activists, an outspoken Rabbi, and, get this," he said with a chortle, "the winner of a Paris Hilton look-alike contest held last month at the Cheshire Club down on Dale Mabry Then there were those two…"

His voice faded in Nicole's ears and she mumbled, "I want my money back…"

Then something on the TV caught her attention and she struggled to sit up. She stared at the flickering screen and gasped. The detective followed her gaze and turned. A deadpan newsman with decoupage hair stared into the camera.

"*. . .as the drama unfolds before us here in Chicago. Eyewitness News has confirmed an obvious terrorist plot at the Art Institute. We have with us a Mr. and Mrs. Bernie Stinitsky from Sheboygan, Wisconsin who were in the Institute when the attack took place.*"

The camera panned back and the reporter motioned to the couple.

"*Could you tell our viewers what happened?*" He shoved the microphone in front of them and the old man leaned in.

"*See, me and the missus here was waiting on line when this young couple stormed in and began to cause a disturbance.*"

"Young couple? The terrorists were a young couple?"

"A good looking couple," the man replied.

"The worst kind," added his wife shaking her head.

"Then they charged through the museum, ripping down paintings, hurling sculptures, destroying statues—"

"And you shoulda seen the Milk Duds," his wife chimed in. *"Boxes and boxes of them."*

"It was a disaster. A real disgrace. That's when the cops came and started shooting up the place."

The reporter leaned into the microphone. *"The two of them did all this? On their own?"*

He shoved the microphone back before the couple.

"No, no. There were dozens of them. An obvious plot. A conspiracy. Insiders involved. Foreigners and traitors. Destroying our history. Our culture."

"It's what 'those' people do," his wife added as she nodded her head for emphasis.

"A real tragedy, I tell ya." the man from Sheboygan continued. *"Now I hear they got them trapped up on the roof."* He removed his hat and pointed off into the distance. *"See?"*

The reporter turned back to the camera and stiffened. *"Now we'll take you back to the parking lot of the Art Institute where my colleague, Jennifer Jones, is waiting with an update. Jennifer?"*

The scene shifted to a blond woman in her thirties. She brushed a wisp of hair from her face and breathlessly related the recent developments inside the museum: untold damage, shots fired, and a conspiracy. Then she stiffened. *"Wait, I have late-breaking news. Let's go to Camille Lambert inside the Art Institute. Camille?"*

The camera broke away to a smartly dressed black woman standing with a tearful teenage girl. *"Tell us what happened."*

"My God," the teenager sobbed. *"He had me cornered. Said he was a scientist. He was talking about mass destruction. It's nuclear, he said. In the wine. He said it's in the wine."* She leaned into the camera *"Mom, Dad. I'm sorry I took the car. I wanna go home!"*

The camera zoomed in on Camille. *"Nuclear destruction,"* she repeated. *"In the wine. Obviously some kind of code. I'm reminded of the Bay of Pigs and Kruschev's Code 49. Sangria. On the rocks. With a twist of lime."* She shook her head. *"If only we had known…"*

Behind her, seven security guards hustled a thin young man with a goatee out the door and to a waiting squad car. *"You can't do this. I'm a Scientist!"* he yelled as he pulled and shrugged. *"A Scientist, I tell ya!"*

Camille turned her attention to the ruckus behind her, and then stared back into the camera. *"It appears they have one of the operatives. A nuclear scientist."* The camera zoomed in on her stoic face. *"The question we have to ask ourselves, Dennis,"* she said with taut-as-Saran-wrap lips. *"How close did we come to complete annihilation? Now back to you."*

"Thank you, Camille," Dennis said swiveling to the studio camera. *"And this just in. The authorities have two terrorists cornered. Could be a possible hostage situation. Jennifer?"* A camera zoomed in on the couple poised on the edge of the Art Institute roof.

"Yes, Dennis. It certainly appears to be a hostage situation." The camera panned back to Jennifer. She brushed another swath of blond hair from her brow and intoned, *"With possible nuclear ramifications."*

Nicole's eyes grew wide. "Billy?" she whispered.

The detective turned around and stared at the prone girl.

"You know this guy?" he asked motioning with a thumb over his shoulder.

"My, my boyfriend."

"Your boyfriend is a terrorist?!" He rubbed his chin. "Mmm. Then that explains the high-powered weapon."

"But..." she said choking on phlegm. "It's not what you think..."

"Young lady, we really need to talk." He pulled a cell phone from his jacket pocket and punched in a number.

"Captain, this is Johnson. I'm at Tampa General. Listen, we need to get the FBI in here. Yeah, you heard me. The Feds."

* * *

Robbie rolled back on his pillow and moaned. His loins ached and his tongue was sore. The blond woman beside him pulled him back on top of her and smiled a dreamy smile.

"Extra innings?" she cooed as she softly drew her nails up his back.

"Again?" he stammered.

Her hungry eyes met his. "Batter up."

CHAPTER 35

Billy tilted his head back and closed his eyes. A gentle breeze tousled his hair and the light of the midday sun warmed his face. He sighed and breathed in the salt air as it wafted in from Lake Michigan.

His eyes jerked open. Hey, wait a minute. Salt? In the air? But this is a lake.

Then Billy realized the salt air he was breathing was from his own perspiration. He ran a nervous hand up over his brow, through damp auburn hair and down his neck.

"What now, Billy?" Eden asked. Her eyes were wide and her voice was trembling.

"There they are!" shouted someone.

Billy glanced back over his shoulder and saw the guards closing in. Then he turned and looked down to the sculpture garden below them.

"I guess we'll have to jump," he replied.

"Jump? But we must be 100 feet up!"

"We'll aim for those tents over there." Billy pointed to the bright canvas below.

"We'll never reach them," Eden said. "They're too far away."

"Don't worry. If we miss them, the ground will break our fall."

"Billy," she said with a scowl, "this is no time for jokes!"

"Sorry."

Za-ping! A bullet grazed Billy's head. He reached up to touch it and the sting made him flinch. He looked at his finger. Blood. Elderberry. Then he stumbled.

"Billy?"

"I'm okay." He regained his footing.

"Well?" she asked.

"We have to take the chance. . . or we'll be shot. These guys are too pumped to take anyone back alive."

She looked over her shoulder at the rapidly approaching throng. "I believe you're right."

Sirens echoed off the neighboring buildings as three fire engines and an ambulance rolled into a nearby parking lot. The wail caused Billy to wince in pain. The rescue vehicles were followed by two TV news trucks and a growing crowd of gawkers.

Another shot zipped by and struck a pigeon in mid-flight. Feathers scattered into the wind as the frail carcass tumbled to the ground below. Billy looked back over his shoulder. Three of the guards were just 20 yards away and closing fast.

"Hold your fire, men," one of them shouted. "We got 'em cornered now."

"OK," said Billy. "Let's go."

They put their arms around each other.

"Are you sure?" Eden searched his eyes.

He returned her gaze and tasted the fino amontillado as Sachiko's playful voice echoed in his mind, *First you jump off the cliff. . .*

"Yeah," he stammered, "I'm sure."

She leaned in close. "It's been a blast, Billy," she whispered as her lips caressed his ear.

His legs began to buckle and he steeled himself. He pulled her close. "I love you, mystery girl."

"And I love you."

He took one last deep breath and held it. A charging guard lunged toward them.

"Now!" Then they leapt off the ledge and out onto nothing.

The guard tumbled across the gravel toward the edge of the roof, his hand grazing Billy's pant leg. He rolled over and came to a halt just inches from the brink. He craned his neck and cautiously peered over the edge. Horror filled his eyes as he watched the plummeting couple.

"They went over!"

A collective gasp exploded from the crowd below. A swat team member with a bullhorn stood on the hood of an armored truck shouting instructions. Four firemen sprinted across the lawn with a net.

The wind rushed past Billy and Eden and they embraced each other tightly. They clenched their eyes bracing for impact. They plunged for more than fifty feet. Then their descent slowed and Billy sensed they were rising. He cautiously opened his eyes. They were rising indeed. He looked down. Two bodies lay in the shadows of the Art Institute. The tableau should have seemed poignant and serene, like two sleepy lovers locked in a deep embrace. But this scene was different. Their limbs were twisted; bent in unnatural ways. The woman's head lay upon the man's chest, black hair damp from the blood flowing from the man's mouth. Yellow Milk Dud boxes littered the ground around them. The firemen dropped the net and raced across the lawn. Startled cries from the crowd filled the air. Three EMTs hauling bulky black medical bags and a stretcher scrambled to the crumpled forms.

Billy shuddered at the scene below him. He turned and searched Eden's face for an answer. But her eyes were still closed and her face glowed with intense concentration. He glanced over her shoulder to see massive, soft-white wings billowing in the late morning sun like the unfurled sails of a South Seas windjammer.

She slowly opened her eyes and met his gaze.

"You knew?" he whispered.

She nodded and let out a giggle. "It's amazing what you can learn when you listen to your dreams."

Her powerful wings found their rhythm and beat the air. Below them, worker-bee taxicabs, sardine-can buses, and the raging waterfalls of steel and glass dissolved into the grey cityscape.

"Always jump off the cliff," she said as her eyes danced. "Then build your wings on your way down."

He furrowed his brow, trying to understand. "Dive?"

She nodded then added, "And fly."

She pulled him close as they pierced swan-white clouds and entered the indigo ether. A large dark shadow veered in front of them and turned diamond bright. They fell into its swirling slipstream and Eden's countenance lit up as if recognizing a long-lost friend. She stretched out her wings and they rode the solar wind into the cosmos, sending joyous clouds and laughing stars to the periphery of their vision.

The sound of wing slicing wind tickled and warmed Billy's side. He'd felt this before. August of '78. Crossing the Carolina pinelands into Georgia low country in the new Mercury. Dad, proud, vibrant and alive. Captain of this Detroit steel ship. And Mom, the sweet Carolyn O'Malley, first mate, beaming and pointing to the distant and mysterious promised land of Miami Beach. Young Billy sat safe and confident in the back seat, head out of the window. Towhead hair and Irish freckles challenging the wind as the billboards flashed by. The promised land. He could feel it, taste it, even then.

He relished the memory then turned his gaze to Eden and her shining countenance. He looked into the eyes of Joy and drank deeply.

"I've never tasted anything quite like this before," he said as a feeling of ecstasy washed over his tongue and filled the very core of his being.

"Boy," she said as her eyes turned to fire, "like I said, you ain't seen nothin' yet."

And they soared.

CHAPTER 36

EDEN tossed the manuscript onto the kitchen table. A smile crept across her face. "Your mom would've liked this."

Billy sipped his Jameson's and thought about the passing of his mother two years ago and a twinge of grief coursed through him. "Yeah, at least the violence was a lot less graphic. But what do you think?"

"I liked it. I really did. Even better than *Zoot Suits*." She paused and glanced down at the manuscript, her finger tracing its edges.

"And...?"

"You need to change the names. After all, this isn't a memoir."

Billy swirled the ice in his glass. "I thought about that. Just seemed natural, that's all. Heck, I am a writer and you and I did meet under unusual circumstances."

"I'd hardly say that meeting someone at a book-signing is unusual."

"But it wasn't my book signing. It was Tim Dorsey's. I was there just to heckle him. Almost did until someone who shall remain un-named jabbed me in the ribs and hissed, "Why don't you shut your fat mouth and let the man speak.""

Eden laughed. "I thought you were such a dork."

"At least you got a drink out of it."

"I'm always up for a free drink. Even from dorks."

"And there was that Scientist guy there. The one who had 11 books for Dorsey to sign. And that Caribbean-looking woman."

"Okay. Lots of similarities. But I'm no angel."

Billy reached across the table and caressed her hand. "You are to me."

Eden rolled her eyes. "Oh puh-lease. What are you going to write next? Hallmark cards?"

"Okay, the names go. Thank goodness for search and replace. Should be a cinch."

"Any ideas for new names?"

"I was thinking Willy and Edith."

"You're still a dork sometimes!" Eden stood. "Can I refresh your drink, Willy?"

He slid his glass across the table. "Please, Edith."

She walked over to the counter and refilled their glasses. "And I'm glad they didn't really die at the end," she said over her shoulder. "That woulda ruined everything." She returned and set his glass down on the table. "Sorta leaves things open for a sequel."

"You mean something along the lines of *Son of Dive and Fly?*"

She plucked a few ice cubes out of his glass and hurled them at him. "You're not only a dork, you're a wise ass."

He ducked and the ice cubes bounced off the wall and skidded back across the floor. Eden bent down to pick them up as the door-bell rang.

"I'll get it," said Billy, rising.

"No. It's for me. I'm expecting a UPS package." She rose and tossed the ice cubes into the sink, then pattered off to the front of the house.

Billy wandered over to the fridge to get some more ice when he noticed something on the floor. He bent down and picked up a small white feather.

Hmm...he thought as he twisted it between his fingers. Perhaps I don't have as much imagination as I thought I did.

He dropped a few cubes of ice into his glass and added a splash of Jameson's. He took a sip then wandered into the living room to see what the UPS man had just delivered.

www.ingramcontent.com/pod-product-compliance
Lightning Source LLC
Chambersburg PA
CBHW072209170626
46813CB00003B/861